COLONY

LEIGH MATTHEWS

Cover Illustration Copyright © 2016 Aimée Henny Brown

Cover design by Michelle Lee, Broadview Designs.

ISBN: 0992022460
ISBN-13: 978-0992022464

To Claire and Caden, for adventures past and those yet to come. And for my dad, whose impression of an atom is still the best I've ever seen.

ONE

They would face at least two winters here. The howling swirl of dust wrapping them in an ever tighter cocoon. It hadn't been like this at first. No windstorms or unexplained power outages. No sense that the planet itself had begun to speak.

Silver drank the last of the water from her canteen and traced her fingers over the well-worn engraving, "*Mais tu ne peux pas cueillir les étoiles.*" She had come here voluntarily. With enthusiasm, even. But, in the last few sols, the solitude and silence she had enjoyed after her arrival had begun to slip away, seemingly lost to the wind. They had been on Mars for less than six months, and Silver was tired. If she was to survive the next two hundred or so sols, she would have to learn to bear the whispering, the incessant, anguished, quiet roar of this place.

Silver slid the canteen back into the large front pocket of her navy overalls and savoured the cool, comforting weight of it against her thigh. She picked up the grey utility belt on the bench beside her and strapped it on, then swivelled it around until it sat firmly on her hips. Checking that she hadn't left anything behind, Silver walked out of the cafeteria and back to the hangar to find the Chief.

At six feet tall, and with a mass of tight brown curls, Aliyaah Diambu cut a striking figure. It wasn't simply her stature that made people pay attention to her, though. Aliyaah was the Chief Flight Engineer on

1

Octavia, and Chief Engineer for Project Arche as a whole. When Silver entered the hangar and spotted a pair of long navy-clad legs poking out from underneath Rover Four, she knew the Chief was exactly where Silver had left her half an hour before, working away on the hulking grey machine. They had been trying to get the rover back in service for almost seven sols, and while Silver had enjoyed the chance to work more closely with the Chief, she was itching to get on with the more creative, less rudimentary parts of the mission.

"Chief?" Silver said, and tapped her boot lightly against the creeper under Aliyaah's legs. "Are we ready to fire her up?"

Aliyaah pushed herself out from under the rover and blinked as her lenses took a second to adjust to the hangar lights. The green of her irises flickered to yellow and narrowed to a cats-eye slit. She smiled up at Silver, who propped her foot against the creeper to stop it sliding, then extended her hand to haul the Chief to her feet.

"As long as she powers up, she should be ready to go," Aliyaah said as she clambered up the side of the rover. "Can you release the clamps, Antara?"

Silver walked over to the control panel by the hangar door and flicked four switches to release the rover from the hangar's grip. She heard Aliyaah manually powering up the rover, so she began climbing into one of the two white Extravehicular Mobility Suits hanging by the airlock. Once she was zipped up, Silver pulled out two tethers from beneath the panel, slung them over her shoulder and waited for Aliyaah.

Aliyaah connected one of the tethers to a hook at the back of Silver's EMS and then climbed into the other suit. Silver buckled her in and then attached both tethers to the fixtures on the hangar wall. It wasn't really necessary to be tethered unless there was a major windstorm outside, but it was protocol, and protocol saved lives. The Chief nodded at Silver, who nodded back, and they both pulled on their helmets and gloves and clicked them into place.

Silver pushed the blue intercom button on the front panel of her suit, and Aliyaah did the same. After they checked communications between themselves and the rover, Aliyaah flicked a series of switches on the control panel and said, "Commencing launch sequence."

Silver monitored the panel for any signs of problems with the rover. It had been out of commission for the better part of ten sols, and this was the fourth time it had malfunctioned in the time they had been on the planet.

"All systems look good," Silver said, and then laughed as Aliyaah tapped her gloved hand against the cold, grey metal of the control panel. She wasn't normally prone to overt displays of superstition, but Silver tried to cross her fingers, and Aliyaah smiled. Despite the impressive mobility of the skin-tight pressurised Environmental Suits they wore most of the time they were outside the station, the gas-pressurised EMS were still cumbersome and inflexible.

"Ten, nine, eight..." Aliyaah counted down to launch as the hangar doors opened and they braced themselves for the onslaught of dust. "Zero."

The rover jolted forward and headed out into the swirl of dust and dim red light. Silver followed it with her eyes for as long as she could, then turned back to the panel to look for any signs of trouble.

"She's out and all systems look good," Silver said as Aliyaah closed the hangar doors, leaving the rover alone outside the station.

They restored pressure in the hangar and Silver watched as the dust settled. Aliyaah pulled off her gloves and unbuckled Silver's tether. Silver did the same for her. They both removed their suits, and Silver hung them back up by the airlock, then pulled the canteen from her pocket and took a drink. The sight of so much dust always made her thirsty.

Silver offered the canteen to Aliyaah, who shook her head and said, "I'll go and let the Commander know our girl's launched. Keep monitoring and let me know if anything comes up." She turned to walk towards the airlock, then paused and turned back, putting a hand on Silver's shoulder. "And..."

"I know," Silver smiled up at the Chief. "I'll pay special attention to the navigation array."

Aliyaah laughed, covering her mouth. "I was going to say good work Antara. But, yeah, you make sure our baby doesn't get lost out there."

Silver watched Aliyaah head out through the airlock, and smiled at the Chief's futile attempt to brush the layer of dust from her overalls, and to shake it from her hair. The red particulate got everywhere, despite the station's air filters. Silver felt like it was part of her now, having breathed it in for sols on end. She would run her hands through her hair and feel the scratch of the planet on her scalp. She felt it in her lungs, her eyes. A thin red film over everything she touched.

A light on the control panel flickered for an instant, drawing Silver's attention. Nothing was lit up that shouldn't be active. Silver held her gaze steady at the panel, unblinking, but nothing else happened. Rover Four was doing just fine, on its way to the quarry fifty kilometres away; from there it would continue to explore beyond their current perimeter. Rover Four carried RIMSE, the Radar Imager for Mars Subsurface Experiment; Equipment that sent radar waves into the ground to look for signs of water beneath the surface.

Most of the red planet's water was concentrated at the north and south poles, but earlier rover models and a series of orbiters had found evidence of deep ice closer to the equator where the colony was situated. Until the planet warmed, the equatorial zone was the only area reasonably habitable by humans, given the sub-zero temperatures throughout most of the year. The only water they had found close by was frozen deep underground, but there were signs that water had flowed on the planet's surface in this region at some point in the past.

Watching the panel, Silver waited another ten seconds before blinking. As the dust cleared from her eyes, she wondered, not for the first time, if she should start using the cats-eye implants like Aliyaah and most of the crew. The lenses had been rolled out to help counteract Astronaut Ophthalmic Syndrome while they were in zero gravity, but had the bonus of being self-cleaning and helping with focus through the ever-changing light of the dust storms. Some models had been fitted with automated blue light filters, programmable to an individual's shift pattern to aid melatonin regulation. Silver found it unsettling how quickly biohacking had taken hold. Almost all the crew had elected to have melatonin pumps fitted back on Earth, to help regulate their sleep and blood sugar, but Silver had held back, opting for just the regular med-pump on her thigh.

She had always had twenty-twenty vision and impeccable physical health. This feeling of infallibility was a source of pride for her, and her good genetic luck and careful stewardship of her health had played no small part in helping her qualify for multiple missions before Project Arche even got off the ground.

While she could appreciate, intellectually at least, the potential advantages of implants like the cats-eyes, she found it distasteful and unnerving to think about exploring a planet through eyes that weren't entirely her own. She had removed the lenses shortly after landing on the planet, and hadn't planned on wearing them again until the return trip to Earth. Cooper would have laughed at such reluctance, pointing out how much technology already mediated Silver's interaction with the red planet. Cooper, who, for years, had wanted every new device and gadget the instant it was released. Cooper, who had turned her back on that childlike wonder and stopped working at the leading edge of technology.

A light flickered on the panel, showing a sudden, brief flare of radiologic activity around the rover. Silver waited for thirty seconds but nothing else happened. She began a full diagnostic sweep. She did not want to lose the rover and have to take the Space Exploration Vehicle out thirty or forty clicks to tow it home manually.

She checked the navigation array and then the comms array on the rover, listening for any odd noises in the craft itself. All she could hear was the low fuzz of static courtesy of the howling dust. She left the line open and checked all the other systems, finding nothing of concern.

As Silver moved her hand to deactivate comms, she heard something that made her pause. She realised that she had been hearing it for the past few minutes, it just hadn't registered as unusual. Faintly audible among the static and dull roar was what sounded like a voice, speaking a language she didn't understand. It had to be a crossed line with the workers at the quarry, Silver thought. But, for a second, the quality of the voice changed and Silver could have sworn it sounded like her daughter, speaking clumsy toddler French.

Silver gave herself a shake. She was tired, that was all. They had been working hard to get the rover back out into the field and she hadn't been sleeping well, waking in a cold sweat most nights with her head full of thoughts about home. She wondered if she should reconsider the melatonin pump, if it would help her sleep better. She should at least make an appointment to see the station's primary physician, Doctor Claire Schiff, and see if her restless nights were a sign of some fault in her biochemistry.

Silver continued to scan the rover's feedback, then laughed at herself. No, what she really needed was to talk to her kid and take a hot shower to wash off some of this infernal dust.

TWO

After the first humans had landed on Mars in 2025, the planet had slowly begun to be populated by astronauts and scientists from a variety of nations. Project Arche marked a turning point, as an international effort to establish a long-term colony on the red planet. *Octavia* was the first rocket designed to bring civilians to the planet, to make it a home and not just an exploratory outpost.

Everyone who had signed up for Project Arche and the *Octavia* mission, including Silver, knew that they would most likely be away for at least twenty-six months, if not fifty-two. There were only ever small windows for timely travel between Earth and Mars, when the planets' orbits brought them closest together. Outside of those windows, flights were too long and too costly, and so would only be undertaken in an absolute emergency.

Silver had been studying Mars for years before Project Arche was announced. Her time at NASA, the European Space Agency, and on board SkyBase, the successor to the International Space Station, made her the ideal candidate for the crew of *Octavia*. Silver had also flown on several civilian space flights in collaboration with the private enterprise SolarEx, so she was uniquely placed to bridge the public and private spheres of space travel.

As a private company, SolarEx had different goals and ideals from the governmental agencies. They also had alternative criteria for candidacy, and it was SolarEx that had insisted on bringing civilians along for this trip. Some critics had said it was too soon to send untrained astronauts, but it made a certain kind of sense to Silver. Aside from bringing in much-needed financial investment from private citizens, opening the flight up to civilians also meant that the crew could bring family along.

One of the hardest things about being in space was being away from family and friends, from people who didn't just talk about navigation arrays and coupling malfunctions even when off duty. Silver and her wife had tried to stick to a rule of not talking shop at home, but their passion for their work had made that hard at times.

When SolarEx made the announcement to her team, Silver had assumed that Cooper would greet the news enthusiastically and sign up right away. Instead, Cooper had stayed silent, then looked over at their daughter, Cosima, who was playing with her trains on the living room floor. Cooper looked back at Silver as if to ask if she had forgotten they had a daughter.

Cosima had been two and a half then, and she sensed the shift in energy as her parents watched her without saying a word.

"You be enjunneer," Cosima said, breaking the silence and holding out a green train. "Oh no! I'm broken!" she cried, waving the train at Silver. "You be enjunneer."

Silver walked over to sit beside Cosima, taking the green train and making a show of scrutinising the toy for malfunctions. "Ah," Silver said, her tone serious. "You have a fuel leak and a dangerous loss of pressure."

"Fix it! Fix it!" Cosima screamed happily, jumping up and down before running over to Cooper with another toy.

Cooper held out her hand and sighed as Cosima placed a tiny rocket in her palm.

"You be the rocket, Mama."

Cooper closed her hand around the toy, feeling the sharp plastic wings dig into her skin.

"Not this time, sweetheart." She looked down at her daughter and then over at Silver, cross legged on the floor. "Mama's going to sit this one out."

Silver took a slow breath, then scrambled over to Cosima and scooped her up, spinning her upside down. "Woah! You're in a space tumble!" Silver said as Cosima giggled and begged to be tumbled again.

"I'm gonna crash, Mima!"

"I've got you, space cadet," Silver said, looking over the top of Cosima's feet at her wife. Cooper shook her head and walked away. From the sound of crashing pans in the kitchen, Silver knew there would be a fight after they put Cosima to bed. She had fooled herself into thinking that Cooper's previous work on Project Arche meant that she would jump at a second chance to go to Mars. Silver could present all the logical arguments she wanted, that they could afford it, and Cosima would be back just in time to start kindergarten, but if Cooper didn't want to go, there'd be no persuading her. Silver watched Cosima playing with her toys and shook her head. Who wouldn't want to be the kid in class who had already been to Mars?

Silver wondered if it would make a difference if Cooper and Cosima saw the transport ship. Cooper was probably imagining a cramped shuttle like the one she had flown in to dock at SkyBase before Cosima was born. Cooper had spent a couple of days at SkyBase, which, while more luxurious than the ISS, was still far from child-friendly.

The trip to Mars was different though. The civilians would spend most of their time in the cryochambers in a carefully controlled sleep programme, and for the time that they did spend awake, *Octavia* had dedicated civilian quarters with a games room, plush berths, and all manner of creature comforts. The launch and landing would be hard on Cosima's body, but not unreasonable, and once they were in space they would have artificial gravity most of the time. They would also have a lot of anti-nausea meds, just in case, and Cosima was young and adaptable and adventurous. If Silver had been given the chance to go to Mars when she was a kid, she'd have had no hesitation, and she reasoned that if SolarEx had any doubts about having children on board, they wouldn't have given her the green light to invite Cooper and Cosima.

Silver didn't know if the rest of the crew had signed up their families, or which civilians had paid to be on the trip. It was possible, Silver thought, that Cosima would be the first child in space, and she felt a swell of pride at that idea. As much as Silver disliked having to perform for the media, she knew how powerful a message that could be for the world at large.

"We're not puppets, Silver. You can't just pick us up and make us dance to make some grand political statement about diversity." Cooper was changing the sheets on their bed, and Silver worried for the future of a pillow as Cooper shoved it violently into a fresh mauve case.

"Oh, come on, Coops. You've got to admit that we're a pretty photogenic family. Imagine the headlines: 'Gays for Space'," Silver couldn't help but laugh.

Cooper glared at her, and Silver realised that humour wasn't going to help her during this particular conversation. She picked up the other pillow case and said, "It's just, it's an amazing opportunity, Coops. Not just for us as a family, but to inspire everyone back on Earth."

"Do you even hear yourself?" Cooper asked, throwing a naked pillow to Silver. "'Back on Earth.' Goddamnit, Sil. You are on Earth right now, remember? With us. Or have you mentally checked out of this planet already?"

"That's not what I mean. You're being...." Silver stopped herself and took a breath. She stuffed the pillow into the case and then held it to her chest and said, "I get that it's a whole load of unknowns. And, yeah, there are risks, but if you just saw *Octavia*, you'd see she's totally different to the shuttles you've flown. Cosima would love it. You'd love it! And you'd get to be in space without even having to push a button or write a status report."

Cooper sat down heavily on the bed and twisted the duvet cover in her hands. "I'm not being unreasonable. I'm not."

Silver sat down beside Cooper, just close enough that their thighs touched. She looked over at Cooper, but Cooper kept her gaze fixed on the floor.

"You're excited. You always are when you're about to leave. But I just can't get fired up at the prospect of you being away for two years."

"So come with me," Silver said, reaching across to put her hand on Cooper's leg.

Cooper looked up at Silver and shook her head slowly. She let the bedding slide off her lap and shuffled back on the bed. "No, Sil. My life is here. Cosima's life is here."

"But, you're my life, you and Cosima," Silver said, feeling the thickness of tears behind her eyes.

"We're not though, are we?" Cooper lay back on the bed, letting her tears fall onto the fresh sheets.

"That's not fair, Cooper. We knew going into this that one or the other of us would be away for long stretches. We both signed up for this life." Silver lay down beside Cooper and gently turned her face so she could kiss her. Then she rested her head against Cooper's shoulder and said, "This is the life we wanted, right? We're so lucky. I just don't understand why you've changed your mind about this."

Cooper swallowed hard and pulled away from Silver. "Things are different now. Since Cosima was born, this is it for me. I don't want to leave. And I don't want you to leave, - "

"But - "

"Please, let me finish," Cooper said. She sat up on her elbows and looked down at Silver, holding her gaze. "I don't want you to leave, but I know you will. I know you have to, and that's OK. But I'm not coming with you, and neither is Cosima."

"What are you saying?" Silver asked, sitting up and placing her hands gently on Coopers face. "Is this, are you...."

"We want different things now. I've changed." Cooper shook her head, and Silver let her hands fall into her lap.

"But it's just one mission. It's just two years," Silver said, looking down at her hands and resisted the urge to pick at the glittery mess of pink polish Cosima had painted her nails with the day before.

"Don't lie to yourself, Sil. Don't lie to me, or to Cosima. We both know it's not just this mission. Even when you get back, you'll be preparing for the next one, and the next. Or maybe you'll end up staying on Mars. Your life is up there, not here with us. That's just how it is."

"That's not true," Silver said quietly. "I can still call it off. I can let the Director know first thing in the morning that he needs to find a replacement."

"But that won't change anything. Not really. You'll just be here wishing you were there. You'll resent me. You'll resent our daughter. I can't live like that, and I can't live every day while you're gone waiting to hear if you're even coming home."

"So, you're leaving me?" Silver said quietly, trying to clasp Cooper's hands to pull her closer.

Cooper resisted, and took a step backwards. "You already left, Sil. You left when you said yes to Mars."

THREE

"Flight Engineer Antara to Hangar Five. FE Antara, Hangar Five."

The announcement blared out of the computer near Silver's bed and jolted her from a dream. Within seconds she was on her feet and pulling on her overalls. She rubbed her eyes and looked over at the clock on the computer, where the emergency signal was still flashing.

4.37 am.

She wasn't due to start her shift until noon. Something must have gone wrong with Rover Four again, she thought, letting out an exasperated sigh. Her EV suit hung by the door and she thought about taking it with her, but surely the alert would have told her to bring it if it was necessary. She left it and slid open the door to her cabin.

She could hear footsteps approaching quickly, so she carefully stepped outside and stuck close to the wall as she closed the door behind her.

Aliyaah appeared around the corner and Silver was relieved to see she was just wearing her overalls.

"What's going on?" Silver asked as she hurried to keep up with the much taller Chief, who had begun sprinting to the hangar.

"An accident at the quarry," the Chief said.

"Why do they need us?" Silver asked, trying to catch a breath and wishing there had been enough time for her to stretch out her sleepy limbs before this early morning sprint down the narrow hallways of the

13

station.

"There's an issue with a refiner," Aliyaah said. "There were injuries. A miner's trapped in the machine."

"Jesus," Silver said as they reached the airlock leading to the hangar.

"Yeah." Aliyaah drummed her fingers against the airlock door and looked sideways at Silver. Someone was already in the airlock, going through decontamination, which would take another thirty seconds or so. Silver was glad of the excuse to catch her breath, and made a mental note to start using the station's gym more frequently.

Aliyaah, who had barely broken a sweat, gave Silver a concerned look, but it didn't seem to be a commentary on her fitness. "I don't know what we're about to walk into," Aliyaah said. "But I'm guessing it's not pretty."

The airlock opened and they ran through decontamination as quickly as they could. When they walked out into the hangar, they were confronted with a chaotic scene. The great hulk of the refiner crowded the centre of the hangar, surrounded by miners and engineers, some of whom Silver suspected had hitched a ride on the machine. A couple of the miners were still hanging onto the side of the refiner, and everyone seemed to be yelling at once.

The refiner, which only just fit in the hangar at some twenty feet tall, was coated in red dust. The air was thick with the smell of it. One engineer was trying to make space in the crowd so that he could get an aerial work platform up next to the refiner.

Aliyaah ran over and took charge, helping to clear a path. Silver followed her and repeated Aliyaah's call for the hangar to be cleared of everyone aside from essential personnel. If this turned out to be a grisly retrieval, rather than a rescue, it was best to limit the number of witnesses.

When she reached the platform, Silver saw that another engineer had already climbed up.

"Yo, Sil," Jaz held out her hand to haul Silver up beside her and Silver reluctantly took it. Jaz grinned at her and said, "Crazy shit, right?"

Silver gave a small nod as her only reply. She had done her best to avoid sharing shifts with Jaz, who she found to be mouthy and arrogant. She suspected that Jaz was tampering with her implants to boost her levels of growth hormone and testosterone, but Silver wouldn't fink on her, not unless she had hard evidence and thought it was affecting Jaz's ability to carry out her duties. There had been an incident a couple of years earlier, where some younger astronaut candidates had been reported for tweaking. They were thrown out of the programme, but were snapped up by private enterprises like SolarEx. The academy had a zero-tolerance policy on tweaking, but that just made folks more adept at hiding what they were doing.

Right now, Jaz seemed amped up and smelled to Silver like a mix of stale sweat, the inside of an old flight suit, and some cloying body spray. The floral scent didn't seem to fit, and Silver wondered if Jaz was trying to mask a T-induced change in body odour. If she was tampering with her med pump to help her bulk up, it was working. Jaz was ripped. Silver tried not to stare, but Jaz had her orange overalls tied at her waist and was wearing just a white vest that showed off some serious muscles. Jaz caught Silver looking and smirked at her. Maybe there was something else driving Jaz to tweak. Maybe she was already working with Doctor Schiff. Who was Silver to judge?

The space programme had been officially opened to trans and non-binary people a few years earlier, but the barriers to education and opportunity for anyone not cisgender had left a legacy that would take decades to overcome. Silver didn't know of any astronauts or even astronaut candidates who were trans or genderqueer. Space remained one of the last few places where the gender binary was painfully persistent, despite the increased access to drugs that were previously hard to come by. Everyone in the space program had been fitted with a hormone implant, but these were closely monitored, so there was little freedom for anyone to figure things out on their own terms.

Silver had no interest in tweaking her own implant, and was well aware that a double standard would apply if she was even suspected of doing so. She didn't like to dwell on it, but Silver knew that her position on the team, as a woman married to another woman, was still an issue for some of her colleagues. No one could question her commitment, expertise, or her physical readiness, even after having had a child, but that didn't always matter, especially for a woman of colour. Still, while she sympathised with those taking advantage of improved access to hormones to help them transition, she was uncomfortable with the potential safety issues for anyone tweaking without proper supervision.

Silver glanced sideways again at Jaz, and worried about her colleague. Jaz looked far from healthy. Her pale, clammy skin seemed almost to glow under the bright hangar lights. Jaz moved closer to Silver and angled a screen her way. She'd located the video footage from the accident at the refinery.

"Looks like a real clusterfuck," Jaz said. "Some explosion, huh?"

Silver nodded and said, "Is that the radiological alarm?"

"Yeah. They'd just loaded a refiner up with rock from the north of the quarry. Guess the old girl didn't like her new diet."

"That area of the quarry hadn't been mined before?" Silver asked, and Jaz shook her head. She worked out there more often than Silver, helping the miners maintain the machines.

"One of the guys got inside to take a look."

"While the radiological alarm was sounding and the machine was still powered up?" Silver asked, appalled at the riskiness of such a move.

"Nah, they're not that stupid." Jaz shook her head at Silver. "It was a false alarm. They scanned again before he climbed down. His suit should have handled the background radiation just fine."

"So, what? The alarm was an anomaly?" Silver asked.

Jaz shrugged. "I guess. Some weird shit happens out at the quarry. Don't even get me started. This one time -"

"So, the machine was powered off?" Silver said, interrupting Jaz. She had no desire to hear about the exploits of the miners. The quarry already had a reputation at the station as the place to go for a little unsanctioned R and R.

Jaz pouted, clearly wanting a better audience than Silver. She looked back at the video footage and said, "I don't know. The guys are totally sure, one hundred percent, that they cut the juice. It just started up on its own, or some shit."

"That's impossible," Silver said, trying not to think about what she was about to see as they reached the top of the machine.

"Well, yeah, but that's what they said happened," Jaz said, eyeballing Silver as the platform juddered to a stop near the top of the refiner. Jaz released the gate at the front of the platform and was about to step out onto the side of the refiner, but Silver put out a hand to stop her.

Silver called down to Aliyaah. "This thing is definitely inactive, right?"

Aliyaah yelled up confirmation that they had cut the lines from the power cells, then tapped her ear to tell Silver to activate her intercom.

Jaz stepped forward and Silver followed her to the rail that bordered the massive hole at the centre of the machine. This was where the quarry workers dumped the extracted rock, to be processed into the elements needed to keep the station functioning; to make fuel and construction materials; and to provide the minerals for the biodomes where they would grow the food they would need for a self-sustaining colony. Now, somewhere in the depths of the machine, there was a lost miner, or what was left of him.

"If he's in there, he's fucked, right?" Jaz said, voicing Silver's own concern. "There's no way this guy's not mincemeat," Jaz looked over at Silver and raised an eyebrow.

Silver shared Jaz's doubts, but said, "We have to operate on the assumption that he could still be trapped. There's a chance he avoided getting, er, processed."

"Ha! Processed. Yeah. But if he fell through those first large blades into the real belly of this bitch, he's just pulp now. And that's if he didn't get crushed by any boulders."

Silver swallowed, not wanting to entertain the images that kept crowding her mind. She stepped up beside Jaz and began a sweep of the interior with the flashlight on her utility belt.

"Nada," Jaz said. "Can't see a goddamn thing."

"Do you have your cats-eyes in, Specialist?" Silver asked.

"Yeah, I'll switch to infrared."

Jaz leaned farther over the railing as Silver held the back of her suit. "See anything?"

"Nope. I can't even make out the blades. It's weird."

Silver frowned. "They're probably just halfway through a rotation, right?"

"I don't think so. It's like there's nothing in there at all."

Silver pulled Jaz back upright and Jaz blinked several times.

"Perhaps you should reset the cats-eyes?" Silver said, and as Jaz began a manual reset, Silver hooked her suit to the back of the platform and then turned her back to the dark void of the refiner. The cacophony of voices from the hangar below grew muffled, as Silver leaned back and took a step to lower herself into the refiner, holding her weight against the tether and the steep side of the machine's innards. Silver held the flashlight in one hand and angled it downward, illuminating the darkness. She could see the large blades below her, but no sign of the miner or even any rock residue.

There was a sudden screech of metal and the tether holding Silver went suddenly slack, causing her to drop her flashlight and tip backward until she was almost horizontal across the top of the refiner. The flashlight danced around on its lanyard, scattering light haphazardly until it stilled, shining its light uselessly against the wall of the machine.

"Sorry, boss!" Jaz yelled from above. "Tether's jammed. You gotta come back up."

As Jaz began to slowly haul her back in, Silver gripped the tether with both hands. The flashlight jiggled on the lanyard, bumped against the metal wall, and clicked off. Silver looked down into the darkness. The emptiness was thick, swallowing light and sound, drawing Silver in deeper. There was something in the dark, though. Silver could feel it. The absence of light wasn't absolute, and Silver saw pinpricks of colour dancing briefly across her vision, almost like spores or dust motes catching the tiniest fleck of light.

Once she was upright again, Silver walked herself back up the inside of the refiner and, realising she had been holding her breath, exhaled. As she breathed in again, Silver noticed that the air inside the machine had a dank odour. The dust on the refiner had begun to lift in slow, soft clouds as it warmed in the hangar air, and Silver's eyes grew itchy. She blinked and turned her head once more to face the dark abyss of the refiner.

After a second or two, Silver noticed a sound, quiet at first, like the tick of a car engine just after it stops running. Then the sound began to change, speeding up until the clicks began to resemble a voice. Silver recoiled, not sure if she could trust what she was hearing.

"What is it?" Jaz said, as she held out her hand to help Silver back onto the platform.

"I think I heard something."

Jaz's eyes widened, the cats-eyes flickering from yellow to red. "Holy crap! You think he's in there? Alive?"

Silver hesitated. That had to be what she'd heard. The muffled sound of the missing miner calling out for help from deep in the belly of the machine. She thought about the light flickering on the control panel for the rover, the brief radiologic flare, and the strange voice she had heard echoing back at her from outside the colony. Silver still wasn't sure that the voice she had just heard wasn't simply inside her head. It hadn't sounded like a man's voice, nor a real cry for help. Had it just been her inner voice, an audio memory?

No, whatever she had heard must have come from the darkness of the refiner. To admit her doubt would be to get a one-way ticket to the medical bay.

Before Silver could say anything, Jaz yelled down to the crowd below. "We hear him! He's gotta be alive!" Jaz grinned at Silver, and slapped her on the back. There were cheers from the few personnel remaining on the hangar deck, and Silver looked down to see Aliyaah smiling up at her, her face questioning but excited.

Jaz had hooked up a new tether, and was already in a harness. "Clip me in, boss. I got this." Silver was about to argue, but then attached the tether to Jaz's harness and watched her step down off the platform. "Let me down slow, Sil."

Silver nodded, annoyed at Jaz's presumption of intimacy. She outranked Jaz, had significantly more experience, and considered such lapses in protocol to be signs of a wider disregard for procedure that could compromise safety and mission success.

As Jaz stepped backward into the dark chasm of the machine, Silver pushed aside her annoyance, and began to feel relieved, and then a little guilty, that Jaz had jumped at the chance to be a hero and rescue the miner. It made a certain kind of sense, Silver reasoned, given that Jaz was a Lidar expert and could interpret the scope's readout faster than Silver could. Silver had fitted Lidar equipment to the rovers; it was what they used to detect organic matter in the dust of the planet. Essentially, Lidar was the tool of choice for finding any signs of life on Mars.

Jaz tugged twice at the tether, and Silver let out a little more slack.

"Do you see anything?" Silver called down. She could see Jaz's face glowing as she held the flashlight in her mouth and slowly walked her feet down the refiner wall.

"Nada."

Silver wondered if she'd sent Jaz on a fool's errand. She had definitely heard something, though, and they needed to check out the refiner to be sure. She let out a little more slack, holding the handle of the winch tightly with both hands.

"I'm on the first set of blades," Jaz called up. "Give me a little more. I'm gonna look over with the scope."

Silver yelled down to tell Jaz to activate her headset then gave her some more slack. When the rope was taut again, Silver held the winch secure with one hand and used the other to check the live feed from Jaz's scope as it showed up on the work platform control panel. Jaz activated her headset and Silver heard her mumbling about needing more hands.

"Are you getting the Lidar feed?" Jaz asked, and Silver confirmed, as did Aliyaah, who was on the same channel.

The scanner showed a diffuse heat signature in the space around Jaz, but nothing indicating a body, alive or recently dead. The heat was likely residual from the working of the refiner. The dense metal of the grinding blades retained heat well, and they also blocked the scanner, meaning that Silver wouldn't be able to pick up anything below or above whichever level Jaz was at. Jaz would have to move carefully around the metal, dropping the scope in ahead of her each time.

Aliyaah let them know that the CP, Command Pilot Andrew Hadley, had arrived and wanted an update. Hadley was second in command of the mission and was watching Aliyaah and her team closely. "Switch to the secure line, Antara. You too, Specialist Viper."

"Yes, Sir," Silver said.

Once their line was secure, Hadley asked if they had found anything.

"Nothing yet, Sir," Silver said.

Jaz's voice cut through the static. "Just a whole heck of darkness and dust. Not even any blood."

"I guess that's a good sign," Aliyaah said, but Silver wondered how the miner could have survived a fall into the machine, even without it being active. If the machine had jumped to life with him inside, there should be some evidence of that, however grisly.

The line was silent for thirty seconds or so, aside from the static, and there was still no sign of the missing man on the scope. After a few more seconds, Silver noticed something odd in the diagnostic array.

"CP Hadley, Chief, is everyone seeing this?"

"What is that, Specialist Viper?" Aliyaah asked.

"Viper?" Silver said. "You there?" There was no reply, just static. "Jaz, come in, or I'm going to winch you up." Silver had never seen the array lit up like this, and she didn't like not knowing what she was seeing.

She studied the scope's feed closely, and watched as a bright cluster slowly coalesced at the edge of the image. It was almost as if whatever was down there was gathering together to form some kind of organic mass.

"Antara, is that thing moving?" Aliyaah asked, incredulous.

"I... " Silver knew it must be, but wanted to believe it was a malfunction with the Lidar.

"Winch her up now," Aliyaah said, her voice shaking. "Viper, get out of there. That's an order."

Silver cranked the handle to reel Jaz back in. When Jaz still didn't answer, Silver turned the crank faster still, not wanting to injure her by banging her against the blades as she hauled her up, but wary of how quickly the image from the Lidar was changing. The tether was still taut, but something was in the machine with Jaz, and she hadn't responded for at least a minute.

Aliyaah and Hadley yelled for Silver to get Jaz out, then they all fell silent at the sound of the radiological alarm, accompanied by a sudden flash on the Lidar feed, showing a huge organic signature. The screen went blank. No static, no voices, no more light, just the sound of the alarm for a couple more seconds, and then silence.

"Jaz?" Silver said softly, "You there?" There was no longer any resistance as Silver turned the crank. The tether twisted itself up towards her, and Silver saw the carabiners dancing free on the ends.

"What just happened?" Aliyaah's voice cut back in. "What was that? Do you have her, Antara?"

"No, Chief. She's gone. The tether... came free somehow." Silver wondered for a moment if Jaz had unhooked it herself, and then her thoughts were interrupted as the refiner groaned, as if the blades were about to start turning. "Cut the power!" Silver shouted, "Turn it off!"

"It is off!" Aliyaah yelled back.

Silver grabbed at the carabiners, thinking for a second that she should go in after Jaz. Her palms blistered, and she dropped the carabiners. The metal was scorching hot.

The metallic groaning stopped abruptly and a fresh plume of hot red dust soared up from the chasm of the refiner. Silver stepped back and covered her eyes until it dispersed. She turned to look at the scope's feed. The screen was blank. There was no signal, and no sign of Jaz or the miner. The machine was silent, dead silent. Jaz had vanished into the darkness.

FOUR

"Come on, people. I want this thing stripped down, now!" Aliyaah
clapped her hands and watched the crew surround the refiner and
begin dismantling the machine. She turned to Silver; "This is so bizarre."

Silver nodded. After she had descended the platform to rejoin the
rest of the crew, the station's Commander had arrived. He pulled aside
Hadley, the Chief, and Silver. When none of them could provide an
explanation for Jaz's disappearance, the Commander had expressed his
displeasure in no uncertain terms. He immediately ordered that the
refiner be decommissioned and taken apart so they could ascertain why
it had malfunctioned and what had happened to Jaz and the missing
miner. "Something happened out at the quarry," he said, "and you're
going to figure it out so it doesn't happen again."

By mid-morning they had removed the exoskeleton of the refiner,
exposing its bones and the inner wall of the processing chamber. The
titanium plates were wrapped in carbon composite fibres and soldered
together at such an extreme temperature that it would be an enormous
feat to cut them apart. They were designed to withstand the pressure of
the liquid helium that was used to power the rotating blades inside the
propellant tanks.

Aliyaah cleared all crew members from the hangar, except for
Silver and the two engineers tasked with breaking the seals. The
Commander had asked to be updated as soon as they found anything,

but Aliyaah had nothing to report.

While the men worked, Silver discussed her concerns about the helium with Aliyaah. If there had been a rupture in the helium tank, that could have caused a massive explosion inside the refiner as the pressurised liquid vaporised. Anyone caught in that cloud of helium gas would have frozen or suffocated rapidly. An explosion could explain the disappearance of Jaz and the miner, but it didn't explain the strange organic signature they had seen on the scope, or the heat and radiation they had detected. A rupture in the tank was the only hypothesis they had that made any kind of sense, though.

Aliyaah had been thinking along the same lines, hence her clearing of the hangar. If another tank ruptured while the machinery was so exposed, it could easily cause an explosion and send shards of metal flying out at them at an incredibly high speed, not to mention the frostbite and other risks of exposure.

Silver and Aliyaah looked over at the engineers, in full protective gear, working on the seals. Silver checked the visor on her helmet and took a step back, gently pulling Aliyaah with her.

After several more hours, the younger engineer turned to face Silver and Aliyaah and said, "We're in, Chief."

"OK. Let's ease this side off and see what we've got." Aliyaah directed Silver, who climbed into the cab of the floor operated crane. She moved the hoist chain over to the refiner and the engineers attached the hook to the inner wall. Silver waited for the men to stand aside and then began to retract the chain as smoothly as possible to detach the giant sheet of metal. The crane struggled against the weight, and Silver shot Aliyaah a look.

"I'm going to have to give it everything, Chief."

Aliyaah nodded, and moved even farther back from the refiner, taking the two engineers with her.

Silver put the crane in reverse and quickly retracted the hoist chain. The metal wrenched away from the refiner, tipping toward the cab where she was seated. She gunned the crane and backed away. When the dust cleared, she jumped out of the cab and ran over to the refiner, to join the Chief and the two engineers.

"I thought this thing had been cleared out at the site?" Aliyaah said, and Silver saw that there was about two feet of red dust covering the bottom of the refiner.

"It was, Chief," said the younger engineer. "We made sure to clear it straight away, so there was a way out through the chute."

"So why is there all this material there now?" Aliyaah asked.

"Maybe it got jammed?" Silver said. "That might explain the heat build-up too. If the machinery was trying to turn and there was something stuck, that's a lot of energy." She stepped forward and climbed onto the chassis of the refiner. Silver picked up a handful of the red dust and let it run through the fingers of her glove. Some larger particulate seemed to shimmer. Silver wondered at first if what she was seeing were ice crystals, caused by some escaped helium, but the ambient temperature wasn't cold enough for whatever this was to have stayed frozen. Silver held out her hand to Aliyaah. "Chief, what does this look like to you?"

Aliyaah stepped up and then crouched down to examine the dust for herself. "What the -?"

Silver used the microscope on her visor to look more closely at the dust. "It's filament-like. It must have been in the rock from the quarry."

"Get a sample, and get it tested," Aliyaah said to the second engineer. "Make sure you use an RMC," she said, gesturing at the containers for radioactive material, and then tapping the blackened radiation detection strip on the outside of her suit. "And, Specialist, this is classified. Got it?"

The engineer nodded and turned to retrieve an RMC.

"I'll inform the Commander," Silver said, but Aliyaah put a hand on Silver's arm and shook her head.

In a voice low enough that the men couldn't hear her, Aliyaah said, "Report your findings to CP Hadley."

Silver nodded, curious as to what Aliyaah was thinking. She barely had any reason to interact with the Commander as the Chief was her direct supervisor. She saw the Commander on occasion in the mess hall and passed him in the corridors. He was every inch the typical gruff alpha male military type, and Silver remembered him being stern and distant, and not the best of lecturers, at the academy.

Aliyaah pulled Silver aside as the younger engineer filled the RMC with a sample of the dust and the crystalline substance.

"Between you and me, Antara, the Commander hasn't been feeling at his best since he went out to oversee the quarry expansion two sols ago. Maybe it's radiation sickness. Or the stress of the power outages over the last sevensol. All I know is that the CP is doing a double shift so the Commander can get some rest. Let's not disturb him until we have something concrete to report."

"Yes, Chief," Silver said, giving Aliyaah a curious look. It wasn't like Aaliyah to mention a fellow officer's state of mind, and Silver could only imagine that she must be more concerned about the Commander than her carefully chosen words let on.

Aliyaah gave Silver a grim smile, then walked over to check on the engineer collecting the sample.

"Chief," he said quietly as he looked at the rock through the microscope on his visor, "I minored in geochemistry, and this is weird."

Silver and Aliyaah looked at each other, and Aliyaah said slowly, "What are you thinking, Specialist?" She crouched down beside the engineer and looked at the rock in the RMC.

"I think we should get the lab to test mineral composition, and... for any organic material. It's just that..." the engineer paused, then stood up and turned to face Aliyaah and Silver. "So, these look like selenite crystals, or aragonite, or tridymite, maybe, but there's something off about them. I just can't place it. And, anyway, you only get those in areas of extreme heat, like in a volcano. And there's no volcano out at the quarry site, not that we know of. The nearest one is Atlas mons."

"Could the explosions from the quarry have caused this kind of crystal formation?" Aliyaah asked.

"I can't say for sure, but it's pretty unlikely, Sir. They just don't form that quickly. Not usually."

"So, these must be from the north end of the quarry."

"Unless..." the engineer hesitated.

"Spit it out, Specialist," Aliyaah said.

"Well, we don't really know what happened in the refiner. Just now, I mean. Specialist Viper just vanished." The Specialist stared into the exposed interior of the machine.

"And now we have this strange, potentially organic material," Aliyaah said, mostly to herself.

"And there was that intense burst of heat," Silver said, and held out her hands, turning them over to show the carabiner-shaped burns on her palms.

FIVE

Silver, Aliyaah, and the remaining engineer worked for several hours, carefully sifting through the material at the bottom of the refiner. They quickly located what remained of the missing headset, which was bent and buckled as if subjected to intense heat.

Silver kept expecting to come across bone remnants or a shred of Jaz's orange overalls hiding in the red dust. In many ways, she hoped that they wouldn't find anything, but they needed answers and Hadley was pressuring them to provide an explanation for what had happened on the hangar deck. During one of several check-ins, Silver overheard Hadley tell Aliyaah that the Commander was running a fever and seemed delusional. He remained in his quarters, and Silver got the impression that this wasn't entirely voluntary on the Commander's part.

Silver and Aliyaah initially focused their search around the spot where they had found the headset, carefully filtering the dust for signs of ash, bone, or anything else organic. Aside from some additional crystals and pieces of misshapen metal that could have come from Jaz's suit, they had found nothing of note. They extended the search outward and were close to completing a first pass of all the dust in the refiner. The engineer ran everything through a secondary scanner, putting into a lead-lined box any material that showed signs of radiation. The crystals and metallic pieces were the only things they found that were larger than grains of sand and these were localised to a half metre zone around the misshapen headset.

This kind of refiner was exquisitely designed to process the quarried rock into a fine particulate for mineral extraction. Silver thought about the two similar refiners still operating out at the quarry. The CP had decided to let them keep working. After all, the colony needed an almost constant supply of new material to function, and having idle miners wandering the station would probably create more problems than they were already facing.

All the workers wore suits that protected them from the level of radiation they had detected in these small crystal samples, but Silver still worried that there may be larger sources of radiation on-site. If, indeed, the crystals had originated at the quarry. When Silver spoke to Hadley earlier, he agreed that the miners should exercise extreme caution as they continued their work, but Silver remained troubled by the idea that the crystals had somehow formed inside the refiner while Jaz was in there. The thought made Silver's stomach lurch, and she shivered.

"You should take a break," Aliyaah said, surprising Silver by touching her lightly on the back. "Go get some coffee and something to eat. There's not much else we can do here."

"That'd be good, thanks," Silver said, getting unsteadily to her feet and dusting off her suit. "My shift starts soon anyway." She smiled and sighed in rapid succession.

Aliyaah waved her hand dismissively. "I'll get someone to cover your shift. Now that Rover Four is back up and running, we'll be OK without you for a while. You should get some rest."

"It has been a hell of a morning, Chief," Silver said. "I'm not sure it's even really sunk in yet."

"Viper?"

"Yeah."

Aliyaah put her hand on Silver's arm and opened her mouth to say something but couldn't find any words.

"We weren't really friends. But in a place like this, well..." Silver looked up as she felt tears forming. She didn't want to cry in front of the Chief, but the weight of the situation was finally beginning to hit now that she wasn't focused on a specific task.

"She was a fantastic engineer," Aliyaah said, "and I heard she could be a lot of fun, off-duty." Aliyaah smiled. "She'll certainly be missed out at the quarry."

Silver managed a smile, and placed her hand over Aliyaah's for a moment.

"Go get some rest. I'll let you know if we find anything else," Aliyaah said, then added, "Make sure you take your anti-radiation meds, Sil."

Silver nodded and turned towards the airlock.

Silver stepped into the airlock and began the decontamination procedure. She was glad of the chance to take off the EV suit and was looking forward to climbing into her bunk for an hour or two.

Decontamination only took a few minutes, but the time quickly added up when switching between sensitive zones like the biodomes and refinery. It would be years before there was greater freedom of movement across the colony.

Back on Earth, the Planetary Protection Agency had been established to oversee the use of vapor disinfectants, radiation, and intense heat to sterilise everything that would land on the planet, with the notable exception of the humans. The PPA had been an important part of ensuring that the equipment brought to the colony did not contaminate the planet. If they found signs of life, past or present, in the dust or water on the red planet, they wanted to be able to rule out contamination from Earth.

On the planet itself, they employed technology like BILI - the Bio-Indicator Lidar Instrument - to almost continually search for life. BILI had been Cooper's main project when she worked at NASA, and although Silver had never fully grasped how the device worked, she had no doubt that if she spent enough time with BILI and the data she'd understand it. While Cooper had been working on BILI, Silver had known better than to become too involved. It was Cooper's project, and they each needed to have their passions and to feel like the expert on something.

The way Cooper had explained it, BILI used pulses of ultraviolet light from two lasers to detect organic material in dust plumes. The glow from the particles and their response to the laser light provided information on the size of the particles, their age, and their makeup.

Basically, BILI was a way to sniff out life on Mars. NASA had sent earlier devices to scan from orbit, and had then installed BILI on surface rovers. There had been some initial excitement over frozen water under the surface, but it had come to nothing. Private enterprise saw this as the all-clear and, soon after, began to send the cargo needed to construct a viable colony on the planet.

Silver's work focused on ensuring the smooth running of the rovers and the Space Exploration Vehicle, but, thanks to her wife, she knew a little about BILI, and the smaller, hand-held, Lidar devices they sometimes used. Cooper had worked on several of the projects designed to look for organic matter from orbit, and had spent months poring over schematics and data, tweaking sensors and making decisions about where next to explore. Silver didn't have much patience for the slow, steady work of data analysis from millions of kilometres away. She liked to get her hands dirty.

Right now, though, Silver was doing her best to rid herself of the red dust from the refiner, and she could see the benefits of being in a lab on Earth looking at a computer screen.

After exiting the airlock, Silver made her way back to her quarters. She walked down the featureless, gray panelled corridor, and was relieved not to run into any of her colleagues as her eyes filled with tears. Shift changes were currently at two, ten, and eighteen-hundred hours. They changed the pattern every three sevensols to help with the adjustment to the longer Martian sol, and senior personnel overlapped with each shift to help keep things running smoothly. It was just after ten now, so Silver figured the mess hall would be full of hungry overnighters, leaving the corridors of the station mercifully empty.

She wiped away the tears with the back of her hand and wondered if the Commander would make an announcement to all personnel and civilians, or if the CP had already done so. She would check her messages once she got back to her quarters to see what they were telling the crew.

As she walked down the corridor, Silver yawned and felt her ears pop. The sound of her boots clanging against the grated floor seemed louder suddenly, and Silver stumbled, her legs feeling heavier than a moment ago. She yawned again and thought about Jaz's family, and the family of the missing miner. Protocol after an incident like this was to place a blackout on off-planet communications. The next of kin wouldn't know what had happened for another sol at least, not until NASA had decided what to say. She imagined Cooper getting that call, and realised that it was possible the miner had family at the station, and that they would be stranded, grieving, on Mars for another five hundred and thirty three sols before they could go home.

When Silver reached her quarters, she scanned her wrist over the entry pad and slid the door open. Inside, she sat heavily on the chair by the door and took off her boots, lining them up neatly under the hook for her EV suit. Silver stripped down to her uniform grey vest and shorts, then slumped onto her bunk and closed her eyes. She could feel the dust scratching beneath her eyelids. It was in her nostrils, her ears, her hair, and she knew it would have been better to shower before getting into bed. No matter how many adjustments they made to decontamination procedures, the dust still invaded the station, but Silver was too exhausted to shower, and her head was pounding. She hadn't had anything to eat since the night before, and had been called to the hangar before her morning caffeine fix. It was probably good that Aliyaah had given her the rest of the sol off, she wouldn't be useful to anyone without some rest and nourishment.

Silver ran her hands over her face and up into her hair, feeling the rub of sand and dirt. She opened her eyes and then jolted upright. There was someone standing in the corner of the room. She blinked and backed against the wall of her bunk. When she opened her eyes again, the room was empty.

She tried to hold onto the image, to make out details, but the figure had already faded from her mind's eye. She was scared to close her eyes to try to bring back the image, not knowing what she'd see when she opened her eyes again. For now, the room looked as it should, but she could swear that someone had been standing in the corner, someone in orange overalls.

Silver pulled her knees to her chest and sat shaking on the bed. There was nowhere in the room that a person could hide. And there was no way they could have been there one instant and have left the next. Her rational brain knew that she was just tired. She was running on empty, had low blood sugar, and had likely had a dose of radiation from whatever had happened in the hangar. What she had seen was just a hallucination, nothing more, but that didn't stop her gut from tying itself in knots. Silver thought about the Commander, and his delusions. She didn't feel feverish, but twice now she had heard what could be described as auditory hallucinations. She needed to take extra anti-rads, eat, and sleep, and then she would feel better.

She moved to the edge of her bed and reached for a protein bar. She pulled the hard square from the packet and began warming it between her hands until she could roll it into a ball. She took a bite, barely registering the taste as she chewed and swallowed. Silver knew that the smart move would be to head to the mess hall for some hot food, but if she left her quarters now she knew she would be wary about opening that door and seeing the figure when she returned. She would wait it out and let the food settle her nerves so she could think straight and reclaim the space. She could not afford to be frightened of the one place on the station where she could be alone.

Silver finished the protein bar and put the wrapper in the recycling chute. She found a vial of anti-radiation medication in her cabinet and fitted it into the med port on her thigh. The drugs would get into her system faster this way than if she just took the regular oral anti-rads. After she removed the vial and placed it alongside the other empties in the cabinet, Silver looked at the clocks on the wall, showing Mars time and Earth time, currently eight minutes apart. The planets were moving further away from each other, making communication harder and harder. Silver typically managed to call home once or twice a month, depending on the ferocity of the galactic cosmic rays. The idea of hearing her wife's voice was especially welcome on a sol like tosol, but the communications blackout probably meant it would be a while before she spoke to Cooper. She checked the screen in her room, hoping that Cooper had called before the blackout began, and was excited to see an alert in the bottom corner of the screen. Silver smiled. It was a message from Earth, not from the Commander or Hadley.

Silver pulled up the message and pressed play, then sat down at the small table and waited for the video feed to load.

SIX

It was almost a year since Silver had said goodbye to Cooper at the Johnson Space Centre. She had walked away in her NASA uniform, illuminated by the flashing lights of the photographers documenting the launch of *Octavia*. Her smile had been both nervous and genuine as she waved to the crowd of people gathered to watch the historic launch.

Their journey to Mars had taken just over five months, shorter than the typical trip thanks to the use of plasma rockets. In the six months that they had been living on the planet's surface, Silver had talked to Cooper only a dozen or so times. Communication felt strained between the two of them, even without the hindrance of technology, time, and distance.

As Silver waited for Cooper's message to load, she thought with a smile about how they had first met. Cooper had quite literally fallen into Silver's lap, tripping while walking across the campus cafeteria, and spilling scalding hot coffee over herself and her colleague. Fortunately, everyone was wearing coveralls designed to withstand significant heat, so the only lasting damage was a small blister on the knuckle of Silver's thumb. Cooper had asked to take Silver to dinner, to apologise, and Silver wasn't sure whether to find the encounter charming or alarming.

Cooper's charm soon won out, and later, when they were tangled in Silver's sheets, Cooper kissed the healing skin and smiled at Silver before looking up at the dark ceiling decorated with glowing stars above her bed. "The Monoceros constellation?" Cooper asked, and Silver kissed her, thinking then that she would marry this woman.

Cooper moved in a few months later, just after the announcement of the first crewed Mars mission. On their first night living together, Silver had looked up at the stars and noticed something new. Cooper had added Mars to the night sky, "So we always remember what brought us together," she said.

The red planet watched over them for years as they slept, together, or alone if one of them was working late or on a mission. After Cosima was born, the stars would keep Silver company as she lay in bed listening fretfully to the sounds of her daughter sleeping in the crib beside her, each breath feeling like a miracle, each snuffle or hiccough a potential disaster.

Some nights, the idea of seeing Earth from the red planet made Silver feel small and insignificant, like she should accept not only her own inevitable slide towards death but Earth's too. On other nights, seeing Mars looking down at her made her optimistic about the future of humanity. If they had the tenacity and ingenuity to get to Mars and build a colony, how could she doubt humanity's ability to reverse the disastrous environmental and climate impacts of the last couple of hundred years?

When Cosima turned one, they moved into a townhouse, and Silver assumed they would duplicate the night sky, taking Mars with them. But Cooper didn't want to paint the bedroom ceiling black. She insisted it was gloomy and that grown-ups didn't do such things. She also vetoed Silver's plan to paint Cosima's room with planets and spaceships, and after some intense debate over wallpaper samples, they finally agreed on a woodland creatures theme.

Despite not going to sleep each night under an umbrella of constellations, Cosima quickly became fascinated with rockets and space. She listened, her eyes wide, to Silver's stories about exploring planets, and demanded to know what Silver did at work each day. It was endlessly charming to Silver how Cosima clapped with delight at photos of the Earth from space. She knew her daughter didn't really understand what the photos meant, but she would one day and Silver wanted her to carry on being excited by space and science.

As a child, Silver had been anything but delighted at the idea of space. She found the expanse of the universe absolutely terrifying. The idea that the Earth was continually spinning, and that she couldn't even tell, was especially scary, not to mention the idea of the universe continually expanding. What else was happening that she didn't know about and couldn't even sense once she knew to look for it?

This desire to not only find answers to the questions they already had, but to find new questions had stuck with Silver into adulthood, finally leading her to Mars.

Silver took another drink of water from her canteen, a gift from Cooper on their first anniversary. She looked at the engraving and wondered if, even all those years ago, Cooper had considered the Mars mission futile. Perhaps the little prince was right, and you couldn't pluck the stars from the sky.

The message was buffering at eighty percent, and Silver shuffled in her seat, impatient to see Cooper's face. It was ten sols since she had heard from her wife. Cooper and Cosima had been sick with colds, and Silver hoped they had shaken it off by now, especially because Cooper was extra cranky when she was sick.

"Hey," Cooper's voice broke through the static before her image appeared. "I hope all's well up there."

Cooper sounded tired, and when her face appeared on the screen, Silver saw that she looked exhausted. She was hunched over, wearing her familiar and beleaguered, beige cardigan. There were dark circles under her eyes, which were rimmed with red.

"Poor love," Silver said, running her fingers across the screen. Her cold must have been keeping her awake at night. She looked as bad as Silver felt right now.

Then Silver realised that Cooper wasn't looking directly into the camera. She seemed to be deliberately avoiding looking Silver in the eye.

"I need to talk to you about something and," Cooper paused and her face contorted. Perhaps something more serous than a cold had been stealing Cooper's sleep, Silver thought. She immediately looked for signs of Cosima playing in the background, and when she didn't see her, Silver's chest began to feel tight.

"Goddamnit, Sil. I don't want to have to do it like this," Cooper said, looking off to the side, her face bathed suddenly in yellow light filtered through the kitchen drapes.

"Do what, Cooper?" Silver said to herself, "What's wrong?"

Cooper shuffled and then drew herself upright, her shoulders and jaw suddenly stiff and businesslike. "I'm filing for divorce, Silver. Lawrence is drawing up the papers and he'll figure out a way to get them to you." Cooper looked directly at the camera, her eyes cold and dry as she said, "I don't want you to fight me on this. It's what's best for us both, and for Cosima." Silver saw now that Cooper had already cried enough over this decision and that there would be no changing her mind. "And I want to sell the house." The hard edge of Cooper's voice broke slightly as she said, "This doesn't feel like home any more."

Silver's mouth filled with a bitter taste, and she tried to swallow it back down. She clutched at her stomach, then ran to the bathroom and threw up the partially digested remnants of the protein bar.

The sound of Cooper's voice continued to fill Silver's quarters, and she heaved again, bringing up nothing but bile.

"I can't do this anymore, Sil," Cooper said, her voice a little softer now. "I need to start moving on."

There was a noise in the background of the video and Silver heard Cooper tell someone to wait a minute. "I've got to go, Sil. I'm sorry. I really am."

Silence filled the space where Cooper had been, and Silver slumped to the bathroom floor. She felt the sharp shock of the cold surface on her bare legs, reminding her that she was just inches away from the swirling, dusty chaos of the planet, with only a thin, inflated pod for protection. For an instant, she was tempted to smash everything in sight, to tear a hole in the one thing that was allowing her to breathe and stay alive.

After Cooper's decision not to join her on *Octavia*, Silver had pleaded with her not to end their marriage. They had worked hard to find some kind of compromise and, eventually, Silver had promised

Cooper that she would only do one rotation on Mars. She would come back on the first major flight, in two years' time. Cooper had made Silver swear that after that she wouldn't accept any missions longer than a couple of months.

She began to wonder, to really think about the point of all of this, of exploring new places, of leaving the home she knew. If she didn't have her family to go home to, why did it matter if she spent years of her life getting to know this unfriendly planet? If they were never going to join her here, what had been the point of Project Arche?

Silver laughed bitterly as the tears ran down her face. By dedicating herself to bringing life to Mars, she'd lost the life she had on Earth.

SEVEN

It was easy to grow complacent at the station. The artificial gravity and climate controls created a false sense of safety, especially for the civilians, who rarely ventured outside the station. Silver was all too aware, though, that they were close to calamity at any given moment. She also knew that to think like that was exhausting and unproductive. A willful ignorance was necessary to get through each sol, and this was something Silver had been taught early in life.

She had grown up in a house full of secrecy and pretence, and while she had been confused about a lot of things as a child, she had been sure that she didn't want to live that way. She wanted something different, a new kind of family and community.

By the time she left for Mars, it had been almost twenty years since she had seen either of her parents. She had come out to them in her early twenties, once she was financially independent, with a full scholarship. Their reaction hadn't surprised her at all. She had anticipated their judgement, their anger, and had reconciled herself to the idea of walking away from them for good. With no siblings to afford her even a simulacra of connection, she wasn't sure if her parents were still in San Diego, or even if they were still alive. Her father would be in his eighties now, and Silver wondered if anyone would think to contact her in the event of his death.

She had thought about looking up her parents when she got pregnant with Cosima, feeling some vague guilt that her child would, like her, grow up without knowing her roots. But, after some procrastination, she had decided against getting back in touch; there was nothing her parents would add to the life she was building with Cooper, other than judgement and stress, so Silver let them go one last time.

Growing up, there had been many ways in which Silver had stuck out in the predominantly white neighbourhood where her family had settled. The colour of her skin and her burgeoning queerness meant that she had learned early on how to make herself inconspicuous, identify her allies, and swallow any anger she felt. Silver's mother, May, was Navajo, and had lived on reserve land in the Arizona desert until she ran away as a teenager. Trying to create a new life in San Diego, her mother had quickly met a white man twenty years her senior; the man who would become Silver's father.

Her mother had only spoken of her birth family a handful of times, as if she didn't quite believe her life had been real before she came to the big city. To Silver it seemed that her father made no attempt to overcome or even try to hide his disdain for May's history.

She had seen her mother's birth certificate once, her name listed as Mai. She signed every Christmas card and birthday card as May, though, and had such fair skin that most people assumed she was a white woman.

When Silver was born there had been no mistaking her lineage. She was much darker than her mother, and it seemed to Silver that her skin had made her a disappointment right from birth. Her parents seemed to have indulged some strange delusion that they were a white couple and would have white kids. So, despite her father going through the motions of parenting, Silver sensed that his heart wasn't in it. Her parents had no more children after her, but Silver could remember hushed discussions about adopting another child, a white child.

Silver had never felt good enough to earn her father's love or respect, no matter how hard she tried, and had the distinct impression that neither of her parents wished to be seen with her in public. So, while Silver had been curious about her Navajo ancestry, she quickly learned that asking questions about her mother's heritage was taboo in their household.

Silver hadn't talked to another Navajo person until she was in college. A visiting lecturer tried making small talk with Silver about where she was from, which had left her feeling embarrassed at her ignorance of her family history. That embarrassment turned to anger at her mother, even though Silver knew it wasn't her fault, not really. A couple of weeks after their initial meeting, the lecturer sent Silver an email with some gentle suggestions for reading, and Silver spent a semester poring over books about her people and her history. When she went home for spring break, Silver tried to reach out to her mom, eager to talk to someone about everything she had learnt. Her mom told her to leave the past where it belonged, and the clipped, pained tenor of her voice made Silver close the books and go back to pretending that nothing was missing in their lives.

Years later, on a geochemistry field-trip in Navajo land in Arizona, Silver thought of her mother and the lecturer. She looked him up, wanting to thank him for his kindness and his efforts to reconnect her with her native ancestry. He had become a professor at Stanford and was teaching a course on Decolonization, Self-Determination, and Space. Silver hesitated. She was thinking about applying for NASA and was doing all she could to quash the misgivings she already had about planetary exploration and the seeming inevitability of colonisation. It didn't seem fair to have her history, her heritage, which was so suffused with loss, become an invitation for this man to critique her dreams.

Silver wondered now if the familiarity of an inhospitable environment was what had drawn her to Mars, and to space exploration in general. There were inherent constraints involved in space travel that meant astronauts and cosmonauts were typically pragmatic, utilitarian, and willing to embrace a degree of discomfort, and those were Silver's kind of people. It also seemed to Silver that a fair number of astronauts were trying to escape something back on Earth, press a kind of reset button on humanity, or both.

When it was announced that *Octavia* would bring the first wave of civilians to Mars, Silver knew it marked a new era. As much as she wanted Cooper and Cosima to come with her, she also felt a certain defensiveness. Somehow, with this announcement, Mars no longer felt like the frontier, the exclusive territory of scientists and engineers like herself. Silver suspected that it wouldn't be long before the red planet began to feel crowded, just like Earth, and she would get itchy feet again.

It had taken a while for Silver to admit this to herself, but as she listened to the message from Cooper, she suspected her wife had figured it out long ago. Cooper didn't want to keep chasing her across the galaxy, and Silver couldn't stay still.

Long before she met Cooper, Silver spent a summer in the desert, far enough away from the city to avoid light pollution. With no classes to TA, Silver would lay on her back porch at night and stare up at the sky with a cold beer in her hand. She calculated distances and travel times, and revelled in the scratch of sand in her hair, thinking of what it would be like on Mars. She should have been working on her PhD proposal, but instead spent hours wandering the desert picking up ventifacts, the sharp rocks hewn by wind and sand over millennia.

Silver turned these dusty rocks over and over in her hands and stared out across the expanse of desert, imagining herself walking on the surface of the red planet. She wanted to see for herself the geological oddities caused by the dry atmosphere of Mars and the slow swirl of dust filing down the rocks.

After that summer, Silver scrapped her initial PhD plan and instead asked to join NASA's Desert Research and Technology Studies team, known as the Desert RATS. Silver helped develop a wheeled rover, where each wheel moved independently. Unlike the rovers with tracks, the wheeled vehicles could tackle the type of tough terrain they would encounter on Mars. Years later, all those hours in the desert paid off when Silver got to pilot the fifth generation Curiosity Rover model as it made its way across the planet surface, gathering more data in just a few hours than they had gathered in all the previous years.

It was hard to fathom, but three and a half billion years before Silver piloted the rover, the surface of Mars was similar to that of Earth: volcanoes and a denser atmosphere; Water at the surface; All the ingredients needed to spark life as we know it.

Eventually, the red planet lost its protective magnetic field, and solar winds slowly stripped away the atmosphere. The stream of particles from the sun destabilised the water on the planet's surface, and Mars cooled to the point where all water retreated underground as ice.

Scientists had once thought that the slow creep of water through cracks in the planet's surface meant that any microbes constituting Martian life had also retreated underground. Every test so far showed no trace of such microbes, however, and the current theory was that the red planet had simply never been home to living organisms. Most researchers had adopted the view that Mars was empty land, prior to the arrival of humans, of course, with their plans for colonisation.

If Mars had once supported life, it wouldn't be photosynthetic. The planet was too far from the sun for plants to thrive, something they knew only too well from their work in the biodomes. Instead, any Martian organism would likely be chemosynthetic, feeding on chemical energy created by reactions between water and rock below the planet's surface.

Silver had taken several biochemistry classes over her years in school, and had learned about the rock-eating microbes found deep in the Canadian Shield. The rock there was as old as the rocks on Mars. Scientists had spent decades of their lives two kilometres underground, poring over rock samples beneath Timmins and Sudbury, breathing stale air and searching for organisms that were over two billion years old.

The idea of being so deep in the Earth, buried in darkness, gave Silver chills. She wanted to be out on the surface, watching the sun rise and set on the horizon. Now, on Mars, she missed the feeling of wind on her skin. Stepping outside without her EV suit or EMS would mean almost instant suffocation. The dryness of the atmosphere would cause all the moisture in her mouth, nose, and eyes to evaporate instantly. Her lungs would go into shock and, if that didn't kill her right away, the freezing temperatures would cause her muscles to solidify and she would die in excruciating pain.

While the thin atmosphere on Mars remained unbreathable for humans, there was growing talk that this might be about to start changing. ESA had been holding international talks to establish protocols for transforming the Martian atmosphere. Giant terraforming projects were being planned, including setting up colossal mirrors in space that would reflect the sun onto the planet's poles to melt the ice there. Once this happened, there would be no going back. The technology was moving faster than the ethicists could handle.

Hundreds of small biodomes, no larger than the size of a beer pitcher, were dropped to the planet's surface over a decade before Silver ever set foot on the planet. These miniature laboratories were designed to screw themselves into the soil and carry out programmed experiments, extracting minerals from the soil and carbon dioxide and nitrogen from the air. Most of these devices were now redundant, having served their purpose of gathering information to support the design of larger biodomes that would produce oxygen.

India sent the first oxygen production plant to Mars in 2020, followed closely by MOXIE (the Mars OXygen In situ resource utilization Experiment), sent by the Americans in 2021. Over the next decade they built a bigger version of MOXIE and by 2032 they had begun building the biodomes. Almost all of the construction was automated, or had been done remotely, with a skeleton crew staying just two sevensols on the planet before returning to Earth.

The original biodomes were carefully populated with plant life that thrived in a low-light environment, taking the carbon dioxide from the planet's atmosphere and releasing oxygen. The geoengineering projects faced a whole host of obstacles over the years, including a mysterious blight that killed off all but a few of the plants.

These disasters set them back years, but as MOXIE was replaced by more advanced models, including an algae farm that produced huge amounts of oxygen, they had enjoyed considerable success. The last mission to Mars had established two large biodomes in just a few sevensols, and the engineers were halfway through setting up the third when they returned to Earth, taking advantage of the planets' alignment to keep travel time to a minimum.

Biodomes One and Two were each around the size of two football fields, and were clustered together at the equator. These biodomes housed algae farms set up to produce a steady supply of oxygen for refilling any rockets that landed on the planet. This capacity massively reduced the cost of journeys to Mars, and allowed the ships to carry cargo instead of the oxygen needed to burn the fuel for the return flight. Any excess oxygen they produced after the ships were refilled was used to make the air in the station breathable for those astronauts who stayed behind.

Increased oxygen production and work at the refinery meant that they now had enough fuel and oxygen to send *Octavia* back to Earth once the planets drew close again. They would leave behind a skeleton crew to support the civilians and to carry on work to expand the capacity of the settlement. They could launch *Octavia* now - in theory at least - but the orbits of the two planets meant it would be a longer, more difficult journey than it had been to get to Mars.

Everyone on Mars had signed up for the trip knowing that if there were ever a need for an emergency evacuation of the planet, they would have to draw lots to see who got on the first ship home. There was no way to get everyone off the planet at the same time, and there were no passenger flights scheduled for another fifteen Earth months, or four hundred or so sols. A small ship, *Octavia II,* carrying mainly cargo, was due to leave Earth in the next few weeks, but this shuttle had only a small crew and wouldn't be properly equipped to transport civilians back to Earth.

By the time this ship arrived, the new crew might be taking their first steps on a planet already undergoing radical transformation. The oxygen production capacity on Mars was now sufficient to comfortably meet existing needs and to begin transforming the atmosphere. The question was no longer whether they could carry out a project of such magnitude, but if they should. If they began geoengineering on a planetary scale, in just a few decades the atmosphere could go from less than one percent oxygen to the twenty-one percent level of Earth's atmosphere.

Unlike some of her colleagues, Silver paid little attention to the discussion around atmospheric engineering, and the accusations of hubris attributed to the various agencies involved in creating a settlement on the planet. She had noticed that the agencies were careful, for the most part, not to use the word 'colony.'

Occasionally, Silver considered the ease with which she had slipped into the role of coloniser, but as with the ever-present danger of the inhospitable Martian atmosphere, cognitive dissonance was a key part of her survival strategy. It wasn't lost on her that her Navajo ancestors had suffered greatly at the hands of colonisers. And, if she was honest with herself, she continued to feel the effects of both cultural and patriarchal oppression, including the legacy of her father's attitudes and behaviour.

She had a nagging sense that her life and her outlook would be very different if she had grown up connected to her Navajo family, culture, and traditions. As an adult, Silver accepted that she could have developed such a connection herself, and she no longer thought it fair to place all the blame on her parents, however tempting that might be. She also recognized, albeit reluctantly, that if she really considered what settlement meant, if she thought back to her time in the desert and the land the white explorers had declared empty so they could justify its theft, she might come to a conclusion about space exploration that she didn't like.

EIGHT

Silver woke with a jolt and quickly scanned the room for the figure she had just seen, again, in her dream. She was alone, and, for a second or two, that was a relief. Then she remembered Cooper's message.

Rubbing the gritty residue of tears from her eyes and face, Silver rolled off her bed and checked the time. She didn't remember falling asleep, or even getting into her rack, but it was almost midnight. She had slept for close to twelve hours, but didn't feel at all rested. Her dreams and reality seemed to have folded into each other.

She looked up at the clocks again. If everything was normal and she was back on Earth, she would have given Cosima her bath, then read at least two books before finishing with *I Love You Through and Through*. That book had become their way of conditioning Cosima to go to sleep with happy thoughts. Cosima would yawn dramatically, as if eating up all the oxygen in the room. Then she would tuck herself into Silver's shoulder, her little hand across Silver's chest, and be asleep within seconds. She had almost always slept well, something that Silver envied now. Once Cosima was settled, Silver would carefully lift her into her own bed before going to the kitchen, where Cooper would have poured her a glass of wine.

With no alcohol at the station, Silver felt a twinge of envy. At least Cooper could dull the pain a little. Silver had to face it alone and sober. All she had now were memories of Cosima. Her baby would be so different now. She would have grown and changed so much in eleven months. Silver felt the phantom weight of her baby in her arms, and the memory felt tainted somehow. It wasn't real. This baby no longer existed, but the longer she spent on Mars, the more precious these tactile memories became.

When she was born, Cosima had weighed just under six pounds, and Cooper had been so scared at first about every little jostle or bump. Silver remembered gazing down at their daughter in amazement, feeling the softness of her hair, her skin. It was like she was barely there at all. At times, Silver had imagined that Cosima was slight enough that she might be whisked away by one of the desert's calmest sand storms.

Silver was so used to handling large cumbersome machines that she had felt a little scared by this tiny baby. She hadn't told Cooper though. She had felt the need to project confidence, to let Cooper see that their baby was robust, and that she could take care of them both. After Silver had returned to work, Cooper had bathed and dressed and put Cosima to bed more times than Silver ever would.

When Silver had gone into labour, Cooper had frozen. The reality hit and Silver had needed to guide Cooper through even the most basic points of their birth plan. In the hospital, Cooper held Silver's hand and cried silent, happy tears as the nurse placed their tiny baby on Silver's chest. Cosima was born with a full head of dark, curly hair, like Cooper, and a darker complexion like Silver. The nurse, an older man, had laughed, presumably remembering when conception still required the involvement of male and female gametes. He smiled at Cosima and her moms and said, "A wonder of love... and science."

As Silver thought back to that day, she realised she couldn't remember the colour of the little hat the nurse had placed on Cosima's head to keep her warm. It wasn't important, but it bothered Silver that this part of the memory eluded her. She focused on the feeling of the weight of Cosima in her arms, the warmth of her little body as she fell asleep on Silver's chest when she had finished feeding in the middle of the night. She had been so tethered to Cosima for that first year, and things between her and Cooper had never been better than in those nine months after their daughter was born.

Silver wanted to keep hold of these happy memories, but her thoughts felt thick and dull. She kept thinking instead of the fights she had narrowly avoided with Cooper in the months leading up to the launch of *Octavia*, while they tried to keep the peace and leave on good terms.

After those first nine blissful months, once Silver announced her intention to wean Cosima and return to work, things had changed between her and Cooper. Silver felt like Cooper began to slowly shut her out of family life. She took over the grocery shopping and cooking, would make playdates and medical appointments without consulting Silver, and would then get angry at her when they clashed with a project meeting she couldn't miss. Silver lost track of the names of Cosima's friends and their parents' names. She couldn't keep up with the music classes, nursery rhymes, or favourite foods, and felt at times that Cooper made things deliberately obtuse as a way of punishing her for having wanted to return to work, for having wanted to have conversations about something other than diapers and breastfeeding, for having wanted her body and mind to be her own again.

Silver felt the heaviness, the darkness, of those memories, and reached out to record a transmission to Cooper. As her finger hovered over the screen, she remembered the communications blackout and was relieved. She needed time to figure out what to say. She needed to respond not just react. Would things have been different if she had decided to stay on Earth? Would Cooper have relinquished some control and let her in? Maybe, if she went back, they could still work things out.

Silver caught herself mid-thought, seeing that the idea of *when* she went back had switched to *if*. What if she didn't go back? What if she volunteered to stay on for another rotation?

What if she just stayed on Mars and never returned to Earth?

Silver clenched her fists and let out a low, guttural roar. What was she thinking? Of course, she had to go home to her baby and wife. Despite everything that had happened, she loved Cosima, and she still loved Cooper. Didn't she?

Silver's thoughts raced and spiralled, her memories mixing with reality. It was hard to shake herself out of this dream-space, where she still thought of them as a family. It was as if the voice inside her head had surrendered all inhibition even while she was awake.

She went to the washroom and splashed cold water on her face. Despite her confusion and sadness, she had to acknowledge that her family had crumbled long ago. She had disappointed Cooper, and there didn't seem to be any way she could make up for that now.

As her thoughts looped around again, Silver rubbed her eyes and snapped herself out of the dangerous spiral. She would type up her report about the incident in the hangar. Then, she would shower and head to the mess hall for some hot food. As much as she hated the idea of having to make small talk with colleagues, the thought of eating another protein bar was too much to handle right now.

NINE

When Silver got to the mess hall she was surprised to find it empty. While it was almost three in the morning, there were usually a few people just coming off shift or who were having trouble sleeping. The cats-eyes and melatonin pumps helped with the adjustment to a Mars sol which was forty minutes longer than a day on Earth, but sleep still evaded Silver some nights and she knew she wasn't alone in that. In the early hours, she often encountered a few bleary-eyed crew members hunched over a cup of steaming tea, willing themselves back to sleep, or making the most of the extra awake time by writing reports.

The relative silence meant that Silver could hear the hum of the refrigeration units in the back. She listened for the sound of pots clanging in the kitchen, but heard nothing to suggest that there was anyone else in the mess hall. As she scanned the room, Silver noticed a chair lying on its side, and a couple of tables holding half a dozen trays, their food half eaten. She righted the chair and her stomach lurched at the sight of congealed porridge in one of the abandoned bowls. The crew was usually tidier than this.

Silver walked past the tables towards the large whiteboard by the serving station. She had hoped that the menu would already be up for breakfast, but the board still showed last night's offerings. The veggie chilli caught her eye and Silver's belly grumbled. The idea of a warm bowl of spicy chilli made her feel a little more awake, so she called out to the kitchen. There was no response, so she leaned further over the counter and called again.

When there was still no answer, Silver lifted the counter and walked into the kitchen. Unless his schedule had changed, Hardeep was supposed to be working the mess hall. He and Silver had recently become friends after discovering a shared love of obscure 2020's math rock. They traded recommendations whenever their shifts coincided, and Silver figured that Hardeep wouldn't mind if she served herself. He was probably on a quick vape break; something he'd do when there was no one waiting to be served.

The kitchen was empty and quiet, but for the remainders of a pot of chilli simmering on the stove top. Silver picked up a small grey bowl and started walking towards the pot. A flash of light made her stop and stand still for a moment. She turned to look toward the far wall, where the light seemed to have originated, but she couldn't see a likely source. Silver waited for a few seconds and then there it was again: The reflection of something flickering intermittently in the aluminium door of the storage unit at the end of the central island.

"Hello?" Silver said. "Is someone there?" She took a couple of steps forward and said softly, "Hardeep, is that you?"

"Shhh, he'll hear you." The voice was quiet, insistent, but with a tremolo of fear.

"Hardeep?" Silver whispered, moving closer.

"Get over here and get down," Hardeep said and reached up to grab Silver's hand, pulling her to the floor.

He was sitting with his back against the end of the centre island, a huge kitchen knife trembling in his hand.

"What the -" Silver began, but Hardeep shushed her, wide-eyed.

"Did you see him?" Hardeep whispered, peering into the hazy reflection in the metal cabinet opposite.

"Who?"

"The Commander."

"Why? What's going on?" Silver asked, more confused than ever.

"He's unhinged," Hardeep said, nodding furiously at Silver. "He's lost it. I'm serious."

"I don't understand. Did the Commander do something?"

Hardeep snorted. Then, slowly, he pointed a shaky finger at the door to the freezer, which Silver hadn't noticed was ajar. Cold air was pouring out and condensing into clouds in the warmth of the kitchen. The cloud blocked her view of the freezer's interior for a second or two, but then it cleared for a moment and Silver gasped as she saw an outstretched hand, still and bloodied, lying on the white tile.

She started to stand up but Hardeep pulled her back down and Silver turned to look at him. "Who is that?" she asked. "Are they -"

"Dead? Yeah."

Silver sat back down and slumped against the cabinet.

"That's Anderson," Hardeep said. "He tried to tackle the Commander but he just wouldn't stop."

"I don't understand," Silver said, unable to stop looking at her colleague's cold, dead hand. It seemed to be reaching out to her, but there was clearly nothing she could do to help him now. She closed her eyes and then turned to Hardeep and said, "Tell me exactly what happened."

"The Commander lost it. That's what happened."

"From the beginning, Hardeep. I need you to start at the beginning."

"OK. OK. So, everyone was just eating, right? It was a totally normal night. Pretty quiet, but normal. Then the Commander came in, and he was sort of mumbling to himself. Like, he didn't really seem to know where he was or even who he was. He started screaming all kinds of things. About being back at the academy, like, thirty years ago, and how it was too hot in here and he was burning up. Then the radiologic alarm went off and he just, he just went ballistic. He pushed right past me and Andersen, yelling about how he couldn't breathe. He wanted to get into the freezer. Like, maybe he thought it was the storm shelter or something. Anyway, Anderson followed him and tried to calm him down, but the Commander... well." Hardeep covered his mouth and shuddered, then gestured with the knife. "There are lots of weapons in a kitchen, Antara. Like, a lot of bad shit can go down real fast."

"Where's everyone else?" Silver asked. "Didn't anyone help

Anderson?"

Hardeep shook his head. "There wasn't time. And we were all terrified that the Commander would open one of the ports. He was shouting about how we were all going to die because the air was too thick. I saw what he did to Anderson and I, I.... It was too late to stop him, so I just hid. Everyone else just took off, I think. I heard one of the officers say they were going to alert Hadley and the others wanted to get suited up."

Silver was surprised that no alarms were sounding and there was no sign of Hadley. She risked peering around the island to see if the Commander had returned, but she and Hardeep were alone. "When did this happen?" she asked.

Hardeep tapped a spot on his wrist and Silver saw the glow of the time readout below his skin. "About twenty minutes ago, maybe," he said. "I've just been sitting here. I don't think I can move." He clutched at Silver's hand and blinked at her. "I mean, what do we even do? He has the codes to everything. Even if we seal ourselves off in a shelter, he can still disable life support, right? And if what he said was true, that we're all going to die -"

Silver cut him off. "We're not all going to die, Hardeep. The Commander is sick. He's running a fever and is delusional is all. We'll find him and figure out what's going on. Restrain or sedate him if necessary. If his delusions lead him to try to disable life support, don't worry, there are numerous obstacles in his way. He needs Hadley's codes for a start."

Hardeep exhaled deeply and his shoulders slumped as Silver took another look around the kitchen and stood up slowly. There was still no one else there, so she pulled Hardeep to his feet and took the knife from his hand, placing it on the island. "You'll only hurt yourself, or me, with that," she said. She gave him a thin smile and added, "Save it for the carrots."

Silver walked to the door of the kitchen and looked into the mess hall. It was also empty, but she heard a shout in the corridor outside. She gestured to Hardeep to join her but he wouldn't move, so she made her way to the door by herself and pressed the button to slide it open.

She quickly moved to the side of the door, her back against the wall, and listened. There were several sets of footsteps running in the direction of the laboratory and someone shouted, "What the hell is going on?"

Silver checked the corridor in both directions and then ran as quietly as she could towards the laboratory. On her way, someone tripped the station-wide alarm, which would cause all crew members and civilians to suit up or get into a shelter. In almost one hundred and eighty sols they had only ever used the system a half dozen times, to run drills to make sure everyone knew what to do in the event of a massive solar storm or some kind of disaster where the levels of radiation would be too much for the magnetic shield that surrounded the station.

Silver knew that she should head back to her quarters, or to the hangar airlock, which was closer, but she felt compelled to keep running towards the lab. As she rounded the next corner, something hit her square in the chest and she fell to the floor, winded.

"Oh god, oh god. Sil?"

Silver came to and looked up to see the Chief leaning over her. Aliyaah was biting her lip, her nostrils flared and her eyes wide.

Silver tried to speak, but she was having trouble breathing. Holding her hand to her chest, she gulped in some air, then coughed as Aliyaah pulled her upright and looked nervously over her shoulder. "I'm sorry, Sil. But we've got to get to the SEV, right now."

"Did the Commander do something?" Silver managed to sputter as Aliyaah helped her to her feet. "I think he killed Anderson."

Aliyaah closed her eyes for half a second and nodded. "Coulter too. He's lost his mind. It's not just a fever, Sil."

"Where is he now?" Silver asked as the two of them began to move towards the airlock and the Space Exploration Vehicle.

The SEV was closer to the mess hall than anything else that could shield them from the galactic cosmic rays and the effects of a solar storm. Silver wondered for a moment how she had forgotten that the SEV was there. She used to know the station's schematics down to the number of panels in a hallway. She silently reprimanded herself for getting complacent. It was vital to remember that she was essentially in a glorified balloon on an inhospitable planet that could kill her in a second, especially if someone popped that balloon in a moment of insanity.

Aliyaah hadn't answered her question about the Commander's whereabouts, so Silver asked again as they reached the pod.

"He was in the east wing," Aliyaah said. "Now he seems to be headed to the civilian wing," Aliyaah added quietly. "Hadley has a team there ready to meet him."

Aliyaah entered the code to access the SEV and they waited what seemed like an eternity before the airlock began to open.

TEN

As soon as Silver and Aliyaah were in the SEV they grabbed headsets and started scanning for communications from anyone else at the station. They were preparing to detach the vehicle from the airlock when they felt a rumble and heard what sounded like a massive explosion.

"Holy shit," Aliyaah said, scrambling to get the clamps loose.

Another explosion rocked the station and Silver's hand shook as she pressed one last button to confirm their release from the dock. The SEV lurched forward and Silver stared out across the Martian landscape. They needed to put some distance between themselves and the station in case the whole thing blew.

"You got this?" Aliyaah asked Silver, who nodded and steered the SEV as quickly and carefully as she could over the rough terrain towards a slight incline to the west. From that vantage point they would be able to see the station, the quarry, and a couple of the biodomes.

Aliyaah switched between communication channels, trying to access the station's internal network to figure out if there was a breach. The intercom crackled and a voice made them both jump.

"This is CP Hadley in the Civilian Wing. Does anyone have eyes on the Commander? Over."

Aliyaah waited, but no one replied. Hadley put out another call, asking for all crew members to respond, stating rank and location.

Aliyaah responded right away, identifying herself and asking for a situation report.

Aliyaah asked Hadley to switch to an emergency frequency reserved for commanding officers. While Aliyaah talked to Hadley, Silver monitored their current frequency for any other contacts. Other crew identified themselves and their locations. Everyone was in the west wing, the civilian wing, or in the hangar. No one reported in from the three biodomes, but at this time of night there wouldn't typically be workers at those sites anyway. It was strange that there was no word from anyone at the quarry. The night crew should have been at work and the sol shift refiners often stayed on site between shifts. Silver wondered if there were problems with communication across the colony. She also wondered why no one had reported in from the east wing of the station. When Hadley next spoke, she found out why.

"There was an explosion in the east wing. The east wing is destroyed. I repeat, the east wing is destroyed. All personnel to head to the civilian wing or the hangar. Suit up and stay on this channel."

Another man, a Corporal, reported that they had apprehended the Commander heading towards the civilian wing. He was carrying explosives.

Silver glanced over at Aliyaah, both of them acknowledging that the Commander must have destroyed the east wing.

"Why the hell would he do that?" Silver asked Aliyaah, realising that if she hadn't run into Aliyaah and gone to the SEV she would have continued on to the laboratory, which the Commander seemed to have just blown up.

Hadley contacted Aliyaah again a few minutes later. He used a secure channel and told her to get Silver on the line. The lack of communication with the quarry, and Chief Frederickson, who was in charge of the quarry crew, meant that Silver was now acting third in command.

Hadley informed them that the Commander had been brought to the civilian wing and sedated. "All we can get out of him is that he was trying to destroy something in the lab. Maybe whatever you took from the refiner. He wasn't making a lot of sense even before we sedated him; he was talking about how 'they' got to him first. He's having trouble breathing and his fever has spiked. If we can, we'll put him in cryo to try to get his temperature down. He won't survive long if he stays like this, at least not without serious brain damage."

"Do you think he intended to blow the civilian wing?" Aliyaah asked.

"I believe so. He was carrying enough explosives to compromise the whole station," Hadley said.

Silver brought the SEV almost to the top of the hill, to a place where they would be able to see the quarry. Before they summited, she asked Hadley if he had heard from those crew still out there. He hadn't.

Silver turned the SEV slightly as they crested the hill, and gasped. The quarry was covered by a giant cloud of red dust, but this wasn't a typical dust storm. It looked like the whole area was on fire, but that was impossible given the lack of oxygen. Some sort of massive explosion must have just occurred, as when the dust cloud began to settle there was little remaining of the gargantuan refiners that should have been sitting in the centre of the quarry. The small outpost where the workers took shelter from solar storms was completely destroyed. All the crew who the Commander had selected to keep working would have been killed by such an explosion.

"He might have blown it remotely," Aliyaah said.

"How is that possible?"

"Ordinarily, it wouldn't be. He would've needed codes from Hadley, myself, or Chief Frederickson." Aliyaah paused, then said, "Unless it wasn't the Commander at all. It could have been Frederickson."

"A co-ordinated attack?" Silver said, then shuddered, wondering what would have happened if the Commander had reached the civilian wing without being detained. "He was going to blow it all," she said, mostly to herself.

Aliyaah shook her head. "Maybe. But why? If he wasn't suicidal and actually wanted to get off the planet, he must've known there's no way he could pilot *Octavia* by himself, even if she's fully fuelled and has enough oxygen for launch. And why would Frederickson sacrifice himself to blow the quarry?"

Aliyaah asked Hadley if the Commander had said anything else about the lab.

"It doesn't make a lot of sense. He's saying that Specialist Viper told him to destroy everything. That the station is infected."

"Jaz?" Silver said, confused. "He saw Jaz?"

"This is insane," Aliyaah said, but Silver thought back to the figure standing in the corner of her room when she had woken up earlier. The figure had been wearing a uniform like hers, like the one Jaz had been wearing when she vanished.

Silver knew she should tell Aliyaah what she had seen, and heard, over the past few sols, but something stopped her. Everything in her training told her to confess to Aliyaah, and to Hadley. If she was infected, she had a responsibility to quarantine herself, to try to keep the infection from spreading. But the Chief would think she was losing her mind like the Commander, and if he was right, and the station was infected, Silver couldn't afford to be sedated and restrained. Her thoughts were jumbled, but from the tangle of thoughts emerged a clear inner voice telling her to stay quiet. If she could just stay safe she could work the problem: the mantra the academy aimed to instil in everyone.

"Antara," Aliyaah said, staring out of the back of the SEV. She reached behind her to grab Silver's arm. "Sil, just look at this."

Silver turned around and choked back a cry. The east wing of the station had been ripped apart. There were pieces of metal and plastic strewn across the planet's surface. Some of the debris was twisting in the dust plumes, catching the light, not dense enough to fall, too heavy to float higher, trapped in a desperately slow swirl of purgatory.

The loss of the laboratory meant that a major part of the mission was all but redundant. They had transmitted data to Earth daily since their arrival, but now they had no way to carry out most of the tests they had been sent to perform. The SEV and the rovers could carry out rudimentary tests, but nothing like the lab was capable of.

Aliyaah was asking Hadley for a headcount. The east wing not only housed the laboratory, a dozen or so crew had been assigned quarters there. Given that it was now the early hours of the morning, most of the crew would have been in their bunks when the charges blew.

"So far, we've accounted for twelve crew, the two of you, and seventeen civilians," Hadley answered flatly. "If there are survivors from the east wing, the biodomes, or the quarry, they haven't reported in."

"Hardeep?" Silver asked.

"From the kitchen? No, sorry," Hadley said. "He might not be able to get here though, given the extent of the blast." He paused, talking to someone beside him. "We've lost contact with those left in the west wing. They should have been making their way here, but no one has arrived. Perhaps the explosions caused some issue with the internal doors and communications. You probably have a better view of the situation than we do right now, Chief. Could you take a look and send us some images? We might need you to transport people from the west wing if they can't get here by themselves."

Aliyaah nodded to Silver, who started the SEV in the direction of the west wing.

A few seconds later, Hadley's voice came back on the line. "Chief," he paused, then said, "Commander Marshall is dead."

ELEVEN

Silver first met the Commander at the academy, when he was teaching a class on microgravity. He was Lieutenant Commander Anthony Marshall then, and Silver found his teaching style brusque and confrontational. He seemed to want the AsCans, or Astronaut Candidates, to learn through fear and spent an inordinate amount of time slamming his fist on his lectern and eyeballing the students before sending them to the vomit comet.

Over her years at NASA, Silver had cause to run into Marshall a few more times, but she was happy not to have been selected alongside him for a mission until *Octavia*. NASA put all potential officers through rigorous psychiatric evaluation and were painstaking about the make-up of every flight crew. Silver always figured that NASA didn't think she and Marshall would be a good fit to coexist in close quarters.

When NASA announced that Marshall would be the Commander on *Octavia*, Silver had already been assigned to the mission. His posting was something of a surprise to her, especially as he would have been part of the selection committee that chose Silver, Aliyaah, Hadley, and other key personnel.

Silver wondered if something had changed in her temperament, but when she met the Commander again he seemed to have mellowed with age. Perhaps the magnitude of the mission, one of the most historic space flights humanity had ever undertaken, was enough to humble him, or at least make him a little less bombastic.

Silver didn't know if Marshall remembered her from his class a decade earlier. If anything, she had done her utmost to avoid his attention back then. She had done the work necessary to get a good grade, and held her stomach in microgravity. In general, Silver had tried not to draw attention to herself. Perhaps that had paid off years later.

Like everyone on the crew of *Octavia*, the Commander would have had to pass a psych eval. He had years of experience in space, with nothing to suggest the kind of acute breakdown he seemed to have just suffered. Hadley had no explanation for the Commander's death either. He had simply stopped breathing and no one had been able to resuscitate him. Doctor Schiff was in the Civilian Wing with Hadley when the Commander collapsed, but she hadn't been able to revive the Commander, even after an adrenaline shot directly into his heart.

No one had died at the station since they had arrived, and now there were mass casualties. They had all undergone training to help them handle a massive solar storm, mechanical failures, and viral outbreaks, as well as the loss of command personnel, but this was beyond any of their training.

Silver and Aliyaah were guiding the SEV towards the west wing of the station to check for survivors. The SEV was big enough to comfortably carry four crew at a time, or six in an emergency, assuming no other cargo was on board.

They were operating on the assumption that something was obstructing passage between the west wing and the civilian wing, and that the crew was trapped. It was strange that comms were down, but they could be malfunctioning due to the proximity of the blasts. Silver was painfully aware that there might be another explanation for the lack of movement, especially as comms had worked just after the explosions. So far, no one had made it to the civilian quarters.

Aliyaah agreed with Hadley that she and Silver would assess the damage to the wing and see if there was a way to reconnect the parts of the station from the inside. As they drew nearer to the station, Silver's hope faded. The SEV began to encounter an increasing amount of debris, including what Silver could only assume were scattered personal effects from the crew's living quarters. A large, bright white shirt danced through the air toward the SEV, its sleeves flapping frantically as if to wave her and Aliyaah away. The howl of the dust storms was blocked by the SEV's dense shielding, making the silent motion even more eerie.

"Take us over to the crosswalk. I want to take a quick look before we try to dock," Aliyaah said and pointed to a section where the west wing looked like it was still connected to the rest of the station. There were dents in the structure, but nothing that looked significant enough to indicate a major breach.

"It seems intact," Silver said. "The debris must be from the east wing."

"Unless there's a problem on the inner side of the west wing, where we can't see," Aliyaah said.

The station had been designed in a candelabra shape, with exterior crosswalks between each candlestick. These were meant to be used in emergencies only. The rest of the time, everyone had to walk through the south side of the station, where the mess hall was located. The hangar was just underneath the mess hall, built into the slope of the planet's surface. The laboratory had been on the southern most exterior wall of the east wing. By blowing up the lab, the Commander had sheared off the east wing of the station.

Silver had seen from the ridge that the hangar had suffered some external damage. That explained why they had felt both blasts as they detached the SEV from the south wall of the station. Whatever had happened in the hangar could also be causing a problem for the west wing.

The civilian quarters formed the central column of the station, where there was the strongest protection from solar winds and galactic cosmic rays. Its position would have also shielded it from both blasts, but the explosions had damaged the station's magnetic shield, so if there was a severe or protracted solar storm they would all be in trouble.

Silver guided the SEV to the docking station and backed it in. The Chief held up her hand to signal Silver to stay still as she connected with the station's computer network.

"Looks like everything's working fine. I don't see a reason for comms to be down."

Aliyaah looked at Silver and shrugged. "Let's suit up and take a look."

Silver grimaced and recognised the irony of the situation. She was usually eager to explore the unknown, but all of the missions she had been on shared a common factor: she was heading away from civilisation and its problems, not towards them.

TWELVE

The west wing of the station was large enough to house a hundred personnel as well as the colony's main recreational facilities. Only a quarter of the bunks were occupied in the west wing, with this set to increase gradually as more personnel arrived on the planet. *Octavia* was the largest shuttle to travel to Mars so far, bringing fifty crew members and twenty-five civilians. With the crew at the refineries, the human population on Mars had stood at almost two hundred. Now, that number had been cut in half, at least. Depending on what was happening in the west wing, there could be fewer than fifty people left on the planet.

Silver and Aliyaah stepped out of the SEV into the airlock at the dock, with no clear idea of what they would find inside the station. They sealed the hatch to the SEV and after going through decontamination in the airlock, Aliyaah pulled the lever to open the door to the west wing. The door slid open to reveal an empty corridor.

Silver stepped out onto the metal lattice that formed the walkway and looked to her left and right. There was nothing unusual, just the same expanse of grey metal and uniform rows of doors to individual crew quarters.

Aliyaah stepped into the corridor beside Silver and said, "let's head east and see if there are any survivors trying to get through to the rest of the station."

Silver nodded and reminded herself that the west wing comms and door mechanisms were out. The crew might be trying to follow Hadley's order but be dealing with an obstruction from the explosion, or a malfunction affecting the interior doors. The airlock door was on a separate system, designed to allow for emergency access to the SEV.

Silver followed Aliyaah down the corridor, checking behind them every few steps. Their boots reverberated on the metal grates. Aside from that, the only other sound was of her breathing, and Aliyaah's.

Silver felt a trickle of sweat between her shoulders. Even with adrenaline coursing through her body, and the effort of walking in artificial gravity, the climate controls in her suit should keep the internal temperature and humidity in check.

Silver was about to check the diagnostic array on her suit when Aliyaah stopped suddenly. She put up her hand to signal Silver to stop and stay quiet. The slight curve of the wing meant that they had no clear view of what lay ahead. Silver listened, but heard nothing other than her ragged breath. After a moment, Silver asked, "did you hear something?"

Aliyaah shook her head. "No. But look at your radiation strip."

The strip on Silver's suit was rapidly turning black, like it had in the hangar just before Jaz vanished.

"I don't like this, Chief," Silver said, thinking now about the intense heat rushing from the refiner and the blisters on her palm from the carabiner.

Aliyaah stepped forward slowly, and Silver felt compelled to follow, drawing level with Aliyaah. As they rounded the bend, they were temporarily blinded by light.

The soft white light of the station's halogen bulbs danced against a vast expanse of brilliant iridescent crystals that lined the walls and floor. Silver blinked and waited for her eyes to adjust. She could make out tiny flecks of colour in the crystals, imperfections where the light refracted at an unusual angle, creating the appearance of movement, slow and languid, like a thick liquid or vapour.

The heat in this section of the station was intense, like they had walked into a blast furnace. It was clearly more than their suits could handle. The metal grating beneath Silver's feet seemed to hum, as if the atomic bonds of the material were at risk of being broken apart.

There was no sign of the missing crew, but it was hard to see beyond the glowing light. The crystals grew larger and more dense, obstructing passage between the west wing and the rest of the station. Unlike the crystals in the refiner, these were several feet in length, and they grew from the walls, the floor, and the ceiling. Aliyaah stepped a little closer, spotting something amid the crystals.

Seeing a tangle of belt buckles, jewellery, and other personal effects, Aliyaah began to back up, bumping into Silver. She turned as quickly as her suit would let her and began to retreat, back to the relative safety of the SEV.

On the headset, the Chief sputtered, "It's alive, Sil. It's got to be. And whatever happened back there, I know a mass grave when I see one."

THIRTEEN

Aliyaah and Silver had met in their second year at the academy, when they were assigned as bunk mates on a week-long retreat designed to build leadership skills. Silver had arrived at their lodgings first and settled into the top bunk, wanting to give herself the option of hiding from whoever she had been quartered with.

When Aliyaah introduced herself, she had thrown Silver off guard. Silver was twenty-eight and had already spent enough time at the academy to see that people typically fell into one of two categories: the militant careerist who would stop at nothing to be chosen first for a mission; and the smart, socially awkward academic who was in it for the sheer joy of science, but who had been blessed with excellent physical health.

Aliyaah seemed neither militant nor awkward. She was smart, attractive in a classically feminine way, and downright friendly. Silver immediately felt uncomfortable. She was much more at home with people who laid out their agenda in plain terms and figured out how they could leverage whatever you brought to the table. She was used to people who were bullish, motivated, and who tolerated little interference with the pursuit of their goals. Aliyaah seemed to be genuinely interested in Silver's life and aspirations, and not for her own career progression.

Silver asked where Aliyaah had originally trained and was relieved when she said Nigeria. The Nigerian space program had produced some of the world's finest astronauts and scientists in the last few years and had been a huge support to NASA after funding was cut by the US government in the late 2010s and early 2020s. Many of NASA's projects had been turned over to private companies that recruited Nigerian personnel. When NASA's funding had been restored, just a few years before Silver had applied, they had been hard pressed to recruit teachers back from the posts they had been occupying in Nigeria.

Now, the US and Nigeria were close allies and shared their expertise. The teachers originally from Nigeria, and others who had taught there, tended to be more pragmatic, approachable, and engaging than the handful who had stayed in the US. The old guard at NASA, Commander Marshall included, had grown increasingly bitter while maintaining an undue sense of patriotism. Some of the newer cadets seemed to be vulnerable to this divisive spirit. She had been glad to be bunking with Aliyaah, especially as Aliyaah didn't seem to hold it against her that she was American.

Silver was only on the leadership retreat to round out her course credits for the term. She didn't really want to manage people. She was too busy thinking up ways to extend the rovers' reach and improve their carrying capacity. Aliyaah was different. She had as much engineering expertise as Silver, but she excelled at finding a person's strengths and putting them to work.

Over the course of the week, Silver wondered if Aliyaah was particularly gifted at identifying a person's weaknesses. Perhaps that was why Aliyaah hadn't asked Silver anything about her family or life before the academy. Aliyaah wore her wedding ring on a chain around her neck and had called her husband once, a couple of days after they had arrived. Silver had excused herself, saying she wanted to give them some privacy. While this was true, she had also found it difficult to hear such palpable love and respect, especially between a woman and a man.

Aliyaah still wore the wedding ring on a chain around her neck. Silver had seen it a few times when they had been in their civilian clothes in the mess hall or rec room, but hadn't asked about it and had never heard Aliyaah mention her personal life. Still, it was common knowledge at NASA that Aliyaah's husband, a French politician, had been killed in the 2031 sarin gas attacks. Aliyaah had flown on her second Mars mission a year later, coming over in the first wave of engineers who would set up the biodomes in just a few sols before returning to Earth.

The biodomes were Aliyaah's passion. She was a farmer's daughter, her mother having taught her how to test soil samples before she could even string together a sentence. In addition to overseeing the maintenance and operation of the SEVs, refiners, and rovers, Aliyaah was the station's Chief Botanist. She was tasked with biodome operations and the success of the small farm that provided food for the station.

Building a colony on the red planet required most people to straddle multiple roles. Silver was a rarity in that her expertise and responsibilities were mostly limited to the rovers, refiners, SEVs, and rockets: basically, anything that had a guidance system and moving parts. Aliyaah was a polymath, a natural leader, and a good friend, even if Silver had deliberately kept her at a distance over the years.

When Aliyaah had turned to run back to the SEV, Silver hadn't hesitated in following her. They needed to get as far away from those crystals as possible. The amount of radiation they seemed to be emitting was reason enough, but Silver knew there were bigger factors at play.

Once they were back in the airlock, Silver turned and put her hand on Aliyaah's arm. They looked at each other for a few seconds, getting their breath back. Silver raised her eyebrows, asking Aliyaah to say what they both already knew.

"It's some kind of life form, yes."

"Any idea what kind?" Silver asked.

"A chemotroph, most likely. Maybe a chemolithotroph. Either it emits or it needs massive amounts of heat and humidity."

"So, the explosion could have been a catalyst."
Aliyaah nodded. "It seems so."

"Do you think," Silver began, but she couldn't bring herself to say the words.

"It reconstituted all the organic material, yes." Aliyaah words were matter of fact, but she turned to look at the control panel as she spoke and there was no disguising the crackle of her voice. When she turned back to Silver to signal that they should enter the SEV, Silver could see tears on Aliyaah's face.

As Silver climbed back into the SEV, she asked Aliyaah what they were going to do.

"We have to inform Commander Hadley of the situation. And then," Aliyaah glanced across at Silver, "And then I think the two of us should head to Biodome Three."

FOURTEEN

Biodome Three was located due west of the station, over the ridge of the Schiaparelli crater. It took seven minutes, and very little energy, to get there using the zipline system, thanks to the reduced gravity on Mars. Such journeys were only possible on clear sols, when crew would strap on a harness and hook themselves to the zipline, then fly high up away from the station, over the ridge of the crater, and down towards the biodome. Their suits protected them from normal atmospheric conditions, but the system was shut down during solar storms and only essential trips were undertaken using the SEV.

While the SEV had significantly better shielding than an EV suit, the crater's steep slopes made for a treacherous journey. The rovers were much better equipped to navigate such terrain, but these weren't passenger vehicles and were typically several kilometres away exploring new areas of the planet.

Silver had driven the SEV to the biodomes countless times to deliver and retrieve supplies. She knew the best route up the crater, taking advantage of plateaus and steppes hewn into the rocks over millennia by whistling winds swirling with abrasive dust.

Silver rarely lingered in the biodomes, but she knew that Aliyaah spent a lot of time there. Even when she wasn't working in the dome, she would head out there to sit among the plants. Some of the other crew did the same, even if they weren't part of the botanical team. The biodomes had a carefully controlled environment, and the impact of off-duty visitors had been factored into their management. NASA planners had anticipated the need for greenspace in the colony, especially amid the harsh, dusty sandstorms of Mars and the uniform, narrow, grey corridors of the station.

When Aliyaah was twenty, she had been part of a team of chemical engineers experimenting with plant nanobiotics. The idea was to insert carbon nanotubes into the vascular system of plants and use these to detect a variety of chemical compounds in the groundwater or air.

Originally, the project had focused on developing spinach plants that could detect aromatic hydrocarbons. These plants could then be used to indicate the presence of landmines or other explosives. Aliyaah quickly realised the potential for these plants to be used in space stations, rockets, and on the surface of other planets as a way of monitoring and searching for select compounds.

Aliyaah had been on one of the first short missions to Mars, and in the single sevensol she spent on the planet, she had planted several of these nanobiotic plants and established an automated irrigation system using recycled water. The lack of surface water on the red planet meant that they had to develop large scale technologies to allow for an almost one hundred percent water reclamation. The rocket that brought the astronauts to Mars had an eighty-five percent reclamation rate, which could sustain them only for the five-month journey from Earth. Once they landed, they established a dozen ground wells, but it had taken several sevensols to determine the safety of the deep subsurface water table. As their water supply decreased, they'd had to make cutbacks, including restricting the crew to one short shower every five sols. This placed even greater pressure on the team tasked with approving the use of well-water for the station.

Biodomes One and Two had been the first parts of the colony to switch to Mars groundwater, and had been operating on a closed system for more than a hundred sols. They took in carbon dioxide from the planet's atmosphere, which accounted for over ninety-five percent of the air, and effectively used the plants to create oxygen. Specially designed oxygen scrubbers then collected the gas, which was stored for use on *Octavia* for their journey home. Five sols before the accident at the quarry, the crew had celebrated as *Octavia's* oxygen tanks had finally been refilled. The oxygen produced at the biodomes had begun to be transported for use at the quarry, and a newly laid pipeline had begun to feed oxygen into the station's climate system.

Silver thought about the biodomes and the recent changes in the colony as she carefully guided the SEV over the rocky terrain. Aliyaah was checking in with Hadley, using a secure channel so she could update him without causing mass panic among the survivors. As Aliyaah spoke, Silver realised that this was how she had begun to see them: as survivors.

Hadley had already contacted Mission Support to brief them on the situation. They hadn't yet had a reply, but this was expected; communication between Mars and Earth was currently delayed by sixteen minutes due to the planets' orbits.

Command personnel on Project Arche had been chosen specifically for their experience and were imbued with the authority to make autonomous decisions, given this delay in communications. The Chief had led over a dozen space missions, as had the Commander. Hadley came from a military background, and had offered the station's inhabitants an approachable alternative to the Commander. Given the Commander's death, Silver wondered if Hadley might deem it necessary to adopt a more aggressive leadership approach to hold the crew together during the crisis. So far, he was listening to the Chief and following her lead.

Like all personnel on Mars, Hadley had received rudimentary training on all the systems used at the station, including the biodomes, rockets, rovers, and refiners. Those in senior positions had also learnt about the planet's quirks: its atmosphere, groundwater, and mineral make-up, as well as the minimal magnetic field. As Aliyaah explained her theory about the chemotrophic life-form that had ravaged the west wing, Hadley listened quietly, asking questions only when he needed further clarification.

"So, if your reasoning is correct, this thing won't have been able to get through the seal between the west wing and the central hub of the station?"

"It doesn't appear so, no."

"So how did it get into the west wing in the first place?"

"It's possible that it wasn't detected in the recycled air from the biodomes when we switched to the new system. Or it could have entered through the groundwater or hitched a ride on someone's suit. With dust as fine as smoke, it wouldn't be surprising, no matter how careful we are about decontamination."

Hadley was quiet for a moment and then confirmed with Aliyaah something that Silver had been trying to figure out for the past few minutes. The east and west wings had been gradually switched over to a water supply from groundwater wells, and oxygen from Biodomes One and Two. The Civilian wing was still on a closed system using the supplies brought from Earth, with a separate oxygen filtration system created using plants brought with them on this mission.

"So, the Civilian wing is the only structure we currently have that is likely to remain uncontaminated, assuming this chemotrophic organism is in the water or air?" Hadley asked.

"Not quite," Aliyaah said, hesitantly. "The Civilian wing draws some gases from the planet's atmosphere, so it's possible that it's also contaminated." She paused, then added, "there is one area that may be unaffected. It's on a separate system. That's where FE Antara and I are headed now, Sir."

"Where is that, Chief?" Hadley asked, as Silver finally realised why Aliyaah had suggested Biodome Three. In addition to the biodomes, there were several solar storm shelters scattered across the planet's surface, designed to harbor any astronauts out in the field and away from an armored vehicle when a solar storm hit. Feasibly, any one of these could have been the supposed safe zone.

"Sir, I'm sorry, but I'm not able to disclose that information," Aliyaah said firmly. Silver glanced over at her as she continued. "Article seven point five expressly states that in the event of an emergency like this the two senior officers should attempt to restore safe operational control from distinct locations."

Hadley paused for a moment, then agreed. "You're right, of course, Chief. Let's liaise remotely until we have a better handle on things and can be certain we're both of sound mind."

Silver wanted to look over at Aliyaah to read her expression, but she needed to focus on getting the SEV down the last section of the crater's wall and onto flat land. With the lower gravity on the planet, it was harder to rely on physical cues and she had to focus on the sensors to determine the SEV's pitch. While she steered the SEV, Silver thought back to what Aliyaah had said about the quarry, and the Commander. To blow the quarry remotely, the Commander would have needed codes from Aliyaah, Chief Frederickson, or Hadley. It worried her that Hadley and Aliyaah had basically just admitted that they weren't entirely sure they could trust one another.

They were all silent for a few seconds, then Hadley said in a calm voice, "Did you deactivate the SEV's tracking system, Chief?"

Aliyaah confirmed that she had as soon as they had gotten into the SEV. Silver hadn't noticed her disarm the tracker, but she saw now that the system was, indeed, disabled. Neither Hadley, nor anyone else, had any way of confirming where Aliyaah and Silver were taking the SEV.

FIFTEEN

Biodome Three was one of the most recently completed and impressive structures on Mars. Construction had begun at the same time as the two larger domes, but had been delayed by dust storms that gathered at the crater's edge, creating shocks of heat lightning. As the other biodomes were completed, sol after sol passed with little progress on the smaller dome.

Once *Octavia* had landed safely on the planet, a specially assigned team had worked quickly to get Biodome Three up and running. The delays had set them back in terms of oxygen production, but there was a silver lining to the enforced downtime; engineers on Earth had designed a new kind of air and water filtration system, which the *Octavia* team had summarily installed.

Biodome Three's closed system was not the only thing separating it from the rest of the colony; its location beyond the ridge of the Schiaparelli crater had the effect of putting it both out of sight of the station and a little out of mind. As a result, Biodome Three had become something of a haven for a handful of personnel.

Biodomes One and Two each covered almost three acres of land, and their huge curved walls rose to over seventy feet tall. In contrast, Biodome Three stood at a height of just thirty feet, covering an acre and a half. The smaller dome felt more intimate, like a walled garden rather than a research facility. Sitting in the middle of Biodome Three, surrounded by greenery, you almost had the sense of being in a desert oasis.

Silver had heard from Hardeep that for some of the crew, Biodome Three had gained a reputation as an ideal spot for romantic trysts, especially late at night for a little stargazing. It was funny how photographs taken from the surface of Mars seem to suggest that you can't see stars from the planet. Silver, Hardeep, and anyone else who had landed on Mars knew better. The lens exposure needed to capture the details of the biodomes, station, or an astronaut on a space walk on Mars meant that the stars remained hidden for the most part, lost in the vast, inky blackness of space. At night, however, when the lights were off at the biodome, anyone gazing up through the clear panels of the sloped roof would be rewarded with a stunning view of the great expanse of star-filled space, as well as the sight of the two moons, Phobos and Deimos. Phobos raced west to east across the sky, while Deimos, the smaller of the two moons, made its way slowly from east to west. Astronauts working at night on Mars had marvelled at first at how Phobos would rise and set twice in an evening. But, as with many things on the planet, even this magnificent sight quickly became routine.

One afternoon, while Hardeep and Silver were listening to *Dance Gavin Dance*, he had mentioned that he and a miner had spent a night under the stars in the biodome. They had seen Phobos eclipse Deimos, and Hardeep asked Silver if she thought it was a sign that the relationship wouldn't work out. Silver had laughed, reminding Hardeep that she much preferred astronomy over astrology.

Silver was tempted to tell Hardeep that the moons were named for fear and panic, after the two sons of the Roman god Mars, but she had kept quiet in the face of his new infatuation with the miner. Now, it seemed awfully apt that panic was pensive in the sky, while fear raced overhead.

As Silver contemplated the fates of both the miner and Hardeep, Aliyaah interrupted her thoughts.

"Without the laboratory, it's going to be difficult to get a clear sense of what's happening with those crystal formations. Aragonite wouldn't crystallise that quickly from that kind of... substrate. It has to be something else: some kind of microorganism with rapid cell division."

Silver grimaced, then asked Aliyaah what she thought the organism might be.

"My guess is that it's something akin to *Thiomicrospira crunogena*. It probably came up in the groundwater and somehow bypassed the filtration system."

Silver tried to remember back to her biology classes, but came up empty and looked over at Aliyaah blankly as she pulled off her suit in the airlock for the biodome.

"*T. cru*: It's an extremophile that lives in deep ocean hydrothermal vents. It grows rapidly and feeds on carbon dioxide and sulfur. Whatever this crystal-producing organism is, it might be similar to *T. cru.* It could be feeding on carbon dioxide and sulfur and other elements." She paused and then added with a grimace, "Basically, I think that whatever this microbe is, the human body may be an ideal food source."

Silver swallowed, thinking back to the crystalline gravesite they had just escaped. She took extra care as she went through the decontamination procedures. When Aliyaah joined her on the other side of the airlock, Silver asked, "So that's why there was such a massive formation of crystals back there; as our people all scrambled to get out after hearing the blasts it must have been like a feeding frenzy for this thing."

Aliyaah nodded, not meeting Silver's eye as she began the process of getting into a similar suit to the one she had just taken off. They didn't normally wear suits inside the biodome, but Aliyaah wanted to be sure the biodome was safe before letting down her guard for even an instant.

"How do we stop this thing?" Silver asked as they suited up.

"I don't know. When the Commander destroyed the lab, he destroyed our best chance of figuring this thing out."

Neither of them voiced their suspicions about why the Commander may have taken the actions he did. Just thinking about all those lost lives made Silver nauseous, which reminded her that she had been violently sick earlier in the night, or yestersol perhaps. She was no longer sure of the time or sol, and the unsettling feeling brought on a wave of exhaustion. She needed to take extra anti-radiation meds, as did Aliyaah, but even those might not be enough to counteract any damage done by the radiation around the crystal formations in the west wing.

Silver asked Aliyaah if there were extra meds kept in the biodome and Aliyaah directed her to a workroom to the right of the temperate zone. "See if you can also find the M-Lab. It should be in there, unless one of the team was using it in a different dome." The Mobile Laboratory offered their best chance of examining the crystal in a contained environment.

"Where will we get a sample?" Silver asked. "We can't exactly ask Hadley to send someone to us, not without compromising our location."

Aliyaah frowned and said, "Our location may already be compromised. There may be crystals here that we can examine." She gestured toward the control panel on the exterior side of the inner wall of the biodome. "I'm going to run a full sweep before either of us enters the inner dome. Go get the meds and the lab and get back here as soon as you can. And keep your suit on, Sil."

SIXTEEN

Silver walked past the doors to the temperate zone and entered the code Aliyaah had given her for the workroom. Inside were empty lab benches and random supplies, including fertilisers and various hand tools for maintaining the gardens. It was exactly what Silver imagined a Martian gardener's shed would look like. Sadly, that didn't give her any clues as to where she might find anti-radiation meds.

A shelf laden with boxes in one corner looked promising, and Silver began to run her gloved finger down the labels. The boxes contained a variety of chemicals that Silver guessed were being systematically tested on the Martian soil to see if they enhanced crop yields. She moved to the second shelving unit and saw a first aid kit. She pulled this off the shelf and found a stash of meds behind the kit.

Silver strapped the first aid kit to her suit and considered taking off her helmet so she could pop a couple of anti-radiation pills. She knew she needed to wait for the all-clear from the Chief, but she was painfully aware both of how long it had been since her normal dose and how this was far from a normal situation.

After stuffing the meds into the top of the first aid kit, Silver spotted a promising looking container. She picked up the box, which held several anti-rad cartridges. They could plug these directly into their ports to inject anti-rads, avoiding the need to compromise the integrity of their suits. Silver opened the seal on one of the cartridges and gave herself a shot. She added the other cartridges to the kit and relaxed a little, relieved that she was once again protected from the worst of the radiation.

Next, Silver looked around for the M-Lab, which was housed on what looked like a glorified dessert cart. After a few minutes puzzling over how it could hide in a room this size, Silver finally located the M-Lab behind a stack of totes in a far corner.

As Silver moved the totes out of the way, she felt a sudden wave of heat rush toward her. A side effect of the anti-rad shot, perhaps? She preferred taking the pills, and only used the shots when she had no other option, such as on a long space walk where she would be in her suit for hours at a time. If it wasn't the anti-rad shot, it could be a hot flash, she thought with annoyance. She'd had a few hot flashes recently, and remembered now how her mother had gone through menopause early. Silver checked the temperature dial on her suit, in case there was a malfunction, and was shocked to see that it wasn't the anti-rads, menopause, or anything endogenous; the room was getting warmer, and rapidly.

Silver looked around with a growing sense of panic, but saw no reason for the temperature change. She grabbed the M-Lab and yanked it across the room to the door. When she was back out in the corridor, she ran a few metres back in the direction of Aliyaah before stopping and checking the temperature again. There was a massive difference between the workroom and the corridor. Something in the lab had caused that rapid increase in temperature.

Leaving the M-Lab where it was, Silver stepped back toward the workroom, unable to suppress her scientific curiosity. When she reached the door, Silver looked through the window, and saw a figure emerge from behind one of the benches. She jumped back as she saw the figure scurry toward the door. The hunched over man was dressed in white, and had raised his head briefly, giving Silver a glimpse of his face, his pallor deathly grey and shiny. His skin was almost iridescent. She backed away, expecting the man to fling open the door. Silver wasn't at all sure what she would do when confronted with the unidentified scientist. The door remained closed, however, and all that happened was a peculiar change in the light emanating from the room. Silver held up a gloved hand to her visor to shield her eyes from the light, then stepped forward again to look through the window.

The man had disappeared. In his place, in the centre of the workroom, was a crystalline growth that formed into an arch that stopped at its apex. Almost finger-like, the crystal seemed to be pointing directly at the door, at Silver.

SEVENTEEN

The area around the central control panel was empty when Silver arrived to meet Aliyaah, pushing the M-Lab ahead of her. She did a quick visual check of the area and then looked at the panel itself to see if there was any indication of Aliyaah's whereabouts.

The biodomes were not Silver's domain, and while she understood some of the functions on the panel, the rest were unfamiliar. She activated her intercom and tried to hail the Chief.

Aliyaah responded immediately, and moved from behind one of the central columns of the biodome into Silver's line of sight. Aliyaah began to walk towards the doors to the inner atrium but Silver held up her hand to stop her.

"I got the M-Lab. But we have a problem."

On the other side of the glass, Aliyaah frowned.

"I encountered the... well, what looks like the same organism we saw in the west wing." Silver struggled to put words to what she had seen. "It, I guess, *consumed* another man right in front of me. I mean, he was there, then there was just heat and crystal and light."

Aliyaah lowered her gaze and Silver could hear her breathing on the intercom. She seemed to be taking steady, slow breaths, and Silver began to do the same, realising that her heart was pounding. She had reached a level beyond terror, beyond her training, perhaps even beyond her ability to keep holding it together. Aliyaah's breathing was calming, reassuring, even if she was on the other side of the glass.

"Chief?"

"I'm thinking."

After a few seconds, Aliyaah looked up at Silver and said, "If you were in close proximity to the organism, you need to go back through decontamination. There's no other way for you to enter the inner dome without risking bringing in the organism with you."

Silver stared at Aliyaah, wondering where this was heading.

"You have to flush the whole system. The whole outer ring. Decontaminate all of it."

"The scientist in the lab wasn't wearing a suit, Chief. And if there's anyone else in here they'll suffocate."

"I know." Aliyaah's jaw was set, and she held Silver's gaze.

"Can we send out an alert to see if anyone else is here?"

"We would have to be on an open channel to do that, and we would have to identify our location."

"What about a system-wide alarm localised to this biodome?"

"The domes aren't set up that way."

Silver nodded, seeing why Aliyaah had hesitated to give the order. There didn't seem to be a way of alerting anyone who happened to be in the biodome to what was about to happen.

Aliyaah and Silver stared at each other for a few more seconds and Aliyaah started to order Silver to begin decontamination, but Silver interrupted her.

"What about a solar storm alarm?" Silver said, and Aliyaah cocked her head and thought for a second, then gestured Silver to continue. "Because of the crater, this biodome might get hit by solar storms before the station, right?"

"I haven't had to use the system, but you're right. There is a separate storm alert that would tell everyone at the dome to suit up."

"So, if we sound that alarm, anyone who is still here would have to come out of hiding."

"Presumably." The Chief frowned.

"We should at least try," Silver said.

Aliyaah nodded and talked her through how to activate the alarm and for a second Silver felt relieved. Then she thought back to the man in the workroom. Had he been running towards the door for fear of his life, or had he been running right at her? There was something about his expression that scared Silver. Not just the grey colour of his skin, but something in his eyes. It hadn't been fear exactly, but something more akin to rage. As she recalled his expression, she felt increasingly certain that he had been running at her, not to her.

When the alarm began to reverberate around the dome, Silver jumped, suddenly afraid of who, or what, it might bring out into the open.

EIGHTEEN

The sound of the alarm rang in Silver's ears as she watched for anyone emerging from other areas of the biodome. Aliyaah waited and watched from the inner dome, and when a transmission came in from Hadley, it made them both jump. Hadley told Aliyaah to check the new message from Mission Support, so she accessed the array through the device attached to her suit. As Aliyaah listened intently to the message, Silver backed up against the wall so that she would have a full view of her periphery.

After a few minutes, Silver began to feel reassured that she and Aliyaah were the only ones left alive in the dome. She moved forward to check the control panel for any signs that interior doors had opened or closed. As she checked the panel, something flickered at the edge of her vision. Something inside the dome, behind Aliyaah.

"Chief?"

Aliyaah didn't look up from the screen, still focusing on whatever guidance Mission Support was issuing.

There it was again. A shadow of movement behind Aliyaah, just beyond a small plot of corn.

"Chief, there's someone in there with you, or something," Silver pointed behind Aliyaah, and the Chief looked up, hearing the fear in Silver's voice.

Aliyaah turned, just as a man in dark blue overalls ran out from the corn and threw himself at Aliyaah, almost knocking her to the ground. Aliyaah recovered quickly, and dodged a second swipe from the man, then jammed her foot behind his ankle and flipped him quickly onto his back. Crouching down, Aliyaah held her knee on the man's chest and pinned his hands above his head.

The man thrashed beneath her for a few moments and then fell perfectly still.

"Chief?" Silver cried, standing with her hands against the glass. "Are you OK?"

Aliyaah leaned over the man and watched to see if the outside of her visor fogged up. After a moment, she stood up slowly, confident that he was at least breathing, then she released him and glanced up at Silver, saying "He passed out." She kept a wary eye on the man while looking around the inner dome. "I need something to bind his hands with. In case he wakes up and is in the same state of mind."

"What's wrong with him?" Silver asked as she grabbed some cable lying nearby. "Do you think it's like what happened with the Commander?"

Aliyaah didn't respond right away. Instead, she used the cable, designed to support the trusses of the experimental tomato plants, to tie the man's hands together around the base of one of the dome's heat lamps. When she was done, she looked up at Silver and said, "Whatever that was, it wasn't just normal fear or panic. He looked like he wanted to kill me. Like he didn't know who I was." "Or maybe who he was?" Silver said, remembering what Hardeep had said in the mess hall earlier. "If he doesn't remember who he is or why he's here, suddenly realising that you're not on Earth could be enough to make anyone come unhinged."

With the man secured and unconscious for now, Silver went back to the control panel. There were no other signs of movement in the dome, so after confirming with Aliyaah, she hooked her suit to the wall of the outer dome and initiated a complete decontamination. As the air rushed out of the outer ring, Silver watched through the glass as Aliyaah started talking, presumably to Hadley.

After a few minutes, Aliyaah opened a line with Silver and said that there had been a further death back at the station. Another specialist had suddenly become disoriented and violent and had needed to be restrained, dying just minutes later after struggling to breathe. Doctor Schiff had set up a temporary medical ward, salvaging what she could from the wreckage of the lab. The Commander's body, and the body of the specialist, had been moved to the medical ward for examination.

Patching herself into the same line as Hadley, Silver suggested that the remaining survivors take extra doses of anti-radiation meds. Aliyaah added that it would be good for Doctor Schiff to perform an autopsy on both the bodies.

"What do you think she'll find?" Hadley asked.

"Well, if they're dying of respiratory failure, it makes sense to look at the lungs and throat first," Aliyaah said. "If something affected their breathing it could be causing hypoxia and confusion. That might explain their behaviour."

"Like the disorientation you can experience with altitude sickness," Silver said, nodding. Then she pointed at the prone figure behind Aliyaah and said, "He's still breathing though, right?"

Aliyaah checked again and nodded. She wanted to pull off a glove and check his pulse, but along with the risk of exposure, there was also a risk he would wake up and grab her. As he wasn't wearing an EV suit there was no easy diagnostic panel she could access while he was unconscious. She wondered if the M-Lab had a first aid kit. It would at least have some diagnostic equipment that she could use to monitor his vital signs. Maybe they could even run some samples and start to figure out what was going on.

Curiously, Aliyaah's sweep of the inner dome had revealed no undesirable or unknown biosignatures. Whatever had affected the crew wasn't showing up on their sensors.

"What if it's something in the brain?" Silver said, interrupting Aliyaah's thoughts. "What if it's just space-brain from massive amounts of radiation? That would kill off neurons in the prefrontal cortex and lead to a loss of control, memory, and executive function."

Silver waited for Aliyaah to respond, but the Chief hesitated. Then, slowly, she backed away from the man and began to remove her gloves.

"Chief?" Silver shouted, and watched as Aliyaah removed her

helmet. "What if it's airborne?"

Aliyaah set her helmet down on the ground and shrugged. "If he's been exposed, it's likely I have too."

Silver considered this, but stayed silent. Aliyaah continued. "If it's airborne, we would have been exposed back at the station and in the hangar. And if it's radiation, the two of us have more exposure than most. Our scans say there's nothing in the inner dome, but you should get in here with those anti-rads and the M-Lab and we should get to work."

"Doing what?"

"We'll wait to see if he wakes up, and then we're going to swab him and see if we can find anything that didn't show up on the sweep of the dome I ran earlier."

"And if he doesn't wake up?" Silver asked, not without hesitation. She saw the way Aliyaah was looking at the man, and the gentle familiarity with which she now pressed her finger to his neck to check his pulse. Aliyaah knew him, as more than a colleague, and maybe as something other than a friend. "Chief, what if he dies too?"

Aliyaah stayed silent for a moment as she crouched by the man's side. Then, satisfied with his slow, but steady, pulse, she stood up and looked Silver in the eye. Without blinking, she said, "Well, if that happens, we'll have no choice but to do an autopsy ourselves."

NINETEEN

With the outer dome decontaminated, Silver moved quickly through the airlock into the inner dome, taking the M-Lab with her. Aliyaah met her with a handful of tomatoes, snap peas, and carrots. Silver fought the urge to laugh.

"We need to eat," Aliyaah said. "It's not much, but we should eat something with the anti-rads, and I'd much rather fresh food than another protein bar."

Silver agreed and bit into a carrot as she handed over half of the meds. Aliyaah gave herself a shot, then helped Silver set up the M-Lab next to the corn patch. They cleared a small workbench and moved it over to the lab equipment.

Silver looked down at the man lying on the ground and recognised him from the mess hall. She looked up at Aliyaah, but the Chief's expression revealed nothing.

"He's one of the biochemists, isn't he, Chief?" Silver asked, and Aliyaah hesitated before looking over at the man.

"A biochemist and botanist, yeah. Mission Specialist Doctor Dominic Watson. He's part of the team running soil experiments here." As Aliyaah spoke, Silver noticed that she was playing with the ring on the chain around her neck.

"Are you close?" Silver asked, then backed off, saying, "Sorry, I shouldn't have asked." She felt the heat rising to her cheeks. She wouldn't normally ask about a colleague's personal life, especially not her boss, but she had known Aliyaah a long time and the events of the last sol had shaken up the normal order of things.

Aliyaah didn't answer right away, but when she did, she looked Silver square in the face and nodded. "We've been seeing each other for a little while now. We were keeping things quiet. You know how it is with a small crew in close quarters. Everything is so unreal here, it's hard to know what will work and what won't."

Silver nodded and changed the subject, asking Aliyaah about the message from Mission Support.

"They didn't have a lot to say, unfortunately. They're as stuck for answers as we are at this point," Aliyaah said. Then she added, quietly, "But they are delaying the launch of *Octavia II*. Until there's a clearer picture of what is happening."

Octavia II was the cargo flight due to launch in the next sevensol, with touchdown on Mars scheduled for five months from now. Once *Octavia II* landed, she would be refueled and readied to return to Earth. The crew would stay on Mars to provide assistance to the current team at the station. *Octavia* was scheduled to launch twelve months after her sister-ship landed, taking non-essential crew back to Earth. Silver was supposed to be on that flight, but she wondered now if they even had the right personnel to get the ship safely home.

If Mission Support decided to launch *Octavia II*, they would have to completely overhaul the crew manifest to ensure they replaced key crew members lost in the explosions and to the organism. Silver wondered if Hadley had provided a list of the remaining personnel. She shuddered as she thought about how short a list that might now be.

Mission Support would need to send people to rebuild the damaged parts of the station, and Silver knew there would be discussion about postponing the next passenger flight. Postponing a launch was phenomenally expensive, and NASA would face pressure from SolarEx and the other private companies invested in their personal vision of the colony. If NASA delayed the launch of *Octavia II*, would there ever be another mission to Mars? Depending on what they found in the samples, and in the autopsies, maybe NASA would reconsider the whole endeavour. Perhaps no one else would be coming to the red planet.

Silver watched Aliyaah crouch down beside Dominic and check his pulse. She was cautious and gentle in her movements, looking at his face while she counted. When she was satisfied that his pulse was regular and strong, Aliyaah rejoined Silver at the workbench. Silver saw Aliyaah tuck the necklace with her wedding band back into the collar of her suit. She moved her hand to feel the reassuring presence of her own wedding ring, smiling as she thought about how lucky she was to have Cooper and Cosima waiting for her on Earth. She was surprised to feel the smoothness of her skin where the titanium band should have been, then reality hit her hard. It felt just like the earlier blow to her chest, when Aliyaah knocked the wind out of her as she ran down the station corridor. Silver focused on her breathing, trying to force the panic back down. She had forgotten that she had taken off the ring, and why.

She couldn't think clearly and as her breath came in fits and starts, her vision narrowed and the edges of the world crumpled into blackness. She put out a hand to grab the workbench and when Aliyaah said, "Sil?" her voice seemed very far away.

Aliyaah took Silver's elbow, holding her up and then gently easing her to the floor. "Sit down. Take a deep breath. And again. In and out. In, and out." Aliyaah crouched in front of Silver and placed her hands on Silver's knees, looking up at her. Gradually, Silver's vision returned and the weight on her chest lifted. "What happened just then, Antara?" Aliyaah asked, standing up and looking down at Silver. Her voice was firm, with a slight edge to it that Silver had not heard from her before. "Do I need to be worried?"

"No. I'm fine. There's no need to restrain me, Chief," Silver said, and felt the prick of tears. Even now that she had remembered Cooper's last message, it didn't seem real. She hadn't had time to process anything. She had never given herself enough time, even when she wasn't in the middle of a crisis.

Silver knew there were more immediate concerns, but it seemed impossible that she could have somehow forgotten something so important.

She blinked and wiped her eyes, then looked up at the Chief and said, "I had some bad news from home earlier, is all. I'd forgotten it for a moment. I think I wanted to forget."

Aliyaah nodded and said, "that makes sense, given everything that's going on." She smiled, then helped Silver onto her feet again. "Want to talk about it? We could be here a while."

Silver laughed. "It's a little early for gallows humour, isn't it?" she said.

"I meant we might be a while waiting for Dominic to wake up. What did you think I meant?" Aliyaah asked.

"Oh! That we're stuck on this planet, with no one coming to rescue us." Silver laughed again. She knew her emotions were getting the better of her, vacillating between despair and disbelief, but she needed a moment to get herself back under control.

Aliyaah nodded, then asked again, "So, do you want to talk about it?"

Silver didn't respond, and Aliyaah didn't push her. Silver was clearly hurting.

After a few seconds, Silver said, "You know, it's fine." If we survive this, I promise I'll talk to you, or to someone at least, about everything."

"OK, Antara, you do that."

Silver thanked Aliyaah and thought about when she would next talk to Cooper. She would be mad at Silver for not having responded to her last message.

Forgetting protocol for a moment, Silver asked Aliyaah if she could send a transmission to Cooper.

"You can't," Aliyaah said. "We can only talk to Mission Support, remember? We can't contact our families, or anyone else."

Silver nodded and said, "Yes, yes. Absolutely." She sniffled and closed her eyes, then let out a long breath.

Aliyaah took Silver's hand in hers and said gently, "Whatever's going on, Sil, I'm sorry. Right now, though, we all need to have our heads in the game to deal with..."

"Whatever we're dealing with," Silver finished the sentence Aliyaah had left hanging.

The two women held each other's gaze for a couple of seconds, then a noise startled Aliyaah into dropping Silver's hand, and they both turned to look at Dominic.

TWENTY

"Ali?" Dominic said slowly and uncertainly as he woke. He shook his head and screwed up his eyes, as if trying to dislodge something. When he realised his hands were tied to the heat lamp, he struggled and then looked up at Aliyaah, his eyes wide. "What's happening, Ali?" He saw Silver and asked again, "Chief?"

"How are you feeling, Dom?" Aliyaah crouched down beside him and touched him gently on the arm. He glanced up at Silver and then back at Aliyaah, who said, "It's OK. This is Silver, Flight Engineer Antara." Dominic was quiet for a couple of seconds, then asked again, "What's going on? Why am I tied up?"

"What's the last thing you remember?" Aliyaah asked.

"I... I don't know. I think I was taking some water samples back to the workroom. Yeah, I had a joke to tell Alvarez," Dominic grinned for a second, but the look Silver gave him made him shake his head and sit up straight, as if he had suddenly remembered he was tied up and being interrogated.

"And then?" Silver asked.

Dominic's eyes darted around as he struggled to grasp at memories. "The storm alarm sounded. Yes, that's it. The alarm sounded and I tried to get into the workroom, but the door was stuck. I had to force it open. I wanted to leave the samples there and then get to a suit."

"And after that?" Aliyaah asked.

Dominic frowned, then looked up at Aliyaah and shook his head. "I don't remember," he whispered.

"Did you get into the workroom?" Silver asked, "Did you get to tell Dr. Alvarez this joke?" she added, trying to avoid any edge in her voice.

"Maybe? I don't really remember."

"Did you see or feel anything unusual when you got to the door of the workroom? You said it was stuck? Could you see why?" Aliyaah asked.

"Why are you asking me about the workroom?" Dominic said. "What happened, Ali?"

"Think, Dominic. It could be important. Did you get the door to the workroom open? Did you get inside?"

He hesitated, then his expression changed and he looked up at Silver. "It was hot. The door. The door was hot to the touch, like there was a fire in the workroom, but that wasn't what the alarm was for, and I couldn't see a fire. I put the tray of samples on the floor and pushed against the door. Alvarez was supposed to be working in there, but I couldn't see him."

Dominic hesitated again, and Silver asked, "Do you know what Doctor Alvarez was working on?"

After a moment's silence, Dominic shook his head and said, "I don't remember. I'm sorry."

Silver and Aliyaah exchanged a look and then Aliyaah explained that he had appeared in the biodome and, as Aliyaah framed it, hadn't been acting like himself.

"I don't understand," he said. "What was I doing here?"

Aliyaah didn't reply. Silver gave her a few seconds, then looked at Dominic and said, "You attacked the Chief."

Dominic stared at Silver in disbelief, then reached out to Aliyaah, groaning as the cable ties prevented him from touching her. He looked into Aliyaah's eyes and pleaded to be untied. "Why would I do that?" He lowered his voice and said, "I'd never do anything to hurt you. You know that, Ali."

Aliyaah brushed her hand against his cheek and murmured something as Silver looked away. He lowered his head and Aliyaah asked Silver to bring over the medical kit. She explained to Dominic that they wanted to take some samples and run some tests to see if they could find a physiological cause for his aberrant behaviour.

He nodded, then asked what had happened to Alvarez. "I didn't hurt him, did I?"

Silver shook her head and said that they weren't sure what had happened. She brought over the medical kit and told Dominic she was going to run a full body scan. He nodded and Silver gave him a small pinprick injection to populate his blood with nanobots. As these worked their way around his body, assessing levels of minerals, cortisol, neurotransmitters, insulin, and other things in his bloodstream, Silver flashed light into Dominic's eyes to check pupil response. Then she asked him to follow the light as she moved it from side to side and up and down. She could see no evidence of nystagmus or any other signs of ocular nerve damage.

Silver also examined his ears, nose, and throat, and saw that some of the membranes were inflamed and thick with white mucus. She asked to take swabs, and he nodded again, watching Silver with a smile she found unnerving. Silver stowed the swabs in sealed containers and then picked up a scanner, placing it in position over Dominic's heart. His heart rate was a little elevated, but Silver would have been surprised if it had been normal, given the situation.

The nanobots began to relay readings to the device Silver had handed to Aliyaah.

"Your cortisol is high, but I think that's probably true for all of us right now. Your insulin too, but that's also a pretty normal response to stress or shock." Aliyaah handed the device back to Silver and pointed at something on the screen. "What do you make of these figures?"

Dominic had extremely elevated levels of dopamine in his bloodstream. There were also elevated levels of a string of substances Silver didn't recognise: NSE, GFAP, and S100β.

Silver shook her head. She couldn't even hazard a guess, so she located the device's diagnostic program, which would suggest possible conditions and any further tests they might want to carry out. The analysis barely took a second, returning a single result: traumatic brain injury.

Silver tried to remember if Dominic had hit his head during the struggle with Aliyaah. She didn't think so, and even if he had, that was probably not long enough ago to have these kinds of biomarkers in his blood.

"Do you feel unwell now, Dominic?" Silver asked. "And have you had any unusual symptoms the last few sols?"

Dominic said that he hadn't noticed anything out of the ordinary. Perhaps a headache, but he had been working long hours trying to determine why some of the plants weren't growing like the others.

"And I guess I've been feeling a little nauseous and sweaty, but I always feel like that when there's something at work that is a bit stressful."

"Do you have a headache now? Or nausea?" Silver asked, and Dominic nodded.

"But... it's not bad. More a dull throb and mild nausea. Nothing that explains how you're saying I behaved."

"Have you bumped your head recently?" Aliyaah asked.

"Not that I remember."

"Any loss of motor control or vision?"

"No. Why? What do you think is wrong with me?"

Aliyaah shrugged. "I don't know. But your bloodwork suggests a TBI, and maybe that would explain behavioural changes."

"Like a stroke?" Dominic laughed. "I definitely didn't have a stroke, Ali. I feel fine, I really do." He smiled at her again and Silver thought she saw him wink at the Chief, but she couldn't be sure.

Aliyaah nodded slowly, then tried to offer him a reassuring smile before asking Silver to contact Hadley and get Schiff to check the others for similar biomarkers.

"What are you thinking, Chief?" Silver asked, but Aliyaah clearly didn't want to lay out her theory in front of Dominic.

He looked back and forth between Silver and Aliyaah, his eyes wide open. Abruptly, Aliyaah asked him which plants were struggling. Without missing a beat, Dominic answered, "Sector Five. The soy, Aliyaah. I'm sorry. I was going to tell you, but I wanted to try to figure out what was happening first."

"It's not growing at all?"

"Oh, it is growing. It's just how it's growing that's odd." Dominic paused, then said with a grin, "I can show you. But...."

Aliyaah looked over at Silver, who shrugged. "Your call, Chief. I will run these samples through the lab and see if anything comes up, but without a head CT or a functional MRI, there's not a lot else I can test for."

Aliyaah put her hand on Dominic's shoulder and said, "OK, I'll remove the restraints, but if you start to feel anything unusual at all, you let me know and you agree to let me restrain you again. Deal?" He laughed, then nodded at Aliyaah and suddenly turned serious. "Why are you both at the dome anyway?" he asked.

As she untied the cables, Aliyaah explained what had happened with the Commander and at the rest of the station. Dominic listened in stunned silence, then took her hand when she offered to help him up. Aliyaah gestured for him to lead the way to Sector Five, and as he moved ahead of her, Dominic asked, his voice cracking slightly, "How many of us are left, Ali?"

Silver didn't hear Aliyaah's reply, but she ran the calculations herself. Assuming no one was taking shelter in a storm bunker or at one of the two other biodomes, and given the three deaths in the last hour, there were now fewer than thirty people left alive on Mars.

TWENTY-ONE

Silver was careful not to reveal her location when she contacted Hadley, saying only that they had found another survivor. She informed the Commander of what she had witnessed in the workroom, and let him know the results of the medical tests she had run on Dominic, who she didn't identify by name.

"I'll let Doctor Schiff know to check for those things in particular. And, Antara, I'm curious, do you and Chief Diambu have any thoughts on what might explain those results and the abnormally aggressive behaviour?"

"No, not really."

"The Chief has no ideas?" Hadley said, pressing Silver again.

"Well, a TBI caused by a blow to the head or a stroke would usually present with more consistent symptoms."

"And it would be odd for all three victims to have incurred a similar TBI in separate incidents."

"Yes."

"And this patient of yours has no other symptoms?"

"There is some inflammation in his mucus membranes, with no obvious cause, and he says he's generally felt well other than a headache and some nausea."

"Could this just be radiation sickness?"

"Perhaps." Silver's voice was clipped.

"Antara, are you holding something back?"

Silver closed her eyes and exhaled. "Sir, I think we might want to focus on the possibility that each of the victims was exposed to something in the environment. An organism, perhaps."

Hadley considered this, then asked, "And, Antara, in your opinion, do you think this hypothetical organism might be linked to the crystal phenomenon you have seen?"

"I'd say that's a distinct possibility, Sir, yes."

"You understand what this means, don't you?" Hadley paused and Silver shuddered as he said what she and Aliyaah had been thinking for a while now. "If the Commander and the others were exposed and are showing symptoms, the likelihood is that we are all infected."

"Yes, Sir," Silver said. "And if there's a chance we're all infected then we can't risk taking this thing back to Earth. There's no point getting *Octavia* ready to launch."

"Let's not give up, Antara," Hadley said, gently chastising her for her defeatism. "Readying the ship will give the crew something to focus on, while you and the doctor try to work out what we're dealing with exactly. We may yet be able to stay on the planet."

"Yes, Sir," Silver said again, but this time there was no conviction in her voice. At the rate this thing was killing the crew, she wasn't sure they'd survive long enough to get the ship off the ground.

After Silver had closed the connection with Hadley, she took another vial from the medical kit and fitted it into the mini-dart. Holding out her wrist, Silver took a breath and then injected the nanobots into her arm. The more information they had on this thing the better, and if they were all infected, at least this way she would have readings on a patient before they became symptomatic.

As Silver considered herself as a patient, she realised that she had already experienced what could be symptoms of cognitive dysfunction in the previous twenty-five or so hours. She had forgotten about Cooper. She had forgotten about the SEV. Her emotions had been all over the place, which wasn't at all normal for her. She could put the memory lapses and changes in mood down to acute stress and fatigue, but she also knew these could be signs that there was something eating away at her prefrontal cortex.

While she waited for the nanobots to start returning results, Silver ran the swabs from Dominic through the M-Lab. If there was an unknown organism in the samples, she might be able to isolate it and study it. She would send the data back to Mission Support and the scientists there could work out what to do next.

The thought of divesting some responsibility was a relief to Silver, and as she let go of some of the tension in her body, she took a moment to look around. The glassy walls of Biodome Three rose high up above the plants, supported by an intricate web of white scaffolding. This network of tubing contained the oxygen scrubbers and intake valves that filtered gases from the Martian atmosphere down into the dome itself. The web also collected and filtered water released as vapor from the leaves of the plants, and was even designed to simulate rainfall.

Silver had never been inside one of the domes during a rain cycle. Unlike some of her colleagues, Silver missed the desert, not a good downpour. Still, it felt good to be surrounded by greenery. It was a reprieve from the utilitarian grey of the station. Silver thought of her garden back home, where Cooper and Cosima had sown lettuce and radish seeds when Cosima was two, and where she had planted an avocado pit just before leaving. Silver had joked that when she got home from her trip, there'd be an avalanche of avocados. She felt a stab of pain at the memory. Cooper was leaving her, and selling the house, their home. With all the death around her now, Silver wasn't sure she could handle any more loss. She suddenly realised what Cooper must have felt, watching her leave, not knowing if she would ever come home.

Silver felt angry that Cooper had given up on her, even though she could understand why. She knew that in some small way she was also angry that Cooper didn't fully appreciate her commitment to Project Arche and to Mars itself, or why, finally, she had decided she had to leave. Cooper seemed to have folded herself neatly into family life, but that hadn't happened for Silver. She loved her family, but that love wasn't everything to her. Cooper hated that about her, but Silver knew she couldn't change. Silver had never been OK pretending to be someone she was not. She couldn't make herself less complicated, less ambitious.

She hadn't met her parents' expectations either. She had chosen to study biochemistry, engineering, and astrophysics, instead of marrying a nice man and having an average life of tedious contentment. Her mother had presented her with a vision where her only pleasure would come from her husband's successes.

She wanted to believe that her parents had followed her career over the years, perhaps even seen her waving and smiling on TV as she made her way to the launch pad and *Octavia*. Maybe they were proud of her after all. Silver tortured herself with the thought that, if she had stuck around for longer, given them another chance, her parents might have loved her even if she hadn't achieved so much. Perhaps her dad really was capable of kindness and love, and her mother better able to stand up to him now.

Silver had tried with Cooper and Cosima to avoid the mistakes she had seen her parents make. She wanted to love them both for who they were, not what they achieved, but it was hard, and Silver begrudgingly admitted to herself that things had changed when Cooper resigned her post at NASA to stay at home with Cosima. With her resignation, Cooper had lost some of Silver's respect, and Silver couldn't help but see Cooper's choice as a rebuke of her own dogged pursuit of her career. Rationally, Silver could see that this assessment was unfair, but she couldn't make herself feel differently about it. She was disappointed in Cooper. Not that she would ever say such a thing to her wife, nor to anyone else, but she knew Cooper could tell she was thinking it.

Now, some two hundred million miles away, Cooper was living her life without any further need for Silver. She was just a memory to Cooper now, and the Cosima she knew had gone, had grown into a much older child who might not even remember her other mom. Silver stared up into the dusty sky surrounding the biodome and found this thought strangely comforting. If Silver never made it home, she wouldn't run the risk of disappointing her daughter over and over again every time she chose to go on just one more mission. Perhaps it was for the best, Silver thought, if she never went back. Cosima wouldn't miss what she couldn't remember.

Her thoughts were interrupted by the sound of the biodome's air filters kicking up a notch, and Silver looked up once more, seeing that the sun was low in the sky. The light was fading quickly and at dusk the biodomes' artificial ultraviolet lighting, used to boost the plants' photosynthesis, would switch off. Silver wasn't sure if Aliyaah had changed anything to keep the dome lit after that.

Silver activated her intercom, intending to ask Aliyaah about the lighting. But, before she had a chance to speak, Silver heard a single, short scream from the other side of the dome. She left the samples in the processor and ran in the direction of the scream. As Silver scrambled to find Aliyaah, the nanobots coursing through her blood began to relay their results. If Silver had still been standing by the lab, she would have seen that, like Dominic, her cortisol was elevated, her blood glucose was low, and she, too, had the unusual biomarkers suggesting something was affecting her brain tissue.

TWENTY-TWO

Aliyaah was face down on the ground when Silver reached her, and Dominic was nowhere in sight.

"Chief?" Silver cried as she ran across one of the vegetable beds, not caring if she flattened any plants. Aliyaah didn't respond, and when Silver crouched down beside her, she saw a ligature around Aliyaah's neck. She assumed it was Aliyaah's chain at first, but that seemed to be missing, replaced by the cable that the Chief had used to bind Dominic's hands. There were scratches on Aliyaah's throat where she had clearly tried frantically to remove the ligature before she passed out. Silver grabbed the utility knife that was attached to her belt and quickly cut the cable, trying not to nick Aliyaah's skin.

With the cable removed, Silver carefully turned Aliyaah onto her back and began CPR. She was painfully aware that Dominic was loose somewhere in the biodome and would almost certainly have heard Silver crashing through the plants to get to Aliyaah.

Silver pushed down hard on Aliyaah's chest and grimaced as she felt a rib crack. She continued compressions and just as she thought it was too late, Aliyaah drew a breath and spluttered back to life.

Aliyaah clutched at her neck, then stared up at Silver, realising the cable was no longer stopping her from breathing.

Silver sat back on her ankles and let out a long sigh of relief as Aliyaah got her breath back.

"Dominic?" Silver asked, once Aliyaah's ragged breathing normalised.

"Yes." Aliyaah's voice was crackly, and after she spoke she let out a single sob, then put her hand to her mouth and fell silent.

Silver stood up and looked around, but could see no sign of Dominic. She turned back to Aliyaah, who was trying to get to her feet. She thought better of it, and sat back down, holding her ribs and grimacing at Silver. "Thanks, I think," she said, attempting to smile.

Silver returned the half smile and said, "We should move somewhere less visible. And find you some painkillers."

Silver helped Aliyaah to her feet and held onto her as she stood unsteadily for a few seconds. Aliyaah was taller than Silver, which meant Silver had a clear view of the angry red welt around the Chief's neck.

"What happened?" Silver asked, once Aliyaah had her breath back.

"He just turned on me. One minute he was telling me about the plant growth, then he started talking gibberish and lunged at me. He had something around my neck before I could react. I couldn't breathe. I couldn't get my fingers under it or fight back." Aliyaah ran her hand over the red raw skin on her neck and realised she was bleeding from the wounds she had inflicted on herself trying to release the cable. "It's like he just became a totally different person."

"And nothing else happened, before he attacked you?"

"No. He just... became someone I don't know," Aliyaah said, then added in a whisper, "and with this awful strength I didn't know he had. Like he was tweaking on something."

"We have to find him, Chief. We have to restrain him properly this time, so he can't do something we can't come back from."

"I know," Aliyaah said. "If he gets it into his head to decontaminate the inner dome, or flush the oxygen system, well... you know."

"Any idea where he would hide? You know this place better than I do."

"We should check the other sectors. I can take one and two, and you can -"

Silver interrupted her. "No. We stick together this time. We've got to have each other's backs." Aliyaah nodded. "Anyway, if he's that strong, it might take both of us to restrain him safely."

Aliyaah walked Silver to the far wall, where there was another control panel. She toggled some switches and suggested that they walk the outer ring of the inner dome, doing a quick scan of each sector for any large heat signatures. "I've deactivated the heat lamps for now," Aliyaah said. Aliyaah also turned all the lights on full, overriding the normal schedule. Silver worried for a moment that the sudden blaze of light would give away their position, but the crater wall hid the biodome from the station and Hadley would be none the wiser.

Silver activated her hand-held scanner and moved the device from side to side, checking to see if Dominic was hiding in Sector Five. They walked slowly around the perimeter, but their scanners did not pick up any heat signatures. Either Dominic was very adept at hiding, was following right behind them, or had already left the inner dome.

Aliyaah stumbled ahead of Silver, who reached out to grab her arm and stop her from falling. "I'm still a little lightheaded, I guess."

"Sit down for a minute and rest. Up against the wall." Silver lowered Aliyaah to the ground, then crouched beside her. She pulled a protein bar from her pocket and broke it in two, handing half to Aliyaah.

"I can't eat, Sil. It hurts to even breathe."

"You need to eat something, Chief. Those veggies aren't going to sustain us for long, and we should take another round of anti-rads soon." Silver rolled the protein bar between her palms, warming it until it softened. She gave Aliyaah a thin smile, and offered the ball to Aliyaah, who laughed hoarsely.

"It makes it easier to swallow," Silver said. "I've eaten so many of these damn things, I've had to figure out how to make them a little more palatable."

Aliyaah shook her head and took the other half of the bar. "What can I say? I'm a traditionalist," Aliyaah said, then took a bite of the bar and started chewing slowly.

Silver had rested her scanner on her knee when she crouched down, and as she finished the last of her protein bar she saw a bright spot emerge on the screen. She nudged Aliyaah's elbow and angled the screen so the Chief had a better view. They both stood up slowly and quietly, the Chief wincing as she put a hand to her ribs.

They kept their backs flat to the wall, their eyes flitting between the screen and the space in front of them. The heat signature was about fifteen feet away and was getting bigger and brighter. It wasn't getting any closer though, and it was definitely not shaped like a human. The focus of the heat seemed to be on the other side of one of the dome's interior struts, demarcating the edge of Sector Five. The strut was narrow, about a foot in diameter, and made of a strong titanium alloy. For the heat to penetrate the metal and create a signature on the scanner, it had to be much higher than human body temperature.

The Chief gestured to Silver that they should investigate. They stepped forward, keeping an eye on the periphery in case Dominic reappeared. The air seemed to hum, and Silver felt beads of sweat forming on her brow. She wiped them away and inched forward.

They were within five feet of the strut when a sharp crack split the air. Silver covered her ears, dropping the scanner into the dirt at her feet. Aliyaah had also covered her ears, and the two women stared at each other for a second. Silver bent down to pick up the scanner and took a breath. As she inhaled, she realised that the dank smell in the air was not coming from the soil. It took her a moment to identify the odour. It was the same as the smell from the refiner, just after they had lost contact with Jaz.

Silver and Aliyaah checked the scanner. The heat signature had diffused. There was now no clear focal point, just what looked like the residue from a small explosion, although there was no smoke. Silver suspected she already knew what they would see behind the strut.

Aliyaah moved first, circling around the strut one way and indicating that Silver should go the other way, keeping their distance just in case. As she rounded the strut, Silver saw a glint of light bouncing off a close packed cluster of crystals flush against the titanium. The plants in the immediate vicinity had wilted, but there were no scorch marks, despite the heat.

Aliyaah drew closer, then clasped her hand to her neck, as if searching for something she already knew was gone. It took Silver a second to see what Aliyaah had already seen. A gold chain hanging on one of the tallest crystals, complete with Aliyaah's wedding band.

TWENTY-THREE

After landing, the crew had relocated *Octavia* to a site two kilometres away from the station, reachable only by hitching a ride on a rover or taking the SEV. Even that short distance on uneven terrain would be difficult to walk in an EMS, and the risk of solar storms was ever present. The crew had spent several sevensols finishing the new launch platform and, while a walkway between *Octavia* and the station was slated for construction closer to the time of their return to Earth, several other projects were scheduled for their next thirteen months on the planet. Given recent events, Hadley wanted to make sure they were prepared to leave quickly. He couldn't help but feel that something didn't want them here.

Hadley worked through a variety of scenarios, focusing on what they knew and what might soon be revealed by the autopsies. Occam's razor told him that there was most likely a link between the strange events of the last few sols: the accident at the quarry, Specialist Viper's disappearance, the organism Chief Diambu had found in the west wing, and the behaviour of the Commander and the specialist who had died at the station. And, after Aliyaah cited Article seven point five, Hadley knew she was already operating under the assumption that, whatever was going on, any one of them might experience the same rapid cognitive decline as the Commander.

If it was true that they were all infected, the journey to Earth would give them months to figure out how to eradicate the organism, assuming they didn't succumb to it first. If that happened, then at least they would have tried to get back home. In the worst-case scenario, NASA could pilot *Octavia* remotely and do what was needed to prevent anyone bringing the infection to Earth.

To get the walkway ready, Hadley needed Aliyaah's insight. The original plan was to build the walkway using materials created from metals extracted from the rocks in the quarry. The hangar currently housed almost all the prefabricated pieces they needed, but with the quarry gone, they were short some materials. Aliyaah not only had the engineering know-how, she also had the respect of the other engineers, both of which they'd need to get the job done.

Hadley considered their other options. The need to transport both personnel and cargo to the ship meant that the rovers were of little use, and it would take too long to ferry everybody over in small groups using the SEV. Once Hadley determined that the walkway was their best option, he contacted Aliyaah to ask if construction was possible with the materials available.

"It's possible, Commander," Aliyaah said, as she sat beside Silver at the workbench in Biodome Three. Silver was preparing samples for the M-Lab following Dominic's death, and the call from Hadley proved a welcome distraction for them both. "The thing is, Sir, I'm not sure we should focus our resources on this yet. We don't have approval from Mission Support, do we?"

"No, Chief. I recognise your concern, but we need to be ready to go when the launch is approved. And, frankly, if I don't give the crew something practical to do, I'll likely be facing a revolt in the next few hours," Hadley said. After a brief silence, he added, "They feel like they're just waiting to die."

Silver looked up at Aliyaah when she heard this, and Aliyaah swallowed hard. The Chief asked Hadley which crew members were with him and he rattled off a list of names. Aliyaah told him who had experience with *Octavia* and then talked him through the process of laying out the segments of the walkway.

"I'll put together a team to check out the ship and get everyone else working on the walkway," Hadley said.

As Hadley was about to close the line, Silver asked, "Any news from

Schiff?"

"She checked the things you mentioned, Antara, and, yes, the Commander had elevated levels of all three biomarkers, and higher than normal dopamine and testosterone," Hadley said.

"And the other fatality?" the Chief asked.

"The same. Elevated testosterone, dopamine, and cortisol. Cause of death appears to be a massive myocardial infarction, which might explain why it was so quick after the onset of aggression, unlike with the Commander." Hadley paused, then asked Aliyaah, "Will you be able to carry out autopsies where you are, Chief?"

Aliyaah hesitated, so Silver responded. "Sir, I don't think you quite understand. There are no bodies, as such. Doctors Alvarez and Watson are, well, they've been sort of... crystallised."

"But you can still get tissue samples, yes?"

Aliyaah glanced at Silver and frowned, then said, "It's possible, if we can find the right tools. But, Sir, the bodies were almost entirely consumed. All visible organic material has been transformed."

Hadley was quiet for a moment, then he said, "Do you have any thoughts on why that didn't happen to the Commander and the other man here? If that's what this organism does, why leave those bodies intact?"

"Perhaps the growth conditions just weren't right, Sir," Aliyaah suggested.

"Commander, did you detect any significant changes in temperature around the time they died?" Silver asked.

"No. At least not that I recall," Hadley said.

"And they were in an open area?" Aliyaah asked.

"Yes, we were all gathered in the rec room."

Silver jumped in and said, "radiation levels were lower when they died, right?" Silver looked at Aliyaah as she spoke, trying to see if the Chief shared her suspicions about the organism.

"Yes, there was less background radiation than usual at the time of both deaths," Hadley confirmed.

Aliyaah returned Silver's gaze, her expression thoughtful. She muted the line with Hadley and asked Silver, "Can you bring up a readout showing background radiation for the last few hours, just at this biodome?" She unmuted the line and suggested Hadley get a similar readout at his location.

"What are you thinking, Antara?" Hadley asked. "That galactic cosmic rays might be a catalyst?"

"The GCRs could be a factor, and so could an enclosed environment, like in the refiner and the west wing," Silver said.

Aliyaah continued the thought, saying, "If it turns out that these factors are contributing to the organism's growth, it will give us more insight into how we can protect ourselves from it."

"But the others still died, Chief," Hadley said.

"It might buy us some time, Sir," Silver said.

Hadley closed his eyes and pinched the bridge of his nose. He exhaled, then said, "Of course. You're right. OK. Be in touch when you've got something."

"Yes Sir," Aliyaah said. She closed the channel with Hadley and turned to Silver. "I want you to do me a favour, Sil."

"Chief?"

"I want you to check my blood for those biomarkers we found in the others."

Silver said nothing, but got a vial of nanobots from the medical kit.

"Use the other bots, the ones that stick around for longer. I want to track any changes in my bloodwork over the next few hours, or sols, depending how long I stay alive."

Silver put the bots back and chose a different vial. "And Sil, we should do the same for you."

Silver nodded, but said nothing. She had seen the readout when they had returned to the M-Lab. She already knew that something was happening to her, she just wasn't sure if she would meet the same fate as the others.

TWENTY-FOUR

The existence of galactic cosmic rays had fascinated Silver for years, even before she put herself on the fast-track to NASA. That these ionised particles, remnants of ancient supernovae, were flying around the universe was at once exhilarating and terrifying.

Galactic cosmic rays could penetrate spacecraft and the human body, and had been a major obstacle for earlier missions to Mars. Exposure to GCRs could break down tissues in the body, and seemed especially damaging to the neurons in the prefrontal cortex, the decision-making centre of the brain.

When scientists on Earth exposed animals to galactic cosmic rays, the effect was like stripping the branches from the neuronal trees of the brain. In humans, pruning the neuronal pathways this way significantly reduced a person's capacity for dealing with the unexpected; the thoughts simply had nowhere to go. Everyone who spent time in space, and strayed beyond the protective magnetic field of the Earth, needed some way to protect themselves from these rays.

As Silver processed the samples she had taken from Dominic, she noticed that a strange separation had occurred in centrifuge. A thin crust of sediment had formed at the apex of each vial, and when Silver held a vial up to the light she saw that the sediment was made up of tiny crystals. She put the sample under the M-Lab's microscope so she could see the crystals more clearly.

Silver called over to Aliyaah, who had been analysing the data they had on levels of galactic cosmic rays in the biodome. Aliyaah showed her the near perfect correlation between peaks in the rays and the two deaths. There were two other, smaller, peaks, which corresponded with both of Dominic's attacks.

"What have you got, Sil?" Aliyaah asked.

"The samples I took from Dominic, they've crystallised in the centrifuge. It's possible that the white stuff I removed from his mucus membranes was substrate for these crystals."

Aliyaah looked into the microscope and then nodded. "If these were in his respiratory system, chances are that whatever this thing is, it's airborne. Which means we're already exposed."

Silver nodded. "Given that the activity of this thing seems to correspond with elevated GCRs, maybe this organism isn't a source of radiation. I think it feeds on radiation, Chief."

Aliyaah frowned, then continued Silver's thought. "So, if other conditions are right, a spike in GCRs would lead to a massive growth surge. That would mean... to stop it growing, we'd need to shield ourselves from radiation."

"Yeah, and that could buy us some time to figure out how to eradicate it from our systems," Silver said.

"Simple!" Aliyaah said, grimacing. "Any thoughts on how to do that?" Aliyaah asked, and Silver shrugged as best she could in the cumbersome space suit. Aliyaah sucked her teeth and shook her head. "Yeah, me either. I've never seen a pathogen like it."

"We should send all of this back to Mission Support and see what they make of it." Silver said. Aliyaah agreed, and Silver asked, "Has Hadley sent anything yet?"

"Yeah. It's the same at the station. A spike in GCRs around the time the Commander started behaving erratically, and the same for the specialist."

"But not when they both died?"

"No. There was a drop in GCRs then."

"So, the organism itself died?" Silver said, then raised her eyebrows and quickly threw an idea at Aliyaah. "Maybe, then, if we just deprive this thing of GCRs for long enough we can kill it?"

Silver's excitement vanished as Aliyaah said, "Yeah, but even if the organism died, so did the Commander and the specialist."

Silver sighed and said, "You're right."

Aliyaah looked at Silver for a couple of seconds, then said slowly, "We have the organism isolated now, right? From the samples you took from Dom."

Silver hesitated, then answered, "Well, I don't know if it's the organism itself or simply what it leaves behind after... after it's done feeding."

"Can you analyse it further using the M-Lab?"

"I'll try, of course, but we'd be better off if we had an actual biochemist working on this. Rovers, rockets, and SEVs are more in my wheelhouse, not microscopic flesh-eating organisms."

Silver laughed as Aliyaah said, "Well I don't think anyone wants to be in that wheelhouse."

"I will check with Hadley to see if there's a specialist who can work with Schiff," Aliyaah said, and moved away to contact Commander Hadley.

When Aliyaah returned, Silver saw that her expression had changed. There was a deep crease in her brow and her shoulders were tight.

"What's going on, Chief?" Silver asked, seeing how the Chief's general exhaustion had been overcome by something acutely worrisome.

"It's *Octavia*. Hadley wants her up and running right away, but the crew are having some issues."

Aliyaah looked directly at Silver, who nodded and said, "You have to go over there, don't you? So, Hadley's asking you to break protocol? He'll know where you are."

Aliyaah smiled thinly, and Silver nodded, understanding that Aliyaah was their best option for getting *Octavia* prepared for launch.

"I won't reveal your location, though," Aliyaah said.

Silver pursed her lips, then said, "You'll need the SEV. And take these." Silver grabbed a handful of anti-rads and passed them to the Chief.

Their hands touched for a moment, and Aliyaah said quietly, "I'm sorry, Sil."

"I know. It's OK," Silver said, and smiled.

"I'll come back, Sil. Once *Octavia* is up and running. I'll come back for you."

Silver laughed. "I'll be waiting," she said, and watched the Chief walk away as she added quietly, "It's not like I'm going anywhere." As Aliyaah entered the airlock, Silver couldn't help but wonder if it was the last time they'd see each other alive.

TWENTY-FIVE

Alone in the biodome, Silver's attention started to wane and she felt herself drift in and out of sleep. She hadn't slept properly in several sols and the hum of the spinning centrifuge was dangerously soporific. Her eyelids grew heavier and her soldreams mingled with snatches of memory from biology classes at school.

As a child, Silver had spent hours in the school library. She had been obsessed with books about stars and space travel, and would hide in the library at recess and lunch, dreaming about rocket ships. While the other kids played outside, Silver had clung to the idea of becoming an astronaut, desperate to feel connected to something greater than herself and to envision a life that didn't resemble that of her parents.

One day, Silver turned the pages of a book on astrophysics and discovered why it was that the barns she saw littering the landscape of America on her travels with her father were painted such a specific colour. As a star shrinks and starts to run out of fuel, the temperature and pressure increase and heavier and heavier elements begin to fuse. Eventually, all that is left is iron, an element so tightly bound that it absorbs energy during fusion, cooling the star until its death. Eons ago, when dying stars finally exploded, the iron in their cores was scattered across the universe, and the resulting abundance of iron oxide in the earth led to its use as a pigment for cheap paint.

To Silver, learning about nuclear fusion in dying stars was as good as reading any book about wizards and magic. Red barns may well be commonplace, but for Silver every barn she saw suddenly felt special, as if the barns had been painted with the stars themselves. After reading the book, whenever they drove by another barn on their way to another town where her father would try to sell farm equipment, Silver felt like she had a window into the past and, perhaps, to her future too.

Despite her father's insistence that she attend Sunday School, Silver's formal education had left her with the feeling that the universe was understandable only as the random activity of atoms and particles careening around space, forming objects, beings, consciousness, and resources for human exploitation. She, like everyone else, would live a linear life, slave to an internal chronology based on her physical form, and her expectations. Without such form, she would no longer be herself, and yet the tissues, cells, molecules, and atoms of her body were almost continually in flux. How she started out life would not be how it would end. Her body would destroy and recreate itself countless times, until no part of her original form remained. Even her memory would be made up of different cells and pathways, recreating itself each time she unfolded a memory.

This rationalisation of life simultaneously comforted and terrified Silver. She wanted to have an intellectual appreciation for the complexity and connectedness of the universe, but to also feel that connection. The closest she had come to really feeling this was when she was pregnant, when her baby was simultaneously part of her and yet growing into an entirely different being. The sudden separation when Cosima was born had been more of a shock than she had anticipated. It hadn't taken long for Silver to accept the severing of this connection, but after the initial shock subsided, Silver sensed that the love she felt for Cosima had changed; it was no less true, but the quality of it had been somehow altered. She wondered if it was the same for her own mother, or for her friends, but she had never felt like it was something she could say out loud.

As a child, Silver had crossed through reserve land on those road trips with her father, and had taken great care not to draw his attention to her origins. She would hunker down in the truck, hiding herself from sight whenever they stopped for gas or food. Her father seemed happiest when she stayed in the vehicle, and the few times when someone did see Silver, she quickly looked away from their curious stares. As an adult, Silver sometimes wondered how her view of the world might be radically different had she grown up immersed in Navajo culture, with people who saw her and accepted her as she truly was.

Day after day, while her father drove in silence down the seemingly endless desert roads, Silver had thought about the barns and felt an unnameable sadness. The farmers had painted these inelegant structures with something as magical as stardust, not knowing what she knew. Such nonchalance, such a lack of curiosity, seemed utterly bizarre, almost blasphemous, to Silver.

Over time, that simple discovery in her school library led her on a path that took her all the way to this biodome on Mars. She dreamed that she was walking from barn to barn, the contrast of the red with the yellow fields, stretching out her future and that of all humanity across California, Arizona, and into the unknown. She sang as she walked, and all space and time became part of her and was created by her. She could always see just a little farther ahead, but beyond that, at the limits of her imagination, she felt the slow slide into darkness, into nothing.

A voice in Silver's mind told her that to keep the dream intact, she had to keep walking, keep singing, but her throat felt dry, her eyelids gritty. When she woke, Silver was confused to find that she wasn't in the school library or laboratory, nor was she in the biodome. Instead, she was standing on the surface of the red planet, the dust storms whispering all around her, singing their own song. Silver took a deep breath and, for just a second, her eyes were open wide to a new world. Then she heard the centrifuge beeping, and she blinked. She was sitting at the workbench, and could see the samples, shimmering with the same white crystals as before.

Realising that she had finally succumbed to sleep after what seemed like sols of wakefulness, and recognising the dangers inherent in being unconscious in the centre of the biodome, Silver decided to move to a safer location to rest. If there was another crisis, the lack of proper sleep would dull her reactions.

Silver spent a few minutes setting up samples for analysis, and entered her clearance codes to bypass the communications blackout and automate the data transmission to Mission Support. She tidied the workbench and looked at the schematic for the biodome, berating herself silently for not remembering the location of the storm bunker. This kind of information should be lodged in her memory, and while she could rationalize the memory lapse as a result of exhaustion, she couldn't help but think that it was a sign of something more sinister.

The storm bunker was the safest place to get some sleep. It was secure and would offer protection if a solar storm occurred. The schematic showed her that the bunker was beneath the inner dome, with the easiest access through a hatch from the outer dome. She picked up the Medical Kit and her scanner, then made her way to the airlock.

The stillness of the empty biodome was unnerving. She had grown used to the sounds of the station, with its busy corridors and the frenetic activity in the hangar. She had always loved the silence in the SEV, but where that solitude had felt like a reprieve, this felt dangerously close to permanent isolation.

It had only been an hour since Aliyaah had left in the SEV. She would have arrived at *Octavia* by now. Silver had an urge to contact the Chief, but she had nothing new to report and felt foolish for simply wanting to hear Aliyaah's voice. She fought the urge to check-in without reason, knowing that the Chief would be busy. She briefly thought about contacting Hadley, just to hear a voice other than her own, but he had enough to deal with and an unnecessary call from her would only make him suspicious as to her state of mind.

It was imperative that they get *Octavia* operational, and coordinate with NASA to ensure a safe exit from the planet. The launch window was shrinking fast, and if they couldn't get the ship launched in time they would be unable to complete the journey with the supplies they had left.

As Silver calculated how much time they had to flee the planet, a voice in her head pointed out that she had failed to factor in recent events: with significantly fewer passengers and crew on the return flight, the remaining supplies would stretch further. While this thought provided brief comfort, Silver couldn't help but think that recent events might simply mean that they wouldn't make it off the planet at all. Knowing she needed to maintain her composure, she told herself to take a breath and work the problem.

Silver entered the bunker, secured the door behind her, and sat down on one of the beds. With her head in her hands, she tried to quiet the tangle of voices in her mind. She was having difficulty unscrambling the threads of thought, as if she was overhearing a confusion of voices, rather than her own consciousness.

At least now that she was in the bunker she was protected from the worst of the GCRs and from any solar flares. If the unidentified organism did feed on radiation, this bunker could be the best place to lay low while they figured out a plan. Silver thought back to what Aliyaah had said about the Commander and how the death of the organism might result in the host's death if the two were already inextricably connected. As Silver closed her eyes, she thought of the nanobots running around in her blood. Did the biomarkers mean that she was already infected? Was the organism now so closely entwined with her own body that its death would mean her own?

Despite that sombre thought, Silver felt the weight of oncoming sleep. Her breathing slowed and the multitude of voices in her mind dropped away, leaving her with a thread of thought resting in a soft silence: when she woke, would she still know who and where she was? Would she even wake up at all?

TWENTY-SIX

The solar storm struck at midnight, lighting up the night sky over the planet's northern hemisphere. Swirling red and purple clouds danced at the horizon, over the lip of the crater, the quarry, the station, the empty biodomes, *Octavia*.

A rapid influx of charged particles crashed into atoms and molecules in the ever-present Martian dust clouds, releasing massive amounts of energy as clouds of hot gas, and knots of magnetism wrenched themselves free from the sun's surface.

All communications were disrupted between Mars and Earth and on the red planet itself. As was protocol when a solar storm hit, inessential technology was powered down and personnel took cover wherever they could. The minutes ticked by, then the hours, and still the sky glowed a fiery red and bruised purple.

Mars SOHO, the Solar and Heliospheric Observatory that predicted space weather on the planet, sounded the alert an hour before the first effects of the storm reached the planet. The coronal mass ejection bombarded Mars with charged particles. The exploding sunspot swept aside huge amounts of GCRs, and deflected the charged particles to significantly lower atmospheric radiation. As expected, the number and intensity of solar storms had decreased since *Octavia's* launch. They were moving away from the solar maximum of 2036, when the sun's activity was at its peak.

Space agencies almost always scheduled interplanetary travel during the solar maximum because this reduced exposure to cosmic rays. The downside was that they had to be on constant alert for solar flares and coronal mass ejections.

This latest storm was an anomaly, lasting for half a sol instead of just a few minutes or an hour. A large coronal mass ejection like this could suppress cosmic rays for several sevensols, but it also disrupted navigational equipment, communications, and power.

Anyone who was outside in a storm like this would be bombarded with high-energy solar protons. To survive a Mars solar storm required getting to a shelter before the storm hit, or having immediate treatment for exposure. Otherwise, the best-case scenario was a quick death as damage to DNA prevented mitochondria from producing the energy the body needed to survive. At worst, an astronaut would die slowly as DNA damage stopped their body from producing functional cells.

The anti-rads helped stave off the worst of the damage, and the colony was protected by shields at the station, domes, and other major structures, but the system wasn't foolproof. Like all astronauts, Aliyaah and Silver had signed up knowing that their time in space was limited and would likely shorten their lifespans. Longer missions like *Octavia* would have an even greater impact. After her husband's death, Aliyaah had felt few qualms about signing on for such a lengthy stay in space. And for Silver, the risk was worth taking, even if Cooper saw things differently.

More insidious than the sun, cosmic rays could penetrate the hull of their ships, the station, biodomes, and even, to some degree, the shelters. These supercharged subatomic particles shot out across the universe, from black holes and stars exploding outside the solar system, and no one had yet discovered how to block them from passing through the human body.

As Hadley organised the crew working on the walkway, Aliyaah hunkered down in the ship itself. The storm meant that they were relegated to working inside the ship instead of on the launch pad. In the bunker beneath the biodome, Silver remained unaware of the storm, sleeping fitfully, waking from one dream and sliding unaware into another.

In Silver's dream, she was standing on the exterior walkway, her head protected only by a simple oxygen mask that covered enough of her face to prevent the moisture from her eyes, mouth, and nose from rapidly and painfully evaporating, effectively boiling away in the dry Martian atmosphere.

An extremophilic fungus spread slowly across the surface of Mars, making its way out of the quarry and towards the station. As the fungus drew closer, Silver felt her tongue grow thick in her mouth, and her eyes become sticky. Her vision clouded over. The air was too thin. The mask was failing. Silver clutched at the mask, but it was no longer there. She clawed at her face and neck, holding her breath against the freezing Martian atmosphere. If she opened her mouth, the moisture in her lungs would evaporate and her body would go into shock. She would decompress and die in excruciating pain.

But Silver didn't die. Her eyes weren't desiccated. In fact, her vision had cleared. Still, she tried to find the mask and glanced up at the station, knowing that she wouldn't have enough time to get back inside before her body gave out. The station had vanished, and Silver looked down to see that the walkway had vanished too. She was alone and naked on the dusty surface of the red planet, and Silver watched as the Martian landscape morphed into limestone cliffs littered with nuclear hazard signs. The fungus drew closer by the second. Its fruiting bodies had a crystalline structure, unlike any fungi she had seen before. The organism seemed to rise and fall, a morass of arms and torsos, heads and faces she couldn't quite place, growing in and out of the earth. This miasmic sea of semi-human forms grew ever nearer.

Paralysed by terror, Silver watched as the figures shrank back into a carpet of spores, then coated her feet and legs, rising up her body and snaking their way into her nostrils, her ears, her mouth. In her dream, Silver gasped, and when she woke, she was standing at the control panel in the bunker. The automatic climate controls had been disabled, and Silver was surprised she could still breathe. She was surprised to still be alive at all.

The weight of her dream pressed down on her, but as she took breath after breath the air in the shelter cleared her mind and the thin sheen of sweat coating her skin started to dissipate.

Silver tried to hold onto her dream, and wondered what, if anything, her mind was trying to tell her. She thought about how the landscape had changed to something reminiscent of England's Peak District. What was the connection between that and radiation? Why the nuclear hazard signs?

Suddenly, Silver remembered back to a biology class she had taken early in college, and how British researchers working near a dumping ground for nuclear waste had found extremophilic organisms. The scientific community had been abuzz with speculation that the organisms had evolved to quench radiation before it could damage their cells. There had been so much excitement about the possibility of creating an internal barrier through symbiosis, but laboratory tests in a simulated human system failed, and some researchers began to reconsider the complete ban on animal testing. Hearing of mutterings in the research community, lawyers representing the personhood of non-human animals moved quickly, reminding the scientists of the law, the lives lost, and the horrors associated with drugs that had been approved for human use based on misleading evidence from animal research. Silver, hadn't paid much attention at the time, and was surprised at how the memory had suddenly resurfaced.

She was trapped in the solar shelter, her synapses firing at an incredible rate. As her thoughts moved faster than ever before, she kept seeing glimpses of memories and ideas that danced away before she could turn them into anything solid. She tried to hold onto the thought about the scientists in England, but the air in the bunker felt so thick and rich, and she was so hot. She was going to suffocate in this tiny box. She needed to get out, to breathe clearer air.

She wiped the sweat from her brow and blinked. Her vision cleared, as if she had dislodged a film covering her eyes. She blinked again and reached out to the control panel. Her body felt heavy and stiff. Her limbs seemed to crack as she moved.

A small voice inside Silver cried out, insisting that she should fight whatever was taking over her body and, increasingly, her mind. Part of her held onto the idea that what she was experiencing was a result of damage to her prefrontal cortex or other parts of her brain; but at a deeper level, she began to accept that she was now host to an extremophilic organism.

She hadn't asked for this. And yet, as she examined the control panel and formed a clearer picture of what might be happening, Silver felt a growing sense of serenity and connection to something bigger than herself. She hadn't invited this process, nor had she expected it, none of them had, but she felt peaceful. In a way, this was what she had signed up for; another kind of exploration. She was on the precipice of something greater than herself or her life's work. Something greater than anything they had imagined when launching Project Arche. Infection with the organism felt less like a hostile takeover, and more like an emerging connection: symbiosis, not parasitism. Whatever was happening to her seemed organic, natural, desirable even.

Silver tried to reflect on how her mind, her way of thinking, had changed, but recognized that the attempt was inherently flawed. The organism seemed to be communicating with her using her own consciousness. Could she still trust what she was thinking and feeling? Despite this ambiguity, Silver was not afraid of the organism, at least not in relation to her own body and mind. In a way, they were both explorers in strange lands: Silver on this new planet; the organism in a new body and mind.

She thought about Aliyaah and Hadley. She should let them know how she had changed, but she wasn't sure how they would react and, anyway, comms were still down. She needed to stay in the bunker until this second storm passed. Without the SEV, there was no way to make it to *Octavia* safely. The radiation from the storm was too strong to attempt the journey in just her EV suit, and the EMS was too bulky.

Silver checked the readout from the control panel. The numbers were frightening at first. The temperature was just fifteen Celsius and oxygen was at eighteen percent. She should be struggling, but instead she felt compelled to reduce the temperature to five degrees and the oxygen to fifteen percent. She stood in front of the air vent, breathing in the fresh, cool air. For a moment, this made her thoughts dizzyingly clear, but she soon lost the feeling and the air hung thickly in her lungs. The adaptation was rapid, and Silver tapped the buttons to toggle the oxygen down to ten percent. She lowered the temperature to zero.

The air in the bunker cooled and the oxygen dropped. Silver's limbs relaxed and her thoughts regained the coherence and clarity she had felt moments before. She looked back up at the control panel and smiled. The current life support settings should have killed her, and yet her breath came easily and she wasn't cold. Silver felt better than she had in hours, sols even.

Sitting back down on the bunk, Silver pulled out her canteen from the pocket of her overalls. She felt the familiar markings on its side and smiled as she lifted it to her lips. When Cooper gave her the canteen she had joked that the traditional gift list was redundant for astronauts: no paper or cotton. Instead, a branched carbon nanotube canteen coated with titanium dioxide nanoparticles represented real romance. If she was going to try to capture the stars, Cooper said, at least she could have a canteen that didn't grow biofilms when she neglected to clean it.

Silver could see Cooper's face with a wonderful clarity as she remembered that anniversary dinner. They had been so happy then. If Cooper could only feel what she was feeling now, this connection to something greater than herself, maybe then she would understand why Silver had needed to leave.

Silver let the memory go and instead recalled the content of her dream with an enjoyable lucidity. She felt each of her thoughts as it travelled from neuron to neuron, racing across the synaptic gaps. Her mind was reconstituting itself, clearing away unneeded pathways to create a cleaner, more efficient roadmap for consciousness.

As Silver calmly observed the changes happening within her, she started to accept the symbiosis as inevitable. She still knew little about the organism, but felt entangled in its need to survive and grow. It had remained underground for so long, dormant and undetected. Now it was out in the open, having been unearthed by the machines, and Silver saw how symbiosis might be advantageous. With the organism's support, she might be able to stand on the surface of the planet. She smiled, thinking about how she might soon be able to breathe the thin, freezing Martian air, and feel a breeze against her skin again.

TWENTY-SEVEN

On board *Octavia*, the half dozen engineers were getting restless. It had been several hours since they had identified an issue with the ship's landing gear, and quickly fixed the problem. As they were about to head back to the station they had received word of the incoming solar storm. Some of them had wanted to make a dash for the station, but Aliyaah decided the risk of being caught outside in the solar radiation was too high. They had been stranded aboard *Octavia*, waiting out one storm as they received warning of a second storm soon to hit. If they were lucky, there would be a big enough break to allow them to scramble back to the station.

Not for the first time, Aliyaah was relieved that *Octavia* was such a large ship. This gave the crew enough space that they could keep out of each others' way while they had little to do. Tensions had already been high when she arrived in the SEV; several junior engineers were itching to get flight-ready as soon as possible, and paid little heed to the more cautious approach of their senior officers.

Two of the remaining engineers raised concerns with Aliyaah about launching the ship on an unscheduled mission with the possibility of an unwanted guest. Aliyaah was inclined to agree with them, but she held out hope that NASA would approve their launch so they could evacuate the planet and reduce their risk of further exposure.

As Aliyaah tried to allay some of the crew's concerns, the residual effects of the first storm abated and Aliyaah saw that communications were back up, at least temporarily. She scanned the data on the incoming storm. There wouldn't be a long enough reprieve to allow for them to return to the station. She was about to tell the men when she saw a flashing light alerting her to a new transmission. There had been no radio contact with Hadley and the station for several hours, thanks to the storm's disruption. She opened a channel, but when the connection was made, it was not Hadley's voice that cut through the static.

Someone whose voice she couldn't quite make out was mumbling intermittently, and Aliyaah tried to clean up the signal as she looked around at the crew. They fell silent as they, too, struggled to hear the transmission.

"Who is that?" one of the engineers asked, and got shushed by his colleagues. The engineer threw his hands up and muttered to himself, "Jeez Louise."

After a moment, the voice became a little clearer and one of the men said, "Is that Lars, maybe?"

"Maybe. But what the devil is he saying?" asked one of the older engineers.

The transmission got louder suddenly, and they could all hear a man shouting, "Gå ut! Gå ut! We must get out!"

There were sounds of a scuffle, and other voices yelling, "Don't open the doors!"

Aliyaah looked around at her team, who were wide-eyed as they listened to the ensuing struggle. The storm had scrambled the time code on the message so she couldn't tell if it had been sent seconds before or hours ago, when the first storm hit. She assumed that the transmission had come from the hangar, and it seemed like someone had tried to open the hangar doors while the crew weren't suited up.

After several seconds of silence Aliyaah moved to stop the message replay. But, before she flicked the switch, a scream shattered the silence and the man cried out, "I can't breathe! Jag brinner!"

There was a loud crashing sound and the man's screams were muffled, then the transmission ended.

Aliyaah avoided meeting the eyes of the men around her and instead scrambled to open a line to the station.

"What did he say?" the men asked, turning to one of the few remaining Swedish-speaking engineers.

The man swallowed hard and sniffled. "He said, he said, 'I am on fire. I burn'."

Aliyaah looked over at the man, and they were all silent. She closed her eyes and tried to dissolve the image of catastrophe on the hangar deck. A beep drew her attention back to the console and she saw that the channel on which they had received the message was still open.

"Hello?" Aliyaah said. "Is anyone there?"

She waited and then heard Hadley's voice. He was commanding the men to stand down, and as the line stayed open she and her engineers heard Hadley ask, "Is he breathing? Is he conscious?" There was no audible reply and several of the engineers on *Octavia* lowered their heads.

"Commander?" Aliyaah ventured. "I'm on an open line, with the engineers. What just happened?"

"Chief Diambu?"

"Yes sir."

"Just a second. I... Doctor Schiff just arrived." Hadley cut the line. A minute or so later, Aliyaah heard the doctor's voice, followed by Hadley.

"Chief, there's been another death. I suspect the same affliction as with Commander Marshall."

"Symptoms of psychosis, paranoia, and aggression?" Aliyaah asked.

"Yes. Leading to acute respiratory failure. At least, that's what it looks like," Hadley said. "Chief, do you have the second storm alert? Can you and the crew make it to the station between storms?"

"There isn't enough of a window, Sir. At least not for all of us to get back," Aliyaah said.

"Are you OK to wait out the second storm?" Hadley asked.

"Yes, Sir. I wouldn't want anyone to get stuck out there when it hits."

Hadley agreed and Aliyaah was about to close the line when one of the engineers asked quietly, "Chief, who died? Was it Lars?"

Aliyaah knew that it was, but she relayed the question to Hadley anyway.

"Groening, yes," Hadley confirmed. "I'm sorry. Yes, Lars is dead."

One of the engineers slammed his fist against the nearest wall panel, shaking some nearby wires, but leaving no visible mark. The other men just sighed and shook their heads. Aliyaah felt her own fists clench, and wondered for a moment if there wasn't something to be said for the satisfying explosion of plaster and plywood when punching a hole through a wall. She caught the eye of the man now holding his hand against his chest. He looked away, his nostrils flared, then he took a breath and returned to his seat.

"He shouldn't have gone out like that," he said.

"No one should," Aliyaah agreed.

"Lars would never hurt anybody," said another engineer, and the men nodded.

Aliyaah took a deep breath and winced at the pain in her chest. She exhaled slowly and looked at the men.

"Whatever this thing is, it makes even the gentlest of men... forget themselves." She put her hand to her neck, feeling the raised welts, and said, "Let's all remember Lars as he would want to be remembered."

They were silent for a moment, and then Aliyaah forced herself to smile at the men and said, "Remember when he made that disgusting birthday cake for Bryce, from his entire sevensol's ration of protein bars and green juice?"

A couple of the men laughed, and several shook their heads and groaned, smiling and clutching at their stomachs.

The engineer who had asked if it was Lars who had died, said, "That thing was so gross."

"But impressive as fuck!" said one of the youngest engineers.

"No doubt," said Aliyaah, smiling at the crew.

"Remember when we stole his ukulele?" another of the engineers asked, grinning. "Do you think it's still on the ship?"

"Shit, yeah! I'd forgotten about that."

"Where did that thing end up anyway?"

Aliyaah watched the crew for a few moments, happy that she could help allay their grief, at least temporarily.

She stood up and stretched, feeling an ache in her chest. Her limbs felt stiff and heavy, but the pain in her rib had lessened, which surprised her. She had had a broken rib before and it had taken months to heal. She wondered what was different this time. Perhaps the lower gravity made a difference, or it could be that her adrenaline was elevated and was helping to numb the pain.

Aliyaah took a step away from her crew, intending to contact Hadley on a secure line, while communications were still possible. As she approached the ladder to climb up into the next section of the ship, one of the engineers mentioned a prank they had pulled on Lars.

"Didn't we stash his uke in the medical bay?"

The question threw Aliyaah's mind into turmoil, and she looked over at the engineer, seeing the black Crew Medical Officer band on his arm. She didn't understand how she could possibly have forgotten that *Octavia* had a fully stocked medical unit, complete with testing equipment.

Aliyaah thought of Silver, alone in the biodome. She hoped that Silver had seen the solar storm alert and had made it safely to the bunker. Once the second storm lifted, she would make contact and ask Silver to send the data from the tests she had run. There were still nanobots in Aliyaah's blood, and in Silver's too if she had followed Aliyaah's order to test herself, but with the storms disrupting communications, there had been no way to see the data. She had assumed she would need to contact the doctor to get access to those results, but now that Aliyaah had remembered the on-board medical unit, she might be able to access the data herself. At least, that is, she could see the data from the nanobots in her own blood. What she didn't have was an isolated sample of the organism, so she was limited in the types of tests she could run. Still, the nanobots might turn up something useful. And, if she was infected she might be able to isolate the organism herself.

The solar storms were also preventing communication with Earth. For all she knew, Mission Support could be trying to get a message to Hadley letting him know that they had a plan to deal with the organism. Or they might be sending instructions for the survivors to remain on Mars, instead of risking bringing the organism back to Earth.

If she could run a sample of the organism through the lab on *Octavia*, they might be able to figure this thing out. First, though, Aliyaah needed to head to the medical unit to check if she was infected. She considered bringing the engineer with his black armband. It made sense to enlist his help in the laboratory, but as Lars's screams echoed in her mind, a quieter voice began to make itself heard, telling her that if she was infected, perhaps it was best to keep that information to herself. After all, she had to lead the crew to safety. If they thought she was infected, they might panic and defect.

TWENTY-EIGHT

Aliyaah climbed up ladder after ladder, through the centre of *Octavia,* heading to the medical unit. Her ribs ached, and her legs and arms felt leaden with fatigue. It was so much easier to traverse the ship in zero gravity. Aliyaah was craving some rack time, but with cabin fever already setting in with the crew, she knew it was safer to stay awake.

Like all the astronauts on the Mars mission, Aliyaah had received at least thirty hours of basic medical training, including a crash course in the use of the diagnostic program Silver had used to assess Dominic. During her studies, Aliyaah had managed to avoid revealing her squeamishness, but the effort of hiding her disgust had detracted from the usefulness of the training.

When she reached the medical bay, Aliyaah located the handheld device that ran the medical informatics software. She searched her memory, knowing that there was a way to tap into the data stream, not only from the nanobots in her bloodstream, but also from those in Silver's blood.

If there was any data, it would likely be several hours old by now, and it crossed Aliyaah's mind that Silver could already be dead. Until communications were fully restored, there was simply no way to know.

Aliyaah tapped the screen and located the feed from the nanobots in her blood. She tried to remember the biomarkers Silver had found in Dominic's system, so she could see if any similar elevations were present in her own body. Her cortisol level was higher than normal, but not dangerously so, and Aliyaah knew she could probably get that in check with some basic meditation, if she got a chance. More worrying was the elevation in NSE, GFAP and S100β: the same three substances flagged as abnormally elevated in Dominic's blood just before he died.

Aliyaah recognised that it was impossible for her to objectively assess her own behaviour, but she was fairly confident that she didn't display any of the symptoms she had seen in Dominic. She was tired and her thoughts were confused, her memory hazy, but there had been nothing normal about the last few sols, so she had no way to isolate causative factors for these symptoms. Mental and physical exhaustion could easily be to blame.

Aliyaah slumped in her chair and wondered why, if she was infected, she wasn't displaying any other symptoms. She wasn't feeling paranoid or aggressive, unlike the Commander, Dom, and now Lars. Little differentiated her from them, aside from her sex. They ate the same food, drank the same water, and she and Dom had often shared sleeping quarters. With Dominic's work focused in the biodome, he had been exposed to different air than Aliyaah a lot of the time, and he would have had more exposure to radiation than those working mostly at the station or on the ship.

This realisation got Aliyaah thinking about what Silver had said about GCRs and the solar storm. She had largely been shielded from GCRs courtesy of her time in the SEV, the station, and on *Octavia*. Aliyaah also knew that Dominic had sometimes been lax about taking his anti-rads, while Aliyaah was strict about her schedule. She had felt the effects of radiation sickness before and, as an experienced astronaut, had already accumulated years of exposure that meant she was not willing to risk more through sheer laziness or hubris.

When communications were restored, she would ask Schiff to test the samples from the Commander, Lars, and the other deceased engineer. She would be able to assess if radiation affected the organism's growth. If so, that gave them something to work with, but Aliyaah wouldn't know until after the storm abated and they could return to the station. In the meantime, Aliyaah gave herself another anti-rad shot before working her way through the ship, ensuring that every member of her crew took their meds.

TWENTY-NINE

Once the storms abated and communications were fully restored, Aliyaah contacted the station and Hadley informed her of three more casualties. Several people had also gone missing, and Hadley was at a loss as to where they might have gone. He was reluctant to send out search parties and risk further deaths, but Aliyaah knew he was making the same calculations she was, working out how many more people they could lose before it became impossible to get *Octavia* off the ground.

They had been trapped on *Octavia* for more than a sol, thanks to a series of intense back to back solar storms. Aliyaah insisted that she ferry the crew back in small groups using the SEV, to minimise radiation exposure. Hadley agreed, even though it would have been faster for the men to walk in their EV suits. It took several trips in the SEV, but they were all accounted for, and none of the men showed any symptoms of infection, so far. When all the engineers had returned to the station, the relief on Hadley's face was obvious. He told Aliyaah about the three most recent casualties. Two of the men had become confused, then aggressive, and had died from sudden cardiac arrest. Hadley suspected that the third man had taken his own life, and he asked Aliyaah to keep his assessment to herself. In a confined and isolated environment, and with a mounting sense of hopelessness, there was a significant risk of mass hysteria and suicide contagion.

Aliyaah confided in Hadley how she was finding it increasingly difficult to determine if the crew's quick tempers were a symptom of infection or simply a reasonable reaction to their current situation. They had all been selected for the mission in part because of their ability to remain level headed. Now, though, after hours cooped up in the ship, with little to keep them occupied but thoughts of their dead colleagues, some of the crew were struggling to keep their emotions in check. They knew they needed to wait for clearance from Mission Support, but they desperately wanted to begin building the walkway to *Octavia* and making a start on pre-flight checks.

When they were waiting on *Octavia,* Aliyaah had overheard the men muttering about Hadley wasting time. She had let it slide until one specialist began questioning Hadley's ability to handle the situation. Despite her fears, she projected a sense of calm, hoping to pull everyone together behind Hadley. The best way to get ready for launch was to do their jobs and work as a team.

Once they were back at the station, Aliyaah summoned Doctor Schiff to the hangar. As she waited for the doctor to arrive, she sent a message to Mission Support to ask for further instruction. Aliyaah tapped her fingers on the communications console, willing the little green light to appear that indicated an incoming message. A growing hubbub drew her attention across the hangar. Hadley was waving his hands in what looked like a calming motion, trying to de-escalate the situation. He was standing close together with most of the remaining crew, including the men who had been with her on *Octavia*. Their voices grew louder as they vented their frustration. Being trapped on the ship and then returning to news of further deaths was trying even the most stoic among them.

One of the younger officers, Corporal Adams, shouted at Hadley, adamant that he wouldn't spend another sol on the planet. He gestured towards the hangar door and said, "You're not doing a damn thing, and there's this... this thing killing us!"

"Corporal Adams, take a breath and watch your tone," Hadley said. "Remember your rank. This colony is still under my command."

The corporal scoffed, then looked around at his fellow specialists, assessing their level of support for an insurrection.

Hadley's expression remained neutral, but Aliyaah observed a slight hesitation, almost imperceptible, before he continued. "Corporal, you were chosen for this mission, like all of us, because of your ability to handle stressful situations. Remember your training. Everyone needs to keep a cool head while we work this out as a team." Hadley paused, considering his next words carefully. "Until we know exactly what we are dealing with, and we get clearance from CapCom to launch, we will remain on Mars. We have to ensure we do not inadvertently transport this organism with us back to Earth. It is not just our lives at stake here, and we would all do well to remember that."

Adams turned back to face Hadley, and Aliyaah watched as he shook his head and narrowed his eyes. "With all due respect, Sir," the corporal said with derision, "we all know what is at stake here, and that means getting off this goddamn planet as fast as *Octavia* can take us."

Adams took another quick look at his colleagues and then walked out of the hangar. Four or five of the men followed him, avoiding eye contact with Hadley as they went.

Hadley watched them leave, then turned to the remaining crew. "Those of you who would like to avoid being court martialled, get to work. You have all been assigned tasks. Go do them. I will let you know when anything changes." He looked over at Aliyaah, then back at his officers. They hadn't moved, so he clapped his hands and said, "Get to it."

Hadley stood still for a few seconds, alone in the centre of a flurry of activity. Aliyaah wondered what he was thinking, and if he would go after Adams and the others who had walked out. Perhaps feeling her scrutiny, Hadley looked in her direction then walked her way. "Any changes, Chief?"

"Still waiting for a response from Mission Support, Sir," Aliyaah said.

"The crew is getting restless," Hadley said, and raised an eyebrow. "You may have noticed."

"I know, Sir. Being confined to *Octavia* didn't help." Aliyaah glanced across at the hangar door, then said, "It's probably good to let the corporal cool off, Sir."

Hadley nodded. "That was my thinking too, Chief. I don't know how he passed the Psych Eval, if I'm honest."

"He can be quite hotheaded, yes," Aliyaah said, then added, "just like his father, General Adams." Aliyaah watched Hadley as he opened his mouth to respond and then promptly shut it again and nodded. She risked a small laugh and was relieved to see Hadley's flat expression crack a little.

"Good old nepotism," he said, and they were both silent for a moment before Hadley inhaled sharply and asked, "Still no word from Flight Engineer Antara?"

Aliyaah shook her head. It was now more than two sols since Aliyaah last heard from Silver. Their confinement on *Octavia* and subsequent return to the station had afforded Aliyaah no opportunity to return to the dome for Silver. Once communications had been restored, Aliyaah had tried to contact Silver, but had gotten no response.

The nanobots stopped sending data as soon as the storm hit, and nothing new had come through even in the brief reprieve that allowed her to contact Hadley. The little information they received had been garbled by the storm, and none would have made it to Mission Support, so they remained unsure as to what they were really dealing with.

Aliyaah held onto the idea that Silver had retreated to the safety of the storm shelter and was now camped out in the relative safety of the inner dome, where there was plenty of food and water. The storm could have knocked out communications and Silver might be working on fixing the problem, hoping that the Chief would come back for her as promised. Aliyaah knew that the longer they went without hearing from Silver, the more likely it was that she had met the same fate as the others.

After transporting the crew safely to the station, Aliyaah wanted to take the SEV to the dome, but on her final trip the SEV jammed as it locked into the station's dock. It took them hours to release the clamps manually. They needed two teams, one working inside and one outside the station, to coordinate a safe release of the SEV. Aliyaah made sure to rotate the two teams to reduce radiation exposure.

As tempting as it was to use brute force to release the vehicle from the dock, the risk of damage was too great. Without the SEV there would be no easy way to get Silver safely back to the station.

While Aliyaah had been stuck on *Octavia*, Hadley had assigned a team to restore the station's radiation shield back to full capacity. The damage from the explosions had weakened the station's magnetic field, so most of those remaining at the station had spent the storms confined to the emergency shelters. The latest casualties were those who had worked outside the shelters the longest during the storm. The missing crew had also spent considerable amounts of time outside the safety of the shelter, working to maintain essential systems at the station.

With the shields almost back at full capacity, Aliyaah's focus was on working with the crew to build the walkway to *Octavia*. She had used her time on *Octavia* to come up with a way of using equipment she hoped was still in the hangar, and parts from a rover, to get around the shortage in construction materials. When she checked the inventory after getting back to the station, she was relieved to see that the equipment was still intact and functional, so she set the crew to work dismantling machinery and building the missing pieces.

With construction underway, Aliyaah hoped she could convince Hadley to let her take the SEV over to the biodome. If nothing else, they could retrieve the samples and the data from the M-Lab.

Aliyaah had only managed to sleep fitfully while on *Octavia*. She had grown wary of her bunkmates and wanted to be ready to move as soon as the storm abated. Patience was a necessity in space. It wasn't like in the movies where everything moved so quickly that you could barely keep up and always had something to keep you busy. Instead, the almost constant waiting and watching led to a restless kind of exhaustion, and as Aliyaah waited for the little green light to flicker she let the voices of her colleagues wash over her. Her head grew heavy in her hands. She desperately needed sleep, but the growing sense of mistrust among the crew made it hard to feel safe even when she was awake. Aliyaah was also worried about her own paranoia. Was it a reasonable reaction to the situation, or was she feeling the effects of .

It was clear that Hadley also had concerns. He knew he was losing control of the crew, and the civilians were barely holding it together. They were all too aware that they were not being told the full story, and in the absence of clear information, rumours abounded. The story of the Commander's erratic and violent behaviour, and of the recent deaths, spread throughout the colony. Witnesses had enjoyed a brief and curious celebrity as they recounted the terror, confusion, and sudden demise of the men, but it wasn't long before the storytellers' proximity to the dead made them seem dangerous. If the deaths were related to an infection, then it might be spread through physical contact or breathing the same air, meaning that those closest to the Commander and other casualties might also be infected. Some of the crew insisted on setting up a quarantine zone, but after talking to Schiff, Hadley quashed the idea. He stressed to the remaining crew and civilians that now, more than ever, they needed to work together, not isolate one another.

Aliyaah was relieved that only Hadley and Schiff knew what she and Silver had seen in the west wing and at the biodome. If the civilians had seen the state of those bodies there would be little Aliyaah and Hadley could do to allay their fears.

Just before the storm hit, Schiff had told Hadley she wanted to begin testing the crew and civilians for signs of infection. Wary of causing widespread panic, Hadley initially opted to wait for a decision from Mission Support, until the doctor suggested running blood tests under the guise of assessing the negative effects of the unusually lengthy set of solar storms. With the shields down, those remaining at the station could have experienced significant radiation exposure. Schiff said she would take blood samples to test for radiation and infection, and would hand out additional anti-rads to anyone who needed them.

The swabs that Aliyaah had taken from her own nose and mouth showed no signs of the crystalline formations she and Silver had seen in Dominic's samples. With the original data made incomprehensible by the storm, Schiff got to work analysing another source of material: the bodies of the deceased.

When the doctor finally arrived in the hangar, she was suited up like the rest of the crew, so Aliyaah didn't pay her any special attention. It was only after a few minutes that Aliyaah realised the newest arrival in the hangar hadn't moved from the door. Instead, the figure seemed to be scrutinising the officers' movements. Aliyaah noticed the medical armband and waved Schiff over, breaking the doctor's focus.

Schiff continued to observe the crew, even after reaching the communications console. She glanced at Aliyaah, keeping eye contact brief, and said, "Chief," before returning her attention to the crew.

"What are you looking for?" Aliyaah asked, and Schiff narrowed her eyes but said nothing. "Can you tell? If they're infected I mean?"

"There are no visual signs in the early stages," Schiff said slowly, still scanning the hangar.

Aliyaah followed the doctor's gaze, which settled on a group of engineers who were dismantling an old rover model to use its parts for their new walkway construction.

The two women remained silent for thirty seconds, and Aliyaah considered Schiff, whose focus never strayed from the group of men. Aside from the medical assessments required by NASA, Aliyaah hadn't needed to see the doctor during their tenure on Mars. She didn't know Schiff well, but found it interesting that someone charged with looking after the wellbeing of everyone on the mission had such a cold and stiff demeanour. Perhaps her bedside manner was friendlier when she hadn't been asked to cut open the body of her now deceased commanding officer.

"Did your autopsy of the Commander reveal anything of interest?" Aliyaah asked, breaking the silence. She half hoped that the tests would show no effect of radiation on the tissue samples. But if that was the case, they would be back at square one, with little idea of how the organism caused such massive tissue destruction so rapidly.

"No clear proliferation of the crystalline growths. Some evidence of the biomarkers you observed, and prefrontal cortex disintegration. That appears to be the most opportune tissue to colonise, and from there, one might assume, to begin to alter host behaviour."

Aliyaah leaned back and fought off her inclination to let out a low, whistling screech through her teeth. This was something she had done as a child and had learnt to temper as an adult working with Americans. She shifted slightly in an attempt to meet Schiff's eye. "That's an interesting way to phrase things, Doctor: 'The most opportune tissue to colonise'." Aliyaah said.

"Yes, well," Schiff said flatly.

"Any signs that radiation affects this thing?"

"My research is ongoing," Schiff said, turning her attention to Hadley and the other men as they moved a section of the walkway across the hangar.

Aliyaah observed Schiff watching Hadley and the men for a few moments, then asked, "Are you OK, Doctor?"

Schiff turned to look up at Aliyaah and blinked. Aliyaah saw her pupils narrow under the bright lights in the hangar. The doctor considered Aliyaah for a moment and then nodded, saying, "Yes. Everything's just fine."

Aliyaah sucked her teeth then said, "I think things are far from fine, Doctor."

"You're right, of course," Schiff said, continuing to look closely at Aliyaah, her scrutiny beginning to make Aliyaah feel uncomfortable. "Chief Diambu," she said, letting a smile slowly take over her features, "the tests on the crew would proceed more rapidly if I had an assistant."

"You need an assistant?" Aliyaah asked, finding the doctor's abrupt change in manner somewhat discombobulating.

"Yes. I could assess the men more quickly with an assistant to process the samples."

"So, you know what to look for in the blood to establish infection?" Aliyaah asked.

Schiff paused, and her smile gave way for a moment. "We should have that information soon." She pointed at the group of men working on the rover. "Those men. Are any of them medically qualified?"

"No," Aliyaah said slowly. "But there is a junior officer with a background in biochemistry. I could..."

Schiff cut her off, saying, "Yes. A junior officer would be ideal."

"OK," Aliyaah said. "If you're sure it's necessary."

"It would expedite things, yes."

"Of course. I can send him to the lab right away, Doctor. And please, once he arrives, can you stress that he keep his work confidential. He should only report to yourself, me, or Commander

Hadley."

"That won't be a problem, Chief," Schiff said, as she turned towards the hangar door.

"Doctor?" Aliyaah said, reaching out her hand to touch the woman's shoulder. "Are you sure you're OK? Perhaps you should get some sleep."

Schiff briefly looked at Aliyaah's hand on her shoulder and then half turned to face the Chief. "There's no time for that, Chief."

Aliyaah watched the doctor walk away, marvelling at how even her gait was stiff and unfriendly. As she considered Schiff's behaviour, Aliyaah saw a green light on the communications console. She looked around for Hadley and saw that he was over by the hangar door talking to Schiff. Aliyaah waved him over and he nodded and held up a gloved finger to ask her to wait a moment.

Aliyaah sat down and cued up the message from Mission Support. Once Hadley arrived, they listened to the message without comment. With a note of resignation, CapCom said, "It has been decided to further postpone the launch of *Octavia II*."

"Until when?" Aliyaah thought, and when CapCom continued, she wasn't surprised.

"*Octavia II* is postponed indefinitely." The officer's voice softened as he added, "We just can't risk sending more of you up there. I'm sorry, Commander, Chief. We'll have more for you soon. Our thoughts and prayers are with you."

Aliyaah sat down and put her head in her hands. What good were their thoughts and prayers? No one was coming to help them, and if they were too scared to send reinforcements, they were unlikely to approve the launch of *Octavia*. Even if they made it back to Earth somehow, they would be greeted by people in hazmat suits, not open arms and happy cheers.

Mission Support hadn't yet responded to their request to launch *Octavia*, other than to say they were considering all courses of action. Aliyaah knew that negotiations would be taking place between NASA, the ESA, the Planetary Protection Agency, and a host of other international stakeholders.

Feeling the panic begin to set in, Aliyaah gave herself a shake. Hadley put a hand on her shoulder and gestured for her to vacate the seat.

"Did Schiff fill you in?" Aliyaah asked as she stood up.

Hadley nodded and took the seat. "She said she's running further tests."

"Yes, and she wants a lab assistant," Aliyaah said. "I approved the request," she added and watched Hadley's reaction.

"If it helps her get us answers, I'm all for it," he said. "Thank you, Chief."

Aliyaah took her cue to leave and went to find the junior officer as Hadley adjusted the microphone and faced the camera. Hitting record, he said, "Message received and understood, CapCom. We have *Octavia* up and running. The walkway is in progress and we will begin loading the ship and taking steps towards launch once we have your go ahead. I am sending you the revised trajectory and flight plan I intend to follow. We understand that the timing is less than ideal, with our launch window closing, but if we leave now we still have some protection from GCRs thanks to the residual solar activity over the next few sevensols." Hadley hesitated, then added in a slow, measured voice, "There are no further cases of contagion. Schiff assures me she has control of the situation. I'm officially requesting permission to continue with launch preparations." He hit the send button, deleted the message, and then studied the console, as if seeing it for the first time. He rubbed his eyes and blinked. The console seemed brighter than usual, and he couldn't quite recall what each of the lights meant. Hadley took a deep breath and tried to gather his thoughts. He had just lied to Mission Support, and he wasn't entirely certain why.

THIRTY

The *Octavia* mission had brought enough supplies to the planet to last the crew at least twelve months beyond their intended return date, but the explosions at the station had destroyed food stores, medical supplies, and other necessities. After the storms, Hadley assigned a team to take stock of their remaining supplies. Using that information, Aliyaah calculated that their remaining rations would last them eight months, possibly more now they had fewer mouths to feed. Their journey to Earth would take at least six months, and while the biodomes had extended the rations brought from Earth, the colony was reliant on resupply from the incoming shuttle.

After NASA cancelled the *Octavia II* mission, Aliyaah knew that they either needed to get off the planet in the next few sevensols or face starvation. The settlement plan relied on each incoming shuttle, whether civilian or cargo, bringing more supplies than it needed, creating a stockpile for current and future settlers through a full twenty-six months, or seven hundred and seventy sols, if they missed their flight window or had other reasons to stay on the planet. The gradual process of terraforming would allow them to build a self-sustaining settlement, but the realisation of that plan was decades away. *Octavia* was meant to have heralded the beginning of Project Arche, not the end of Mars exploration.

Aliyaah knew that impending food shortages weren't the only concern. The biodomes and the station relied on material mined at the quarry and processed by the refiners. By destroying those machines, the

Commander had also destroyed their ability to create new construction materials and to add minerals to the soil they were building up in the biodomes. To survive, they either needed to leave the planet and head back to Earth soon, or dramatically alter the way they interacted with Mars.

While there had been more deaths at the station during the solar storm, no one on *Octavia* had succumbed to the organism. The shielding from GCRs and solar radiation was more effective on the ship, which gave Aliyaah a sliver of hope. If Silver was right and the GCRs acted as a catalyst for the organism, they might be able to slow down the progression and spread of the infection if they got everyone on board *Octavia* and off the planet.

Aliyaah knew this might be wishful thinking, and even if the theory proved true, there was always the worry that killing the organism would also mean killing its host. Aliyaah considered this for a moment, in light of Schiff's findings. Perhaps it was only once someone was symptomatic, and had suffered serious damage to their brain tissue, that eradicating the organism would prove fatal for its human host.

One thing was clear to Aliyaah: There were too many unanswered questions to allow her, Hadley, or Mission Support to make informed decisions. Schiff was adamant that she study the bodies of all the deceased more closely, and had also requested that she personally assess every crew member. To do that, they would need to retrieve the bodies from the biodome, along with the data Silver had collected, and perhaps Silver herself. They would first have to repair the SEV, as the residual radiation from the storms made it unsafe to use the zip line system to reach the biodome.

Schiff suggested that she could go and retrieve the samples, but Hadley wouldn't risk sending the only fully qualified physician they had left. Aliyaah also had reservations. Her interaction with the doctor in the hangar had made her wary of breaking protocol to reveal Silver's location. Silver was now third in command, and Aliyaah felt a nagging concern over Schiff's odd demeanour; was her research truly motivated by a desire to help the crew?

Hadley quickly shot down Aliyaah's concerns about protocol.

"We've already contravened policy by both being here at the station instead of at separate facilities. I need you here to oversee the walkway construction, and, you're the only one who has seen this thing up close. It might be helpful for you to be here while the doctor carries out the autopsies."

Aliyaah nodded. She didn't relish that task, nor did she want to reveal Silver's location. She considered voicing her concerns about Schiff, but worried that it would make her sound paranoid.

"Where is FE Antara, Chief?" Hadley asked. He waited for Aliyaah to answer, but she stayed silent as she thought through various scenarios. Hadley gave her a few more seconds, then said pointedly, "Chief, there are few places left to hide on Mars. The rest of the crew will figure out Antara's location eventually. Your travel time in the SEV. A slip in comms." He shook his head. "We no longer have the luxury of keeping certain information classified."

Aliyaah reluctantly agreed. "She's out at Biodome Three."

"Thank you, Chief. Now, can you draw up a list of who we have left who can pilot the SEV?"

Aliyaah frowned and said, "Sir, there's just you, me, and Corporal Adams."

Hadley looked dumbfounded and began to check the list of remaining personnel. "That can't be right. Can it? We had ten qualified SEV pilots and now -"

"I know, Sir," Aliyaah interrupted him. "Assuming Antara is alive, we still have four, but the others are either dead or missing."

"Well, I clearly can't send Adams." Hadley shot Aliyaah a look of exasperation, thinking about the potential insurrection the Corporal was creating.

"It might get him out of the way, Sir. Prevent him from stirring up more trouble."

"No. Adams can't be trusted. There's only one option. I'll go," Hadley said, frowning.

Aliyaah was about to disagree, but realised it was futile. She nodded, then retrieved some sample containers for radioactive material. "You'll need these, for tissue samples. And you might want to take a hatchet, or something similar."

Hadley grimaced and said, "Where are the bodies, Chief?"

Aliyaah told him where to find Alvarez and Dominic, then added, "Antara probably set up camp in the inner dome, where there's food and water. That's what I would do." She hesitated, considering the situation, then added, "But, if there are any issues with comms in the dome, she might not know the storm is over. She could still be in the shelter." Aliyaah's voice hardened and she said, "That's assuming she was still alive and thinking clearly when the alarm sounded. It's been three sols with no response from the biodome, Sir. We should consider that Antara has succumbed to the organism."

Hadley nodded, hearing the edge in her voice. "Antara is one of the smartest, most resourceful officers I've known, Chief. If anyone can survive this, she can."

Aliyaah swallowed hard before saying, "Yes, Sir. And, be careful. If Antara is still alive, she might be infected like the others." It felt like a betrayal as Aliyaah reluctantly added, "Antara is strong and could take you by surprise. She'll know the biodome much better than you by now, and she knows how to drive the SEV. If this thing is affecting her behaviour, she could leave you stranded, or worse."

Taking the sample containers from Aliyaah, Hadley thanked her for the warning. "I'll be back, Chief. You worry about the walkway, and I'll worry about Antara."

THIRTY-ONE

Aliyaah, with the help of two other engineers, lifted a section of the walkway onto the scaffold and felt it click into place. Turning to pick up the next piece, Aliyaah took a moment to catch her breath. The dull ache in her ribs had subsided. All she felt now was general fatigue as the last few days caught up with her.

Aliyaah looked out across the dusty, rust-red planet in the direction of the biodome and thought about Silver. With no contact from the FE, Aliyaah was losing hope that Hadley would find her friend alive. The last few sols had brought home to Aliyaah how removed she was from most of her female colleagues, and how much of herself she had hidden from her crew. Silver was the exception, given how long they had known each other, but even their friendship hadn't been close.

Aliyaah was one of just five female engineers on *Octavia*, including Silver and Jaz, and there were only around a dozen women in the entire first wave of Project Arche, including Doctor Schiff. Aliyaah had known better than to assume that she would find common ground with the other women on *Octavia*. Still, she was surprised that, despite having spent hours working together, she barely knew anything about the women's personal lives. She knew their qualifications and experience, of course, as she was responsible for organising work crews and schedules.

Come to think of it, Aliyaah wasn't even sure if Jaz had identified as a woman. They had only ever talked about work-related things. What she did know was that Jaz had a background in biochemistry, was an expert on Lidar, and would have been damn useful right about now.

Aliyaah felt guilty for thinking in such a utilitarian way, but their time on *Octavia* and on Mars was mostly filled with tasks specific to their skillsets. Aliyaah provided oversight but otherwise trusted her officers to do their work, whatever their personal circumstances. It didn't matter if you didn't particularly like all your crewmates, you still had to trust them.

Aliyaah's thoughts turned back to Silver. Aside from Dominic, Silver was the only other person on the planet who she actually considered a friend. Still, Aliyaah could probably count on one hand the number of times Silver had mentioned her life back on Earth, and her family.

The male engineers had always been more open than their female colleagues when talking about their lives back home. Aliyaah wondered if it was because the men felt they had less to lose, and maybe even something to gain, if they showed a side of themselves that wasn't purely logical, hard-nosed, and professional. A woman who talked about her kids or her partner ran the risk of being seen as overly emotional and perhaps unreliable as a result.

While they were cooped up in the ship with little to do, many of the men talked about their wives and girlfriends. None of them mentioned a male or genderqueer partner, which didn't surprise Aliyaah. Anyone who did so would likely fall prey to the same biases affecting women in the military. Some of the men passed around pictures of their kids and shared cute stories, but the atmosphere was bittersweet. Thoughts of family so far away were inherently tainted with the idea that they might not make it home, and speculation over what might happen even if they did.

Aliyaah had stayed quiet while the men talked about their lives. If she had been reluctant to mention Dominic before, there seemed no reason to reveal their relationship now. As far as she knew, Dominic had never discussed their closeness with anyone else on the crew, nor with his family back home. Silver was the only other person who knew, and she might also now be dead. Aliyaah felt a sudden urge to publicly acknowledge that she and Dominic had been more than just colleagues. It seemed so unfair that she had no allowance to grieve. Under ordinary circumstances she would have informed NASA. There would have been a report, a thorough debriefing, and mandatory counselling, but these were not ordinary circumstances, and Aliyaah had to postpone her grief. There was no time for her to fall apart and stitch herself back together, even if her stoicism felt like a betrayal to Dominic's memory.

Knowing that she was thinking about Dominic's death at a necessary remove, Aliyaah thought back to Silver's loss of composure in the biodome. She knew that Silver was married, and Aliyaah had even seen Cooper a few times at NASA functions, although it was hard to say whether Cooper was there as a plus-one or in her own right. Aliyaah had actually met Cooper before Silver, when they worked together on a project some years before Silver joined the agency. As Aliyaah remembered, Cooper had brought a refreshing, quiet humour to what was a rather mundane project. She was very good at what she did, and Aliyaah considered how she would have been an asset to Project Arche, especially given that they had now lost Jaz, their only real Lidar specialist. NASA didn't usually approve the assignment of couples to the same mission, for obvious reasons, but Cooper was eminently qualified and if she had wanted to be on the crew Aliyaah didn't see any real obstacle. It was a long time to be separated, and Aliyaah wondered why she had chosen to stay behind.

As she helped position the next piece of the walkway, Aliyaah suddenly remembered that Cooper and Silver had a child, a girl. The thought caused her to lose her grip on the smooth metal plate in her hands and she was fortunate that it was already in place and dropped down to catch on the adjacent section. She glanced at the men beside her, who didn't seem to have noticed her slip. For the briefest of moments, before her thoughts turned back to Silver's family, Aliyaah wondered what thoughts were racing through the minds of the men working by her side. They must surely be battling their own demons. Had it helped to pass around those photos and to say the names of their partners and children?

Aliyaah couldn't remember Silver ever talking about her child. She knew the girl's name was listed in Silver's personnel file, but she couldn't recall the details now. That must be why Cooper had stayed on Earth. Space was no place for a child. Aliyaah felt mad at herself for playing into the double standard, but she couldn't stop herself from judging Silver for leaving her little girl for such a long, and potentially dangerous, mission. Aliyaah wanted to believe that she would make a different choice to Silver, that she would stay on Earth like Cooper, but she didn't have children of her own, and didn't plan to, so she would likely never know how she would feel in a similar situation.

For Aliyaah, the decision to come to Mars was simple. She was leaving behind friends and family, but she had no partner, no children to whom she felt obligated or who she'd miss while she was away. Aliyaah couldn't imagine how Silver endured being away from her wife and kid. Perhaps that was why she never mentioned them. If she didn't admit their importance to anyone else then maybe it made it easier to survive the distance and time.

When Aliyaah had lost her husband, Ben, it had been both tragic and newsworthy. She hadn't been able to escape the attention, and had been forced to grieve quickly and publicly. At times, she had felt as if she were performing the part of a widow of terrorism rather than actually feeling what she professed to be feeling. Perhaps this was why it had taken her years to let anyone else in after Ben's death.

Now, Aliyaah considered how Cooper would feel if Silver didn't return to her. She would also be a widow, and she, too, would have to grieve in public. What was worse, she would be expected to have accepted that by marrying an astronaut she had signed up for this possibility. It seemed desperately unfair to Aliyaah, but she could see now that she had once asked Ben to accept the very same thing.

Aliyaah thought back to the conversation with Silver in the biodome and regretted not having done more. It seemed like a lifetime ago that she had helped to steady Silver, and she wondered about the news Silver had received from home. She should have been a better friend, and now she might never get the chance.

Friendships between astronauts had always seemed fraught to Aliyaah, especially between minorities. Everyone was so motivated, and resources and assignments were finite. The agencies didn't want to admit it, but the odds were against you if you weren't straight, white, and male. Tokenism was alive and well, despite extensive diversity directives.

Aliyaah considered her marriage to Ben, remembering how happy they had been, both in their demanding careers and in their life together. They had rarely quarrelled, and had been loving and happy even when Aliyaah was away for months on missions. Aliyaah hadn't expected, or desired, to get romantically involved with anyone after Ben had died, but then she had met Dominic and long forgotten pieces of her began to re-emerge. Dom had given her a chance to feel playful again, to feel sexual and engaged. Being with him had allowed her to open up a little, not that she had let that show to her crew.

Aliyaah had worked harder than ever after Ben's death, becoming the youngest Chief Flight Engineer in the history of the space programme. It had been clear from the start that she would be selected for Project Arche and for *Octavia*. She was the most qualified astronaut to lead the engineering team, and she had been heavily involved in selecting her crew for the mission to Mars.

Part of Aliyaah's remit had been developing the refiners and she had played a significant role in the design of the station itself. This mission was the culmination of years of her life, but the events of the past few sols had left Aliyaah questioning a whole slew of decisions. If they had used different materials for construction, would they have been able to detect the organism earlier and contain it before it spread across the fledgling colony? Would they have fared better, been less vulnerable, if the fundamental shape and structure of the station had been different? The Commander should never have been able to destroy the refiners and the east wing, even if he had received help from Chief Frederickson. And now, with Hadley heading out to the biodome, Aliyaah was in command at the station. These people were relying on her, and she wasn't at all sure she could get them safely back to Earth.

Looking around at the crew, Aliyaah saw a group of exhausted men who were using their last reserves to build the walkway to *Octavia*, taking advantage of the brief period where GCRs were low thanks to the solar storms. In the last few hours, she had gone over her plan with the crew to devise a workaround for the pieces of the walkway yet to be built. She recalled Rover Four to the station, and assigned crew to cannibalise it for parts. They were using these alongside pieces from the earlier rover models in hangar storage to construct the missing parts of the walkway.

Now, with the first of three sections of the walkway in place, Aliyaah motioned to the crew to lock it down and take a break. Her limbs were burning from the manual labour and even with her suit's internal climate control, her skin still felt damp with sweat.

The lower gravity made things easier, but lifting the giant metal grills into position still required intense physical effort. While she rested, she was briefly tempted to alter the settings on her hormone pump. If she gave herself a corticosteroid boost right now, and a shot of testosterone, she could continue working through the pain and exhaustion into the night. She wondered how many of the men had thought something similar, and if any of them had acted on the thought.

Leaving her hormone levels to regulate themselves, Aliyaah activated her headset and contacted Schiff at the station, requesting an update. Schiff didn't respond, so she tried a different channel, hoping to get her lab assistant. There was still no response, and she was about to switch to another channel to contact Hadley when she heard someone whispering her name over and over. For a second, she felt hopeful, thinking that Silver was finally making contact, but then the voice grew louder, pleading with her to come back to the station. It was one of the men she had left working in the hangar.

The specialist yelled, "Chief! Chief!", then fell silent. Before she could respond, the line filled with screams, then abruptly cut out. Aliyaah was left frozen in place as clouds of dust lifted slowly from the ground, coating her, the crew, and the walkway in a fine red powder.

THIRTY-TWO

As he clambered into the driver's seat of the SEV, Hadley felt some of the tension of the last two sols fall away. A farm boy turned Colonel in the US Air Force, he had been flying planes and guiding shuttles for decades, and couldn't remember a time when he didn't know how to handle an ATV or drive a tractor. The familiarity of the machine was reassuring and Hadley felt a renewed sense of hope. Maybe it was still possible to save what remained of his crew, and salvage something from this mission.

Hadley ran his gloved fingers gently over the array of switches and buttons and took a deep breath. He checked that the SEV's tracking system was active and released the clamps to separate the vehicle from the station. He had only piloted the SEV a handful of times since arriving on the planet, but he had spent hours at the test site in Nevada, working with Silver and the other engineers to figure out adaptations to the vehicle that would enable it to better navigate the tough terrain on Mars. He had also spent a summer in the Canadian north, working on developing deep water submersibles to investigate stromatolites and microbialites on the ocean floor.

Piloting the SEV was a little like guiding one of those remotely operated vehicles. Its slow, lumbering motion was vastly different from that of an F-35 Lightning fighter jet, but he knew that this torpidity was deceptive. All too quickly, the wrong decision could incapacitate the vehicle and leave him stranded.

He had almost twenty years of experience as a test pilot, flying over California, working on pitch control margin simulation and training the greenest of pilots as well as some of the best in the world. Throwing planes into a spin and pulling them out of crisis wasn't a game to him. He knew the risks he took as a test pilot and astronaut, having lost friends and colleagues over the years through human error, mechanical failure, and simple bad luck. Hadley wasn't immune to the feeling of terror as a plane plummeted to earth. If anything, it was this that fuelled his ongoing fascination with flight. His fear metamorphosed into something akin to the weightlessness of mind, if not body, Hadley felt when he meditated. He would experience a startling clarity of thought, as if time stopped and expanded, freeing his mind to explore myriad possibilities simultaneously. The resulting insights simply weren't possible without living the experience. This is what kept Hadley in the air, year after year.

Hadley's commanding officers recognised this capacity for almost beatific calm early in his career. They fast-tracked him through promotion after promotion, and assigned him projects where it was almost guaranteed that complex machinery would spiral out of control. As he rose in the ranks of the military, Hadley's technical abilities continued to impress. When his career trajectory threatened to take him away from the cockpit and into boardrooms, Hadley made the decision to apply for NASA, where his calm demeanour was also highly sought after.

In almost every other way, Hadley flew under the radar. His relationships with his fellow officers, pilots, and astronauts were only remarkable in how unremarkable they were. Where astronauts and officers married, divorced, and married again, Hadley remained unattached. It wasn't that he was unlikable, but he did appear to be a little aloof, and he hadn't put in any particular effort to form close bonds with anyone he worked with, or anyone outside of work for that matter. His colleagues couldn't mistake the rapport Hadley had with machines, but this facility only highlighted how little he seemed to connect with the humans around him.

A few of his senior officers had observed this quality in Hadley, but no one had questioned his command capabilities. He had an exemplary safety record and every project he led had been a success, even if it produced little fanfare.

When he was selected as second in command for *Octavia* it was the first time in his career that Hadley had considered turning down an assignment. He had just quietly celebrated his sixtieth birthday, and while he was committed to the mission to Mars, he wanted to focus on the experience and technical challenges without the distraction of having to manage a crew. He was still in excellent physical, but he knew he wouldn't be able to meet the standards required for the refinery crew. His only other option was to go to Mars as a civilian, but that would grant him few, if any, opportunities to pilot the rovers or SEV, let alone *Octavia* herself. So, in the end, he accepted the assignment and tried to reframe the responsibility as just another challenge to be met.

With the Commander's demise, Hadley had been thrust into a leadership role he had never wanted. Maintaining order among the crew and keeping the civilians calm was proving to be a challenge for which he felt unprepared. When technology malfunctioned, he could seek a solution. Managing people was a more nebulous problem, and Hadley was grateful both for Chief Diambu's assistance and to have this brief respite in the SEV.

This gratitude wasn't uncomplicated, however. Hadley couldn't avoid feeling a little disappointed in himself at having felt such relief when it became clear he would have to pilot the SEV this time. The desire to escape from the station, from the very people who now trusted him to guide them to safety, was not becoming in a Commander.

Hadley was sorely tempted to go slower than necessary in the SEV and, perhaps, to linger at the biodome, but he resolved to find Antara, collect the samples and data, and get back to the station as quickly as possible. He needed to redirect the crew's nervous energy into more productive channels. They would need discrete tasks to keep them occupied and engaged while Mission Support figured out the next steps. He had every confidence in the Chief, but he should still get back to the station as soon as he could, before there was a full-blown mutiny.

Realising that he had been focusing only on the terrain

immediately ahead of the SEV, Hadley took a moment to look around, making sure that the route he had chosen to the biodome was still the most efficient. The surface of Mars was barren; intensely dry dust storms blew across the landscape and carved strange and delicate shapes in the rock. Millennia of this subtle sculpting created geological formations not seen on Earth. Sometimes, the rocks seemed to form the strangest of objects: a floating spoon, a coffin, a fossilised iguana. Faces jumped out from the planet's surface. The sides of the craters loomed and danced with ever-changing patterns.

The lip of the Schiaparelli crater separated Hadley and Biodome Three, and he watched the swirling dust form faces and bodies against its steep walls, like the russet-coloured ghosts of actors long since dead, playing out their parts on a colossal movie screen. Hadley resumed his journey, guiding the SEV carefully up the foothills of the crater. What he was seeing was classic pareidolia, apophenia; his mind was simply finding patterns where there were none. The surface of the red planet was not changing before his eyes, nor taking human form. It was just shadows from dust dancing in the dim sunlight.

Knowing that it was against procedure, Hadley removed his helmet and gloves and ran his hands over his face. His skin was rough and dry. Two sol's worth of stubble snagged against the callouses on his hands. Hadley rubbed the sleep from the corners of his eyes and was thankful that he had stopped wearing the cats-eyes a few sols before. Suspecting a malfunction in the implants, he had removed them and sent them to the lab for testing. When the Commander destroyed the lab, he also destroyed any way of confirming Hadley's suspicion that the implants had caused a drop in his melatonin production, affecting his sleep cycle. Given the events of the previous two sols, a disrupted sleep routine was hardly his top priority.

Hadley put his helmet back on and locked it into place, then pulled on his gloves and started the SEV moving again. As he drew close to the lip of the crater, the SEV's radiological alarm tripped then quickly fell silent again. He carefully brought the vehicle to a halt as soon as he reached a flatter stretch of ground. This high up on the crater wall, where the surface was steep and littered with scree, any abrupt movement could cause the SEV to lose traction.

He checked his sensors and scanned the area ahead for radioactive material. The monitors showed nothing unusual. He did a second sweep just to be sure, but the result was the same. Something must have passed on the wind. He took a breath to compose himself, then put the SEV into gear and gently pushed the lever. The vehicle crawled forward and he looked at the screen showing the feed from the roof-mounted camera, which now had a view over the lip of the crater.

Biodome Three looked no different than usual. It's great white walls curved up to form the dome, lit from inside by the banks of ultraviolet lights. Hadley blinked and checked the cameras again, then the radiologic scanner. Everything looked sound, if a little more brightly lit than was usual for this time of sol. He wondered if Antara had changed the sollight settings at the dome. Or the Chief may have adjusted things before she had left for *Octavia*.

Making his way down the inside wall of the crater, he followed the tracks left earlier by Aliyaah and Silver when they took the SEV to the biodome after the explosions at the station. When he arrived at the biodome's SEV dock, Hadley took a moment to check-in with Aliyaah.

"We're laying out the last of the walkway now, Sir," Aliyaah reported. "GCRs should remain low for the next little while, so I have most of the team heading to *Octavia*. I assigned a skeleton crew to finish up salvaging rover parts in the hangar. If we go in shifts, we should have everything done within a sol."

Hadley thanked her and then asked about Schiff, saying, "I haven't been able to get in touch with her, or her assistant. I wonder if there's a problem with communications in the temporary lab. Have you heard from her, Chief?"

"No, Sir," Aliyaah said. "I tried earlier and couldn't reach her. I was going to check in once I got back to the station. Or I can send one of the hangar crew now to find out if there's an issue."

"No, no. She's probably just engrossed in the task. There are multiple bodies now, of course."

"Yes, Sir. I'll let you know what she has to say when I get back shortly. Hopefully she has determined a more accurate cause of death."

Hadley heard Aliyaah shout something to one of the crew, then she came back on the line to ask, "Any sign of Antara, Sir?"

"Nothing yet. I did a quick scan of the systems at the dome. Life support is still functional, as are comms."

"Be careful, Sir," Aliyaah said.

"You too, Chief. Over and out."

Hadley brought the SEV in close to the dock and activated the clamps to create an airtight seal. He made sure his space suit and helmet were secure, then released the door at the back of the SEV. The airlock was empty aside from the two suits hanging at either side, which looked disconcertingly corpse-like. Hadley chastised himself for such thoughts, but found it hard to shake the uncomfortable feeling that death was all around him.

After sealing the door to the SEV, Hadley deliberated over adding extra security clearance at the airlock. This would prevent anyone but him from accessing the vehicle, but it would also slow him down. He decided to leave security as it was. Depending on what he found in the dome, he might need to leave quickly. He started the decontamination process and then switched to one of the EV suits hanging inside the airlock. After locking his helmet into place, Hadley opened the door to the outer dome and stepped through.

THIRTY-THREE

The ambient temperature in the outer dome was colder than Hadley remembered from his previous visits to the biodomes. He checked the oxygen levels and saw that they were only at fifteen percent. The temperature stood at zero, making the inner atmosphere just a little warmer and slightly more oxygenated than conditions outside of the dome.

This perplexed Hadley. The life support system showed no malfunction, which meant that Antara, or someone else, must have manually reconfigured the dome's environment. Hadley checked the atmosphere and temperature in the inner dome, figuring Antara must be holed up there, perhaps waiting for help and unable to leave if she didn't have a space suit.

The readings showed that the inner dome had also been reprogrammed. Oxygen was at ten percent and the temperature was down to minus five degrees. It would have been impossible for Antara to survive the last few sols in such conditions. Hadley began to think that the Chief was right. Antara must have become infected and grown confused like the Commander, leading her to reprogram the environment and unwittingly bring about her own demise. The only way for Antara to still be alive would be if she had remained in the bunker beneath the dome.

Hadley approached the control panel just outside the inner dome and began a system sweep. He knew that Lidar would be useless inside the dome. Any scan for signs of organic life would be confused by the plant life and imported microbes they were using to enrich the soil. Instead, he checked for any large heat signatures, thankful that the lamps in the inner dome had been disabled so they wouldn't throw off the scan. Nothing unusual emerged, but Hadley did notice that the UV lights were turned way up.

He hadn't spent much time at the biodomes, and was surprised to see the extent to which some of the plants were thriving. Many of the plots were empty, or contained plants that were dead or in serious trouble, but some of the beds contained dense foliage, which made it hard to see any real distance across the inner dome.

A scan of the bunker showed the same conditions as the inner dome. It was highly unlikely Antara was still in there, oblivious to the storms having passed.

Hadley searched for any open comms channels in the bunker, but there was no sign of activity. Aliyaah had reminded him of the lack of a PA system in the biodomes, so he knew he had no way to let Antara know he was there and to ask her whereabouts. That problem seemed redundant now anyway; he wouldn't expect her to respond even if he could send out a message.

He listened intently for a moment or two, but all Hadley could hear was the noise of the dome's air filters high above him. They were louder than he remembered, and their typically steady hum had been replaced by a staccato whining and clacking sound. The filters seemed to be labouring, as if clogged with something. Ordinarily, Hadley would have climbed up to take a look. He was firmly of the mind that problems should be addressed immediately, but dysfunctional air filters were far from his top priority, and Hadley no longer had any desire to linger in the biodome.

The Chief had told him where she had last seen Silver with the samples in the inner dome, and where the two bodies were located. Hadley decided to enter the inner dome first, so he walked towards the airlock and ran the decontamination procedure. Once it was finished, he stepped into the inner dome.

Every metallic surface glowed with a peculiar phosphorescence. Not only was the plant life triffid-like, the floor was covered with a strange growth of white flakes, a carpet of glowing mulch that amplified the light from the UV lamps overhead.

The effect rendered Hadley snow-blind for a few seconds. After his eyes and the light shield on his visor adjusted, he took a step forward and watched as the flakes beneath his feet rippled outward. It was as if he was walking on water. He took another step and the same thing happened again. Mesmerized, he watched the ripples make their way towards the centre of the dome. The movement was languorous, and not really liquid-like. Instead, it was as if the floor was made of millions of tiny interconnected hairs reacting, in turn, to the impact of each of his steps.

Hadley didn't know what to make of the phenomenon. It had to be connected to the crystalline organism, but the Chief and Antara hadn't reported anything quite like this. The mulch beneath his feet certainly didn't seem benign, but as long as his suit remained intact, he didn't feel like he was in immediate danger.

With nothing indicating that Antara was still in the dome, Hadley decided that he should just get the samples and get out as quickly as possible.

He moved forward and found the workbench where Antara had been carrying out the tests on the swabs taken from Dominic. He needed to retrieve samples from both bodies. Hadley was curious to see the phenomenon first hand, but felt some reluctance too as he remembered the haunted look in the Chief's eyes. To quell any sense of fear, Hadley focused on the task: find both bodies, take samples, and get back to the SEV.

It was likely that Antara was also dead. He would need to locate her body and collect samples for analysis, but he didn't want to have to search the entire biodome. Every second he stayed in the dome left him exposed, and he couldn't shake the feeling that the mulch beneath his feet was getting thicker.

Knowing that Dominic's body was close to the workbench, Hadley used his scanner and located a residual radiation signature. As he followed the readings on the scanner, Hadley drew closer to the body and felt a shift in the air around him. The mulch was thicker here, and the plant growth even more lush. He had to fight through some foliage to find the remains of Dominic's body, slumped against one of the dome's struts.

At first, Hadley could barely recognise the body as that of a human, but with effort and some guesswork, he could just about make out what looked like Dominic's limbs. Where his head had been there was simply a mass of crystalline filaments, static in the still air of the dome.

Faced with the reality of the corpse, Hadley wasn't sure how best to obtain a tissue sample. There was no visible human tissue. It was like Dominic's body had been rapidly digested and extruded through his skin, exploding in a proliferation of crystals with a vaguely humanoid shape. He approached cautiously and leaned over what had been Dominic's head, scraping a sample into the radioactive material container.

The hair-like crystals broke away easily from the central mass, making Hadley think of dandelion seeds blown in the wind. Digging down, Hadley held his breath, knowing he would likely hit flesh the deeper he went. As he scraped away more of the crystals he felt his knife plunge through something softer. He cut a vaguely circular section and then leveraged this into another container. As the sample came away from the body, Hadley saw that what he had extracted was a fragment of Dominic's skull, the bone reformed as a sponge-like tissue. There were crystals growing on both the outer and inner surfaces of the skull, and where there should have been grey matter, there was just a tangle of what looked to Hadley like enoki mushrooms. The organism appeared to have sprouted from Dominic's brain, feeding on the fatty tissue and eating through the bone to explode in a frenzy as it pierced the skin.

Hadley sealed the containers and stepped back, keen to get away as quickly as possible. He moved back to the workbench and put the RMCs and samples from the M-Lab into a tote, then he turned around and began to make his way back to the airlock.

After a few steps, Hadley felt the floor getting more and more slippery until, finally, he lost his footing and tipped forward, dropping the tote with the samples. With the weight of his suit, Hadley struggled to stay upright, and his gloves plunged into the mass of mulch beneath him. He pulled his hands free as quickly as he could and tried to shake off the white flakes, but they clung to his gloves. He looked around for something to wipe them on, but almost everything was covered by the growth. A splash of green caught his eye and Hadley quickly moved towards a row of plants with withered blue flowers surrounded by a mass of small green leaves. Hadley broke off a handful of leaves and rubbed the vegetation between his gloves to remove the white mulch. When he was satisfied that his gloves were mostly free of the organism he used the pulpy mass to wipe away the label standing beside the plants: *Clitoria tenatea,* Butterfly Pea.

Hadley pulled the label from the ground and grabbed another handful of the leaves. The floor had begun to pulse at his feet, and the flakes seemed to be getting thicker every second. He ran back to the airlock, clutching the leaves and label in one hand and the samples in the other. He reached the exit and put out his hand to press the airlock release, then stopped. Someone, or something, was standing on the other side of the glass, watching him from the outer dome.

THIRTY-FOUR

The creature entered the south airlock close to the storm shelter and saw Hadley moving around inside the dome. As he headed in the direction of the corpse, the creature stood silent and still, watching.

When Hadley cut into what was once Dominic's flesh, the creature recoiled. The filaments of crystal caught the light from the inner dome and the creature twisted in pain. Once the knife was out, the crystals quickly closed around the wound. The pain receded and the creature took a step toward the airlock door.

The creature's gait was human-like, bipedal, but alternately stiff and languid. It was as if its limbs were held together by muscle memory alone. As it moved toward the control panel, it left a trail of red dust, which lingered for a moment, then paled and began to coalesce into a sea of white flakes.

Reaching the control panel, the creature, an excrescence of a wider consciousness, surveyed the switches, then looked up at the blank screen. Catching her reflection, Silver calmly considered how her appearance had changed. Her skin was now finely coated with small, almost fluid crystals, creating a luminescent complexion that altered with every movement or change in light. Silver could feel the metal under her feet and the switches beneath her fingers, but she also felt the ground beneath the biodome, and the rock of the planet itself. She was more deeply interconnected now with the other symbiotes.

Hadley moved inside the dome, catching Silver's attention. He took the samples to the workbench, where he would be able to see the readouts from the nanobots Silver had injected into her blood sols before. She had scrambled the information transmitted to *Octavia*, afraid of what Aliyaah would do with the results. Now, though, Hadley would be able to see the raw data as well as her calculations and experiments with the plant extracts.

Silver couldn't know for sure if Hadley would understand what she had been working on, but if he took her test results back to the station someone might be able to decipher the data.

The samples taken from Dominic were now highly suggestive. The microbialites had formed fruiting bodies in the test tubes, almost cracking the glass. Once their connection to the wider organism was severed, however, they had grown dull and grey, then died, leaving a fine residue of crystals.

Silver watched Hadley closely. She saw him stumble and was glad he had not removed his space suit when he entered the inner dome. If he had, Silver wasn't sure that she could stop the rapid colonisation of his body. He was infected, as were they all, but the organism's growth was slow in him and the excrescence had not yet formed a strong connection.

Silver watched as Hadley looked around in desperation, holding his gloves out in front of him. As he clutched at the Butterfly pea plants, Silver felt relieved that he was beginning to make the connections in his own mind. She didn't yet have a clear grasp of his consciousness, but it would come.

Silver's own consciousness, while entwined with the wider organism, retained a certain independence. The organism had fought for full control, but Silver had held fast, slowly adjusting the environment in the dome to match conditions outside, on the planet's surface. In this environment, Hadley's body would be an ideal substrate. The residual GCRs would likely catalyse an unstoppable reaction if he were fully exposed. Silver respected Hadley, liked him even. She didn't want him to die unnecessarily, but she couldn't let him take that data back to Schiff, not until she knew more about Schiff's intentions.

THIRTY-FIVE

Hadley didn't recognise Silver at first, seeing only a pale distorted figure through layers of glass. With his glove hovering over the airlock button, Hadley studied the figure, wondering if he was delusional.

For several seconds neither of them moved. Then the reality of the burgeoning mass around his boots broke through his stupor and Hadley began to back away from the airlock.

Silver pushed the button on the door from the outer dome and Hadley stumbled backwards, realising now that he was looking at his officer, or what remained of her, and not some ghost he had conjured from the recesses of his sleep-deprived mind.

Part of Hadley's consciousness whispered to him to stay, that everything would be OK. But he pushed the voice aside, and turned back, running as quickly as he could to the other side of the dome. He hoped that his memory of the dome's schematic was correct and that he was heading towards the south airlock and not a dead end.

Silver walked into the inner dome and took a moment to let her feet sink into the mass covering the floor. She started towards Hadley, barely lifting her limbs, as if she were being carried by the fibrous morass now rising in the dome.

Hadley fought through the growing sea of what he now saw were tiny crystalline filaments like those he had taken from Dominic's remains. It felt like he was running through a river bed. The organism rose to clutch at his legs as if a damn had burst. It wasn't until he finally reached a clear area of the dome that Hadley allowed himself to look back. Just a few feet away the floor undulated in a frothing sea of limbs, torsos, heads, like a raging river rushing drowning people towards him.

The excrescence was now barely ten feet behind Hadley and gaining fast, rising above the undulating morass. He dropped the samples and the plants and ran faster. He had little hope that he would make it to the airlock and get through the door before Silver reached him, but he didn't want to think of what would happen if he couldn't get out of the dome in time.

As he passed through a sector clear of plant life, Hadley bolted right and cut through two irrigation structures dripping with crystals. The visor of his suit grew cloudy with the white material and Hadley wiped it away with his glove, making a futile effort to flick the gunk to the ground as he ran.

Hadley was no longer in Silver's line of sight, but he didn't need to be for her to sense where he was. She felt his feet hammering against the floor as if he was tapping at her skin. Every footstep was a blow against the wider body of the organism. She followed his progress and moved right, along the edge of the plants. Then the footsteps stopped. Hadley was still. Silver struggled to figure out where he was hiding, then she heard a popping sound and turned around.

Silver saw Hadley holding something in front of him, but before she could make out what it was she was felled by a sharp, freezing pain. She twisted on the floor, clutching at her limbs. She dragged herself forward, trying to reach Hadley to make him stop. As she drew closer, her body became cold and numb. Her movements slowed until she couldn't go any further. She struggled to look up and saw Hadley's boots emerge from the receding wave ahead.

Hadley stood just ten feet away, holding a fire extinguisher. He had covered the ground around him with suffocating foam, underneath which the excrescence turned grey, then black and still.

Silver tried to crawl towards him, and Hadley stopped for a moment, hoping to see a glimmer of humanity in her eyes. The pain spread through her body and beyond, and Hadley saw that Silver's eyes were no longer hers alone. The crystalline organism had created a new lens through which she saw the world.

Hadley held the canister aloft and pointed it at the excrescence. Silver waited for the last of her consciousness to die away, for the freezing foam to cut off her body from the air on which she still relied. She waited and waited, but the cold, suffocating sensation of death did not come. Hadley had backed away and was already in the airlock, and Silver watched helplessly as he ran out, holding the samples and her data in his arms.

THIRTY-SIX

Aliyaah stepped through the outer airlock into the upper hangar, gesturing for the crew to stay behind her. They were just as on edge as she was, having overheard the desperate call for help back at the station.

Inside, there was no sign of the remaining crew, or Rover Four. The emergency lighting system had been activated and the life support system appeared to be malfunctioning. The oxygen levels were dangerously low, as was the temperature. Aliyaah assigned two men to work on the climate controls and told the rest to go through decontamination ahead of her.

She checked the rover's location using its on-board guidance system. It had arrived at the hangar an hour earlier, well before the transmission that had caused Aliyaah to rush back to the station. By now, the engineers should have been well on their way to disassembling the vehicle.

Despite the transmission having devolved into screaming, there was nothing out for the ordinary in the hangar, aside from the malfunctioning climate controls and the missing machine and crew. If something had happened to the life support system in the upper hangar the crew may have taken the rover to the lower level for disassembly. While this made sense, it didn't allay Aliyaah's growing concerns. The crew should have kept her apprised, and she wondered if something had happened to prevent contact until that last message.

She checked the climate inside the rest of the station to see if it was a system-wide issue. The temperature and oxygen levels appeared normal everywhere else, but she kept her suit on and her breathing apparatus connected as she exited the airlock into the station's inner hallway.

The crew was waiting for her inside the station and, as she joined them, she pulled one of the engineers aside and ordered the rest of the men to go to their quarters to get a couple of hours of rest. Payload Specialist Barclay had logged a lot of hours with the rovers, and when she asked him to stay behind he didn't wait to ask why.

"What's going on, Chief? Where is everybody?" Barclay said, triggering a volley of questions from the other men, who hadn't moved.

"Yeah, where are you going? Why the suit?"

"Should we suit up too, Chief?"

Aliyaah shook her head. "Go to your quarters, lock the doors, and get some rest. Barclay and I will track down Rover Four and the rest of the crew. Report back to the hangar in two hours and we will get to work on the last sections of the walkway."

"What do you think happened to the crew and the rover?" asked one of the younger engineers. Aliyaah looked at him and saw that he was sweating profusely. He was smiling at her, grinning almost. He looked almost euphoric, not terrified, and the effect was distinctly unsettling. She wondered if she should take him with her to find Schiff, in case he needed medical care. She hoped his odd demeanour was an effect of tweaking. That would be bad enough, but was better than the alternative: that he was infected and symptomatic. She hadn't seen how the organism manifested in the Commander or other men at the station, but she had witnessed the strangeness in Dominic's eyes when he had attacked her.

The men were waiting for Aliyaah to answer, but she was at a loss for what to tell them. She didn't know much more than they did, but understood that the lack of information would allow their imaginations to run free.

"We all heard the distress call, which may mean that the rest of the crew is holed up somewhere with Rover Four. I'm going to do a sweep of the station with Barclay, and I'll see you all back here in two hours, when I'll have more information." She paused, then added, "Some of you don't look so good. Go eat a couple of bars, get some sleep, and make sure you take your anti-rads. And no dosing of T, got it?"

Some of the men didn't move, and Aliyaah glared at them. "Dismissed!"

Still the men didn't move and Aliyaah glared at them. The men looked at each other and then at Mission Specialist Ansen, the most senior member of the crew. After a moment, Ansen stepped up beside Barclay and said, "Chief, there's safety in numbers. I'll go with you."

Aliyaah saw that of all the men, Ansen looked to be in the best shape. She nodded at him, reluctantly admitting to herself that it was probably good to have back up, even if she couldn't entirely trust that the men would act rationally. "OK, Ansen and Barclay you're with me. The rest of you, get some rack time."

As the men walked away, Aliyaah turned to Barclay and said, "Go check the rover's nav feed. It might be that we can track it down by looking at its last movements. If the speed is off, it's possible that the rover malfunctioned before arriving at the station. They might have had to hand-bomb parts to the lower hangar. Suit up before you go down there, and keep me apprised."

Barclay nodded and headed down the corridor to the hatch for the lower hangar stairwell. As he walked away, Aliyaah gestured at her suit, then at Ansen. "You'll need to suit up too. We're heading to the new medical bay, and there may be bodies in there that pose a risk of contagion. We need to minimise exposure."

"There's another suit right by there, Chief. In the airlock," Ansen said.

Aliyaah nodded. "OK. Let's go."

As they made their way down the corridor, the artificial gravity kicked back in, making her suit an even greater encumbrance. She began to fall behind, but Ansen didn't notice and rounded a corner far ahead of her. She had a feeling they were walking into trouble, but she needed to find Schiff and see what was happening in the medical bay. There had been no communication from inside the station since that last frantic call, and it was almost a full sol since anyone had heard from the doctor or her assistant. It had also been several hours since her last check-in with Hadley. She tried to hail him as she continued her slow walk down the corridor. If something bad had happened at the biodome, she might now be first in command, making her responsible for the remaining crew as well as the civilians who had been under the doctor's supervision in her and Hadley's absence.

Aliyaah rounded the corner and stepped past the pod where Ansen was getting into a suit. She saw the door to the improvised medical lab just a little further down the corridor, and noticed a whitish-grey patina covering the floor and walls. Stepping closer, she saw that there was condensation on the door to the lab, as if the inside were much colder than the air in the corridor. Peering even closer, she noticed that the whitish-grey coating glowed, as if the door was lit within itself, with the water droplets doing more than just reflecting the dim emergency lights in the corridor.

Aliyaah traced a gloved finger across the door, then held up her glove to her visor; this was not just water. Like the samples taken from Dominic, the liquid held tiny crystalline filaments.

She shook her glove and craned her neck to peer at the condensation, watching as the droplets coalesced and ran down the cold metal door to the floor. She looked up again and saw that where the water had run from the top of the door, it had left behind a flaky white residue. To the naked eye, this residue looked like lichen, but as she toggled the settings on her scanner to activate the microscope, she saw that the flakes were composed of thousands of tiny strands, like mycelium. As she stared into the scope, the cells all split at once, instantly doubling their mass. She jumped back, almost dropping the scanner. The organism was reproducing rapidly.

She looked up again at the top of the door. The area that had been visible just moments ago was now entirely covered with the lichenous growth.

"Chief?" Ansen's voice came through her ear-piece, and Aliyaah turned to see him emerging from the airlock in the bulky EMS suit.

She held up a hand to guide the Specialist's eyes to the door, and said, "Whatever is going on in there, it's imperative we stay suited up and on an open channel. Got it?"

Ansen nodded and stepped to one side of the door, his hand on the release button. Aliyaah took the other side, then gestured to him to open the door.

THIRTY-SEVEN

A blinding light emanated from the medical lab and it took several seconds before Aliyaah and Ansen could see much of anything.

"What the," Ansen whispered and looked over at Aliyaah. "What is this stuff?" He took a step forward, but she put out her hand to stop him.

"Wait. I want to scan for life first." She held up her scanner and then added, "Human life."

Ansen looked down for a second at the scanner attached to his own suit, then said, "Surely nobody can be alive in there? It's almost zero degrees and the air is thinner than at the top of Everest."

Aliyaah agreed, but continued her scan anyway. "There might be bodies. The doctor. Her assistant. This thing might be feeding on them."

Ansen resisted the sudden urge to retch. He studied Aliyaah for a few moments, then said, "What is this thing?"

She looked up from the scanner and surveyed the room before answering. The walls and floor were thick with the lichenous substance. It pulsed as it grew, causing the walls to close in, inch by inch. There were patches of larger crystalline filaments in places, including on the workbenches and in the far corner. Aliyaah could make out a radioactive hazard sign on an upright cabinet, partially covered with a layer of the white flakes. She figured it was the storage freezer where Schiff would have been keeping the radioactive samples before she tested them.

There were no signs of the doctor or her lab assistant in the room, but Ansen told her that the doctor had commandeered the adjoining room as a medical ward where she could treat patients away from the lab samples: it was possible that the doctor and missing crew were hiding in there for some reason.

Aliyaah turned to look at Ansen and said, "This is what happened in the west wing, only it was worse there. The organism appears to rapidly metabolise organic material, and the faster its growth, the larger the crystals."

"Biology ain't my strong suit, Chief, but even I know there aren't many organisms that behave like this," Ansen said as he followed Aliyaah into the room. He looked at the materials on the workbench, noting the larger crystals and wondering what lay underneath them. "It's gotta be fungal, right? But I'll be damned if it's from Earth. I've never seen anything like it, and I've seen a lot of weird shit."

"I don't think it's something we brought with us, no," Aliyaah said. "My best guess right now is that it came into the station through the refiner and is Martian in origin. It likely evolved to survive such conditions."

"This thing is doing more than just goddamn surviving," Ansen said. He moved towards the freezer and ran his hand over the door, knocking a series of crystals to the floor, where they shattered silently before disappearing into the sea of white. "This thing is thriving."

Aliyaah was about to reply when she saw something shift behind him. She shouted for him to back up and he stepped away just as the cabinet door swung open and something large and heavy fell to the floor.

Aliyaah tensed, ready for action, but whatever it was lay unmoving on the floor. Ansen stepped aside as she approached, and they both assessed the object. Its size and weight meant that she already suspected that this was the missing lab assistant. She bent down to clear some of the crystalline growths, and revealed what was left of a human head, the flesh now nothing but a gelatinous substrate being devoured by the organism.

Ansen turned away and started retching, and as Aliyaah stood back up she saw Ansen unclip his helmet.

"Ansen!" she said, but it was too late. He dropped his helmet to the floor, and vomited against the wall. She walked over and picked up his helmet, then turned him in the direction of the door. "Suit up or get out."

He wiped his mouth and nodded at the Chief. She handed him the helmet and he took it with a shaky hand.

"Sorry, Chief. It's different when you're on solid ground. Easier to forgot."

She nodded. There was something odd enough about zero gravity that it made you think twice about taking off your helmet. In the station, that feeling simply wasn't there. She helped him to put his helmet back on, knowing it could already be too late, then moved back to the body and wiped away enough of the material to access the med port on the suit. The readout told her it was the engineer she had assigned to Schiff as an assistant. She took a moment, then left what remained of his body on the floor and moved back to the workbench.

After clearing some of the debris, she located the control panel and the data that the doctor had been working through.

"It looks like Schiff tested herself and several others," she said, recognising the biomarkers that she had seen in her own blood and Dominic's.

Ansen came over and stood beside her. He rifled through a stack of papers and said, "Looks like the doctor was pretty old school." He found a notepad covered in pencil marks. "It looks like some kind of shorthand." He flipped through the pad and saw that the penmanship devolved as the notes went on.

He read several notes that Schiff had underlined. "Fungal growth. Chemosynthetic? Rapid growth upon exposure to radioactive material. Prefers acidic environment. Chemotaxis?" he said, then held up the pad. "It's illegible after that. Can you make sense of..."

Aliyaah interrupted him, asking, "When did you last take anti-rads?"

"Just before we started work on the walkway, Chief."

"Orally, or by pump?"

"Pump. Why?"

"Take a double dose, now," she said, and handed him two of the four remaining vials she had taken from *Octavia*.

He nodded and took the drugs, passing her the notepad so he could use both hands to open the pump interface in his suit. He gave himself a shot, then another a few seconds later.

"Are you on any stims? Any T?" she asked, not looking up from the doctor's notes.

Ansen stared at her, wide-eyed and silent.

Aliyaah looked up and said, "I'm not kidding. If you are, tell me. I don't care about writing you up."

"No, Chief. I don't touch that stuff."

"You're absolutely sure?" she said. "I know some of the older guys T-up to keep up. And it was hard work out on that walkway."

He shook his head vehemently. "No, Chief. I've always kept my T low. Helps me think more clearly, unlike some of those young hotheads."

"You mean like Barclay?"

"Chief?"

"Just tell me, Ansen."

"Yeah, Barclay, a couple of times maybe. Yeah. I dunno about the others, but some of them tweak for sure." He held her stare for a second, then pointed at the dead engineer and asked, "What's that got to do with this guy though?"

She looked down at the body and felt a stab of guilt for having assigned the engineer to the lab. Looking back up at Ansen, and tapping the notepad, she said, "The doctor listed every casualty. Those deaths linked to the organism are all younger males or those on T."

"You think it's just attacking men?"

"I don't know if it's attacking as such. But there's a pattern to the infections and deaths, however you look at it."

"But, Chief, there aren't many women on the planet. You know?" Ansen raised his eyebrows at her and said, "It's probably just sheer bad luck that it's picking off us guys first, yeah?"

She shook her head at Ansen. "I already did that math. We know of at least forty casualties, and they're all men. That's statistically improbable, Ansen."

"What about Viper?" he asked, cocking his head.

"I suspect Jaz was tweaking. Probably T, and maybe some other stuff I don't know about."

"Shit," Ansen said, closing his eyes and shaking his head. "But what about the Commander? You said it was all young guys."

Aliyaah shrugged. "I said that the casualties so far have mostly been younger males, yes, and those on T. But not all. And the Commander didn't die like this engineer. He died of a heart attack," she paused while she checked the doctor's notes, "brought on by a serious electrolyte imbalance. Looks like it was the same with the other early casualties."

"OK, OK. So, this thing's like some kind of mushroom that feeds on testosterone?"

"Perhaps. Whatever it is, it grows faster at a lower pH, invading the skin and membranes first and then digging deeper into tissue." She held up the notepad again to show Ansen more of the doctor's notes. "And GCRs catalyze its growth."

"So, what, the younger guys, the ones who 'forget' to take their anti-rads are sitting ducks?" Ansen said. "I told them they were being stupid. They've never felt real radiation sickness, so they think it's some big joke and us older guys are too serious about all that shit." Ansen shook his head and added, "We should've put the damn things as standard in the pumps".

Aliyaah nodded, thinking with anger about the anti-anti-rad'ers back on Earth who had protested the development of the pump technology, citing pseudoscience and anecdata. "It looks like the doctor was running experiments to test similar conditions to those out at the quarry, where there's minimal shielding from GCRs."

"And where they've been digging up god knows what," Ansen said, "radioactive mushrooms and all."

She didn't bother to correct his hyperbole as she studied the doctor's notes, trying to piece together the timeline of her experiments before she resorted to a shorthand Aliyaah didn't understand. "So, under certain conditions – high T and radiation – the organism colonises so rapidly that it devastates the host. But, when colonisation is slower, it seems to cause behavioural anomalies, likely by destroying or remodelling parts of the brain that control executive function, just like Silver suggested and like we saw in the Commander, and Dominic." She turned to a page of notes that seemed to show a half dozen numbered human outlines, complete with basic identifying characteristics, "Male, 31, Caucasian, 1 hr. Male, 29, Caucasian, 2 hrs."

"It's a goddamn man-eater," Ansen said. "So, what, I'm infected and you're immune?"

Aliyaah thought back to the readouts from her nanobots and hesitated. Then she looked up and said, "I think we have to operate on the assumption that we are all infected. Those of us who appear healthy may just be lucky so far, in that we've avoided high levels of radiation and don't have a lot of T in our systems. It may take longer to become symptomatic under such conditions." She almost added that it was possible they were already symptomatic and just didn't know it. After all, how would she, or anyone else, be able to tell if their own cognition was compromised?

"So, the doc could be alive somewhere?" Ansen said, and Aliyaah nodded. "Well, I'd say she's damn symptomatic," he added, pointing his thumb at the lab assistant. "I mean, she shoved this guy into a cabinet and then ran off god knows where."

"Yes," Aliyaah said, "I think it's safe to assume the doctor is alive and has a much clearer idea than us about how this organism operates and maybe even how to stop it." She had a growing suspicion that instead of working out how to eradicate the organism and protect the civilians and the men in her charge, Doctor Schiff had been working with, or perhaps for, the organism.

THIRTY-EIGHT

Barclay whistled as he walked along the corridor to the lower hangar stairwell. He was confident he would find the rover, along with the missing crew. Everything would work out just fine.

He was vaguely aware that it was odd to feel so cheerful when all around him was chaos and death, but he couldn't seem to shake the optimism. It was good he was alone. It was so hard to stop smiling, even though he knew it wasn't appropriate.

As he reached the door to the steps, he remembered that the Chief had told him something important. There was something he was supposed to do before going down to the lower level. He laughed. It couldn't have been that important. He reached out to press the door release and felt suddenly dizzy. He held onto the wall and tried to steady himself. He was sweating profusely and his breathing was ragged. He tried to compose himself, but began to feel angry. What was happening to him? Why was he laughing and smiling? It wasn't right when his friends and colleagues were dying.

Barclay's mind raced, and he began to feel as if he were observing himself from outside his body. His earlier optimism had dissipated. He was spinning out of control.

Clawing back some rational thought, Barclay checked his med pump, wondering if there was a malfunction. Maybe his blood glucose was dangerously low. Or his system could have flooded with excitatory neurotransmitters. He had been tweaking a lot lately, so it would be his own damn fault if it had started malfunctioning.

Barclay's fingers slipped on the pump's controls and sweat dripped down his face, mixing with tears. He hadn't realised he was crying, and now the readout on the control panel became too distorted for him to read clearly.

The low-level emergency lights in the corridor made it even harder to see the blurred readout, so he opened the door to the stairwell, hoping for better light.

A blast of cold air came rushing up from the lower hangar, and it had a momentary sobering effect. He stepped forward, glad for the cool air as he descended the steps.

The handrail was cold against his bare skin, and Barclay remembered too late that the Chief had told him to suit up before entering the hangar. The rail also seemed wet, and he shook his hand, then wiped away his sweat and tears. As he took another step, his boot slipped and he clutched at the rail again to stay upright. He didn't think to turn back, but he couldn't quite remember why he was heading to the lower hangar.

The metallic grey steps seemed to glow beneath his feet, and Barclay rubbed the back of his hand over his eyes, hoping that he could clear his vision and see the ordinary grey of the metal steps. When he opened his eyes again he knew he wasn't hallucinating. This was real.

He stopped whistling, and while he felt somber now, his facial muscles remained pulled tight in a garish grin. He imagined what his face must look like and started to laugh and laugh. He couldn't stop, and as the tears snaked down his face, he felt his chest grow tight. His muscles began to cramp and spasm as he hyperventilated, and he clutched his hand to his chest, letting go of the railing.

His body wracked with laughter, and he lost his footing and slipped down a couple of steps. He tried to right himself, but fell forward, still laughing. As he reached the bottom step, he put out his hands to try to break his fall, and his fingers plunged into a soft, gelatinous mass. He lay there for a second, the shock of the impact halting his hysterical laughter. The mass around his fingers twitched and seemed to latch onto his skin.

Barclay tried to pull his hands out, but they were stuck, held by this strange material that seemed both fluid and crystalline. Flat on his belly, He pushed himself upward and craned his neck. He could see someone sitting perfectly still and silent just a few yards away. A bright light emanated from the hangar, silhouetting the figure, so Barclay couldn't make out who it was.

He called out as he tried to free his hands, and something moved, blocking the light from the hangar and plunging him into darkness. He heard machinery, and when the light returned it flooded the stairwell, illuminating the carnage.

The figure ahead of him was the body of one of the engineers, and behind him was another body and another. He looked out across the sea of limbs and torsos, but began to doubt that these were in fact corpses. The hands of the men seemed to be reaching out to him, their faces contorting. He couldn't tell if they were really moving or if this was an illusion, created by the rapid dissolution of their flesh, and the growth of crystals from their arms, their heads, their eyes.

He closed his eyes, not wanting to look at what lay beneath him. He tried once more to free his hands, but they were stuck fast. The light shifted again, as if a vehicle was moving away, its headlights receding. He tried to remember why he was down there, in the lower hangar. He had been sent to find something. A vehicle perhaps? He tried, but couldn't remember what it was. He became furious with himself, and thrashed about in a rage. Finally, he got one hand free and tried to stand, but his feet were trapped, as if they were being held down by something heavy.

His upper body was cold, but he felt warmth covering his feet and spreading up his lower limbs. The sensation wasn't entirely unpleasant. It almost felt like a slow massage by a thousand tiny fingers, and Barclay's rage slowly subsided. The creeping warmth lulled him and he laid his cheek against the floor. His breath came softly now. The only sound was the low whistle between his lips, and as the hangar door opened and the air thinned, he closed his eyes, forgetting about the rover, the Chief, Mars, Earth.

THIRTY-NINE

Aliyaah and Ansen stepped over the body of the engineer towards the door to the improvised medical ward. As much as she wanted to get out of there, Aliyaah had to find out what the doctor had been doing in her absence.

The door was almost completely covered with the organism, and when Aliyaah pulled the handle the door didn't budge. She tried it again but with the same lack of success.

"Here, try this," Ansen said, unhooking his utility knife from his belt. Aliyaah ran the knife around the edge of the door frame as Ansen used his gloved hands to scrape away the material below the handle. After a moment, he could see the red stripe that indicated the door was locked. He slid open the catch and smiled up at Aliyaah, but her expression killed his smile instantly.

"She locked them in," she said quietly, more to herself than to Ansen.

"What's that, Chief?" he asked. "Should I open it?" Aliyaah nodded and he wrenched open the door. As the seal broke, frigid air rushed toward them. The temperature in the medical lab was only five degrees, but even this was significantly warmer than the sub-zero temperature of the ward.

The ward was lit only by emergency lighting, and it was impossible to see to the end of the room. Perhaps the doctor hadn't been treating patients here at all, Aliyaah thought. Maybe it was being used as a morgue instead.

She quickly scanned the room, but saw no evidence of the organism or the doctor. "This is very odd," she said, mostly to herself.

"Relative to what exactly?" Ansen said.

"Do you have cats-eyes?" she asked, and he shook his head.

"I'm too old school for that. I like to see what I'm actually seeing."

Aliyaah entered the room and turned on her flashlight to get a better look. There were a dozen beds on either side of the room, and while those closest to the door were empty, it was hard to tell if any were occupied at the farthest end of the room.

As she inched forward, she saw that the sheets were crumpled and soiled. There were the tattered remains of restraints tied around the beds. Someone had been holding people there against their will, and Aliyaah had a horrifying suspicion that she knew why.

"Chief?" Ansen said, beckoning her over to one of the beds. "What does this look like to you?"

She took a closer look at the sheets on the bed and then looked up at him with a frown. "I think it's blood," she said softly.

"But blood doesn't normally congeal like that," he said, and she murmured agreement, seeing how the blood rose from the sheets in little geometric nodules, like stalagmites.

He moved to another bed and said, "Same over here, Chief. But more of it, and the growths are larger, with clear facets." They both took a side of the ward and moved quickly from bed to bed. Each one had the same strange residue.

As she reached the middle of the ward, Aliyaah stopped and held up a hand to make Ansen do the same. She pointed to a bed near the back of the room, where something moved in the beam of her flashlight.

"Hello?" she called, activating the speaker on her suit. "Identify yourself."

Whoever it was didn't seem to respond, but as she listened more intently she detected a whimper. She moved closer and saw one of the crew she had assigned to work on dismantling the rover. The man was tied to the bed and was naked except for a thin covering of the lichen-like organism.

"Corporal Finlayson? What happened here?" Aliyaah looked down at the red welts on his wrists and ankles, where he had fought against the restraints. She wanted to release him, but who knew what the doctor had done to the man.

Finlayson seemed feverish, but his eyes finally settled on her face as she repeated her question.

"Chief?" he said, his voice scratchy. He looked up at Aliyaah and his eyes caught his reflection in the visor of her helmet. He screamed and started tearing at the restraints.

Ansen and Aliyaah held him down, and asked again, "What happened? Where's the doctor?"

Finlayson struggled against them, then gave in and fell back onto the bed, closing his eyes. He whimpered unintelligibly and Ansen shook him gently. "Fin, what happened here?"

The whimper turned into a moan and Ansen released his grip, allowing Aliyaah to cover Finlayson with a sheet from the adjacent bed.

The corporal opened his eyes and spoke so slowly and quietly that Aliyaah had to bend down beside him to hear. "Mandatory testing. Just routine. Mandatory testing." His voice trailed off into silence as he stared at her, then he tried to sit up again, hit by a flash of memory. "No! Where are they? What did you do to them?" He thrashed against the restraints, and Aliyaah realised he thought she was the doctor. "You killed them!" Finlayson screamed, over and over.

She backed away and said, "Corporal, Finlayson, I'm the Chief. I'm not going to hurt you, but I need you to tell me what happened."

Finlayson looked at her with suspicion, but then seemed to recognise her again and after a moment said, "The doctor infected us all. Made us hosts for the thing. To grow it and test it. The others...." He trailed off as he tried to look around the room.

Ansen lifted his flashlight and shone it across the rest of the seemingly empty beds. "Is anyone else here? She took some of them." Finlayson said. "So why am I still alive?"

Ansen nudged Aliyaah as he spotted two beds that seemed to still have occupants, albeit unmoving. She nodded at him and pointed for him to check out the one closest to them.

He approached the bed slowly, and carefully lifted the white sheet. "Is there another survivor?" Aliyaah asked, and he shook his head.

The body beneath the sheet was also naked, like Finlayson, but the clothing piled neatly by the side of the bed suggested that this was a civilian, not a member of the crew. Ansen checked the ID badge that lay beside the clothes and saw that the body was most likely that of a thirty-five-year-old man. The corpse was almost entirely covered by the organism, making a visual identification impossible, especially as there was significant tissue damage in the face. The man's head was barely recognisable as human. Where his eyes should have been, there was now only a cluster of crystal, and the rest of his face seemed to have become a garish crystalline caricature of itself.

This was different from the lab assistant. It was as if the growth had been directed, following the contours of the man's face.

Ansen let the sheet drop to cover what was left of the man, and went to check the second body. Again, the corpse showed signs of controlled, systematic colonisation. This man's head had a similar pattern of organic growth, but he also had symmetrical patches of the fungal organism across his arms and legs. "Chief, take a look at this."

Aliyaah left the Corporal's bedside and went to join Ansen. As she surveyed the second corpse, she noticed a tray of lab equipment beside the body. The equipment included an empty RMC, and when she checked the label she saw that it was one of the radioactive samples from the refiner. It seemed that something had survived the Commander's attack on the lab, although all that was left inside the container now was a little red dust. She looked again at the body, then back at the tray. There were seven spent syringes beside the RMC, and she could count seven distinct sites of fungal growth on the man's body.

Aliyaah shivered, realising that the doctor must have been planning her experiments even before the Commander blew up the medical bay. Had the Commander known? Was that why he had taken such drastic action? He hadn't been in his right mind, but if he had thought he was saving his crew in the long run, it might explain why he had tried to destroy the samples and destroy quarry operations. The doctor had saved at least one sample though, and as Aliyaah thought back to her notes she wondered if the Commander had really died of an electrolyte imbalance.

"I know what the doctor was doing," she said. "She was deliberately seeding them. Monitoring the spread of the organism to see what factors affect its growth in human flesh."

"Why in god's name would she do that?" Ansen said. He lowered his voice and added, "This guy must have still been alive, and the others too." He glanced at the Corporal, who began to cough violently.

They rushed back over to Finlayson, but the Corporal had already fallen silent, his body still. His eyes were wide open, and Aliyaah watched as the dark brown of his irises slowly clouded over with a film of white. Finlayson's whitish-grey features were spattered with blood, and they watched as the carmine spray turned a dark grey, then lighter grey, before fading to the same shining white of the rest of his skin.

FORTY

Rover Four skipped over the surface of the planet, with its radioactive cargo safely strapped to the roof of the vehicle. Wearing just an EV suit, Doctor Schiff walked beside the rover, her steps light, but keeping pace with the machine. Like Silver, her gait was loose, but strong.

In the distance, the doctor could see Biodome Two: a nearly perfect blank canvas for the next stage. The weak sun had almost dipped below the edge of the Schiaparelli crater, and the doctor smiled, feeling the drop in temperature. Everything was going according to plan. The oncoming night would help her to acclimate more quickly as she walked.

She opened her visor to the Martian atmosphere, then closed it after just a second or two. Breathing in the extra oxygen from her suit, the doctor checked her vital signs and was pleased at her progress. She wasn't quite ready, but it wouldn't be long before full symbiosis occurred and she could do without the suit.

The doctor glanced at the station behind her, considering the evolution of the colony. The reallocation of life was unfortunate, she thought, but every new discovery had a cost. With the Antara excrescence overseeing the seeding of Biodome Three, and Chief Diambu still alive, if not yet symbiotic, it shouldn't be long before they had full control.

It is a shame Chief Diambu is so resistant to metamorphosis. The thought slid across the doctor's mind and she turned to the woman walking beside her. The civilian looked at her, and the doctor saw that the woman's visor was open and her skin emitted a pale, iridescent light.

Perhaps I should have stayed at the station to study Chief Diambu more closely, the doctor thought.

The nanobots will track her progress.

Yes, the doctor conceded, *and our priority is to seed Biodome Two, before the samples decay. Once the men are all immobilised and subsumed into the body, Chief Diambu will begin to see things more clearly.*

The woman beside the doctor smiled, and another voice added itself to the mix.

It will be wonderful to examine Diambu's physiology more closely.

Yes.

Yes.

Yes, said the doctor. *We will see why she has been so resistant to joining with us.*

I am excited to learn.

Yes. And it will make us stronger.

Yes, but we have work to do first. The doctor walked on and turned to look again at the twelve men marching in silence by her side.

FORTY-ONE

"Chief Diambu, this is Hadley. Come in, Chief. Chief?"

"Sir, this is Mission Specialist Ansen. I'm with Chief Diambu now. Where are you Sir?"

"Ansen, good to hear your voice. I'm heading to - "

"Sir?"

Hadley was quiet for a moment, then he turned the question around and asked, "Where are you and the Chief, Specialist?"

Ansen paused, unsure whether or not to answer. He looked over at Aliyaah, who was staring in disbelief at two small children who were huddled together in a corner of the station's gym. It seemed that the officer left in charge of them had vanished hours before, and the children had been hiding in the gym, eating snacks from the vending machines.

The children had no idea what was happening across the colony, nor where their parents were. One of them, a little Russian girl who was probably no more than three, had whispered to her that she thought it best if they went back to Earth now. Aliyaah, whose Russian was a little rusty, had wondered at first if she had misheard, but the little girl repeated herself and she could do nothing but nod at the child.

When Ansen finally got Hadley on the line, Aliyaah was clutching at long-forgotten Russian vocabulary to try to find a way of asking the girl, without prompting panic, what had happened to them. Given the enormity of the situation, the two children were remarkably calm. The other child, a small boy she guessed was around four year's old, was sitting against the wall eating a bag of apple chips, looking as if he hadn't a care in the world. Perhaps it was quite normal for these children to be left to their own devices in strange, militaristic buildings.

When she had listened to the crew talk about their families, Aliyaah felt relieved that she didn't have kids of her own to worry about back on Earth. She had forgotten for a moment that SolarEx had allowed children to come along on this mission. The idea had never sat comfortably with her. There were so many potential risks, their current circumstances being a case in point.

"Sir," Ansen interrupted her and pulled her aside, out of earshot. "Hadley wants our location but isn't saying where he is."

She dragged her eyes away from the two children and looked at Ansen. "Did he say anything about the dome? About Antara?"

"No Sir. He just said it was good to hear my voice."

"OK. I'll talk to him. You..." she gestured at the children. "Er, you look after the kids."

Ansen raised his eyebrows, then walked over to sit beside the boy. He introduced himself first in Igbo and then, once he realised his mistake in assuming that the boy was Nigerian, he began to speak in Russian.

Aliyaah activated her headset. "Commander? It's Chief Diambu. Did you find Antara?"

"Chief, where are you?"

"Sir, I need to know that you're not infected."

"Damnit, Aliyaah. Tell me where you are."

She took off her helmet and rubbed her eyes. "Sir, I want to trust you, but given the circumstances, I'm not sure I can."

Hadley was quiet for a few seconds, then he said, "I understand, Chief. I understand all too well."

"Where are you, Sir? What happened at the dome?"

Hadley exhaled audibly before he spoke. "I'm in the SEV. I'm heading to *Octavia*. We need to get all remaining survivors the hell off this planet."

"Agreed, Sir."

"But we can only do that if we trust each other," he added. "I'm asking you to trust me, Chief. Can you do that?"

Aliyaah took a breath, then asked again, "What happened at the dome?"

Hadley didn't repeat his question and instead said quietly, "I'm sorry, Chief. Antara is as good as dead. I don't know how to explain exactly what I saw at the dome, but Antara is no longer herself. The place has been overrun by the organism, and Antara seems to be connected to it somehow."

Aliyaah leaned back and whistled through her teeth. She wondered how it was that she had been spared, so far. "Sir, I understand. I think the doctor might be helping the organism. Judging everything we just saw in the lab, she may even be behind the events of the last few sols. I'm fairly certain she was experimenting on the men, Sir."

"Experimenting how, Chief?"

"It looks like she was trying to figure out how to control this thing, not to cure it, but to keep it from killing its human host outright. I'm not sure why."

"Just the men?"

"Yes, Sir. The adult males. It seems to affect male and female physiology differently. We found some of the doctor's notes, and some... evidence. From what we can tell, higher testosterone levels, coupled with radiation exposure, fuel rapid and uncontrollable growth. It looks like the doctor was attempting to control that growth and direct the organism to invade certain tissues."

"Which tissues, Chief?"

"My hunch is that the prefrontal cortex is key. I suspect that this is why we've seen the paranoia and aggression; the weird behavioural changes could be the organism taking control."

"So, it's parasitic, perhaps. But the doctor and Antara haven't displayed those symptoms."

"No, Sir. They may have developed a sort of immunity, or a symbiosis with the organism. It's hard to tell. Schiff is missing, Sir, along with most of the crew and the civilians." She glanced over at the children. "The adults at least."

"And you, Chief?"

"Me, Sir?"

"Are you also... becoming symbiotic?"

"No Sir." She looked over at Ansen, who had stopped talking to the children and was watching her closely.

"But you can't be sure, can you Chief?" Hadley said quietly.

"No Sir."

"Any sign of the civilian women?"

She looked over at the children and said, "No, Sir. There are just two children here."

"Good god. What were we thinking bringing children to this place?"

"I don't know, Sir. But now that they're here, what should we do with them?" Aliyaah paused, then decided she had no choice but to trust Hadley. "We're in the gymnasium, Sir. That's where the children have been hiding. The rest of the crew are in their quarters, except for PS Barclay, who I sent to check the lower hangar."

"OK. Round up everyone left at the station and prepare them to move to *Octavia*. I'll head back in the SEV and begin transporting people to the ship. When the walkway is done, we can load her up."

"Yes, Sir. I'll keep you apprised of the head count. We may be just fine with the supplies already on *Octavia*."

"Thank you. And, Chief..." Hadley hesitated.

"Yes Sir."

"Once we're on board, we should consider quarantining all but essential personnel, for the duration."

Without thinking, Aliyaah asked, "Sir, do you think we stand a chance of getting home?"

He hesitated, then said firmly, "Work the problem, Aliyaah. Always work the problem."

FORTY-TWO

Silver woke to the sound of voices, half expecting to be lying in bed beside Cooper or Cosima. Her body was numb, but she wasn't afraid. It had taken Silver a little while to consistently maintain her sense of self, but once she had drawn her boundaries, she had experienced a profound feeling of comfort at this new connection.

Silver felt cradled in a soft, warm space. She knew she could open her eyes if she wanted, but she was content for now to explore her changing reality using her other senses.

The body she had grown accustomed to was no longer her own, and while she had an idea of how to get it back, she wasn't certain that she wanted to. She was no longer a single entity with a discrete mind, and the wider consciousness brought with it a euphoric sense of belonging, of home.

Silver couldn't yet make out individual voices inside her mind, but she gently pushed at the boundaries she had drawn and allowed herself to filter through the cacophony.

The voices weren't memories or her imagination. Not like before. She had been joined by others, some she knew already in their original form, and some were new to her, civilians with whom she hadn't previously interacted. Silver isolated the doctor's voice and let herself fall into step with the woman's feet, feeling the planet's surface with each of the doctor's footfalls. She heard a woman speaking Russian, talking about Biodome Two. Then another voice, speaking Igbo. She had never mastered the language, but she understood everything the woman said. She knew that they were all aware of her presence in their minds as she listened to them talk about Aliyaah.

Silver's connection with the women wasn't as strong as it was with the biodome and the area of the planet close by, but she knew that their link would grow as her body healed from the damage inflicted by Hadley.

Reminded of Hadley, she became momentarily confused and thought for a few seconds that she could also hear his thoughts. Paying closer attention, she realised that what she was experiencing were the slow, subdued voices of the men walking behind the doctor and the other women. She could feel the soft, insistent swirl of dust and wind blowing across their naked bodies. The men's minds seemed dimly lit, functional but unaware of their purpose, or the wider life of the planet.

Suddenly, a sharper voice cut through the murmur of the others. A fearful, cold voice of terror echoing in the cool, dark air of the hangar.

Silver felt Barclay's fear as if it were her own at first, then she drew back and considered it for a moment. She didn't want him to be afraid, but there was no way now to prevent what was happening to him.

Silver began to sing one of the many lullabies she had sung to Cosima when she woke in the middle of the night. After a few lines, the voices of the other women joined hers, and, finally, Barclay hushed. Silver felt an infusion of warmth as what was left of his consciousness joined theirs, his body now part of the wider organism, an excrescence under the control of the collective mind as his higher order functions collapsed. The doctor smiled and Silver, having rediscovered her edges, her self, smiled with her, seeing now what she had to do.

She rose from the floor of the inner dome and saw that the collective had managed to repair most of the damage caused by Hadley. The viable components had been resorbed and reformulated beneath the suffocating foam, growing around and through it, consuming useful chemicals and extruding the rest.

Her own body had needed time to heal too, and Silver knew as she looked down at the strange mass that was once her legs that she was never going to make it back to Earth. She closed her eyes and shut herself off from the voices, allowing herself a single, mournful scream.

Continuing to hold firm the edges of her self, Silver considered Hadley and the remaining resisters. The doctor had succeeded through duplicity and force. Silver's attempt to engage with Hadley had failed. He had been scared into violence, even as she tried to show him the means of their survival. Silver had absorbed enough of the experiences of the men by the doctor's side that she now knew how she must have looked to Hadley. She couldn't fault him for being afraid.

The collective needed a different approach, something that didn't look so unfamiliar, so confrontational as its current excrescences. Silver knew that the wider consciousness saw the doctor's methods as viable, scalable. The collective was merely trying to survive, and had quickly learnt some very human lessons about coercion and colonisation.

Silver held herself steady as she moved through the morass to the control panel in the outer dome, gradually wrenching her body free from the wider body covering the floor. She was not yet sure if it was wise or possible to add a dissenting voice to the greater consciousness, but she could at least help those who weren't beyond reach to get off the planet to relative safety. This would buy the crew some time until Silver could either reign in the doctor or they could use the information she had already given them to protect themselves against re-infection.

From the control panel she accessed the live feed from the SEV's camera and saw that Hadley was travelling along the edge of the crater's rim, following the route back to the station. She closed her eyes and let the sounds of the planet wash over her. Then she focused on the idea of Hadley, the general shape of his being, his calm inner voice, until she saw the station from inside the SEV. Hadley looked briefly at *Octavia* and Silver felt his desire to save his crew, and his strength. As he surveyed the horizon, Silver became aware of an approaching dust storm. She intensified her focus and, after a few seconds, she could feel the heaviness of his limbs, and together they brought the SEV to a halt.

Holding Hadley in stasis, Silver focused on one of the quietest voices in her mind. She drew herself into the body of the other, feeling what they were feeling. She could still see *Octavia*, but from a different perspective now. Silver let herself sink into the physical form of this excrescence, and after a few minutes she began to feel the cold, hard metal under Aliyaah's feet.

Aliyaah's mind felt different, sharp and inhospitable. She couldn't relax into it like with the others, and after gently probing Aliyaah's mind, Silver felt a hardness there. It was as if a whole area was closed off, even to Aliyaah herself. Silver saw that this had slowed down the spread of the infection, but as she traced the folds of Aliyaah's mind it slowly dawned on her what the hardness meant. Silver was contemplating what she should do with this knowledge when she was suddenly jolted by a startlingly familiar sensation. A child had slipped their hand, her hand, into Aliyaah's, and as Aliyaah hoisted the child into her arms, Silver knew that she needed to get *Octavia* off the ground as soon as possible.

FORTY-THREE

The engineers loaded the last of the wagons with supplies and exited the hangar after Ansen. Aliyaah waited until they had gone, then looked down at the children beside her. The girl, Sofia, and the boy, Ari, had been bundled into space suits that Ansen had tracked down in a rapid reconnaissance through the civilian quarters. As Aliyaah checked the hangar one last time and looked out at *Octavia* in the distance, she felt Sofia take her hand. She bent down to pick up the little girl and held her for a moment, feeling a confusion of emotions that didn't seem entirely her own.

Giving herself a mental shake, she settled Sofia into a wagon already loaded with supplies. The girl had dropped her glove, so Aliyaah retrieved it, crouching as best she could, given the pain in her ribs. She secured the glove so Sofia wouldn't be able to remove it on the way to the ship, and gave the little girl a smile she hoped was reassuring. After lifting Ari into the wagon beside Sofia, Aliyaah checked his suit. She had already explained that they were going to *Octavia*, where they could all get some sleep while they flew home. Sofia looked questioningly at her, but demurred, and Ari seemed to go along with whatever Sofia did. Aliyaah was thankful that neither child had asked about their parents. She wondered if they had witnessed their deaths, but didn't feel at all qualified to being such a line of questioning. She also wondered at the peculiarities of their childhoods and at what kind of friendship they had struck up while on this mission.

Before they were cleared to leave Earth, the civilians had

undergone hours of training to ensure they could suit up quickly, open airlocks, and walk in a reduced gravity environment. Sofia would have been just two or so when she set off on the journey to Mars. There was no question that she would have been placed in stasis for the takeoff and landing, and Aliyaah worried that they wouldn't have enough time to repeat this process properly. Still, getting them to *Octavia* and off the planet was the priority. As with so much in space, comfort would have to take a back seat.

The children's helmets had visors that could only be opened by an adult. Aliyaah told them once more, in fractured Russian, how they could activate their headsets to talk to her, then she closed their visors. If they had been adults, she would have reminded them not to give into the temptation to open their visors, even to try to wipe away sweat and get out of the stifling suit. She would have let them know what to do if they felt like they were going to be sick, to hunker down into their suits and release just a little bit of vomit at a time if they could, so it would stick to the skin for easier clean-up. It frightened Aliyaah that she couldn't think of how to explain such things to Ari and Sofia without scaring them. They were too young for this.

Long before they had left Earth, the adult civilians had been told what would happen if they removed their helmets, the pain they would feel and how they would wish for death even in the few seconds it would take before their lungs boiled inside them. Aliyaah looked down at Sofia and Ari as she pushed the wagon towards the outer airlock and wondered if they had any concept of the danger they were in.

When they exited the airlock on the other side, she could see that Ansen had hurried the engineers along and was making good progress towards the ship. Almost all the remaining crew were pushing wagons loaded with supplies.

The ship loomed over them as they made their way along the walkway. *Octavia's* shadow stretched out all the way back to the station and in the rapidly failing light Ansen turned to see Aliyaah at the rear of the group. Fifty yards ahead of him, the first of the crew were almost at the launch pad. They had all been assigned tasks before they left the hangar, and he was hopeful they would be able to prepare for launch calmly and efficiently. What took months, if not years, on Earth had to be done as quickly as possible. They had no margin for error.

When Aliyaah reached *Octavia*, she helped lift the children up to waiting arms above and then checked in with the crew working on the launch pad. She gave herself a moment to look back at the station and sighed. What had possessed them to try to make this planet home? A quiet fury began to grow inside her as she turned to climb up into *Octavia*. Then, seemingly without reason, Aliyaah's anger subsided and she felt serene. She could swear that someone was singing to her, but her headset wasn't active. She knew this was unusual, but she didn't feel alarmed.

Aliyaah had an urge to look one last time out across the Martian landscape, in the direction of the crater's ridge this time. She spotted the SEV, just a speck on the horizon, backlit by the last of the sun and seemingly stationary. She climbed the ladder into *Octavia* and felt sure she could hear her mother's voice, singing her a lullaby in Yoruba. The sound soothed her as she calmly climbed through the ship and passed into the sleeping quarters. Knowing exactly where to find them, she retrieved an RMC from each berth, closed the hatches, decontaminated the units, and opened them up again to allow the crew to settle the children and ready them for launch.

As she passed back through the medical bay, Aliyaah picked up four vials of anti-rads. Then she carried the RMCs back out of *Octavia* and joined Ansen on the launch pad. He looked at her strangely, but said nothing as she handed him the containers.

"These shouldn't be on the ship," Aliyaah said calmly, "We should leave them here". She looked up in the direction of the ridge as a light flashed intermittently.

"Hadley?" Ansen said, and she nodded.

"How long until the ship is ready for launch?" she asked, and this time Ansen was wary.

"Chief, it will take at least another hour, if not three."

"Oh good. Long enough for me to go and get Hadley."

"Chief?"

She turned to look at him, her expression flat, her face pale and ghostly in the light from the ship. "He's running out of time, Specialist. He will be out of oxygen in less than an hour and won't make it down here before he asphyxiates. Not without help at least."

"How do you know?"

"I just do."

He frowned, but didn't press her. "Does Hadley know?" he asked, his attention flitting between Aliyaah and the SEV's futile journey over the red planet.

"Not yet," Aliyaah said as she dug around in the last of the supplies yet to be loaded onto the ship. She stood up and swung something onto her back. "If I'm not back in two hours, take our people home, Ansen."

He watched, open mouthed, as she stepped down from the launch pad carrying the oxygen canister. "Sir?"

"It's an order, Ansen. Get them back to Earth, with or without me and Hadley."

With that, Aliyaah set off in the direction of the ridge.

FORTY-FOUR

The SEV stopped abruptly, jolting Hadley back into consciousness. He had been in a stupor and chastised himself for having let his exhaustion get the better of him. In what felt like a waking dream, he had heard Silver's voice, Aliyaah's too, and he could have sworn he was inside the biodome.

For a moment or two he allowed himself to believe that this was merely a manifestation of extreme exhaustion, but the relief didn't last. This was no hallucination. He wasn't sure he could entirely trust his own mind, but he had no choice but to try and keep going.

The SEV sat high on the ridge of the crater, and Hadley could see *Octavia* ahead of him and Biodomes One and Two just off to the east. Biodome Three lay behind him, but he couldn't quite remember how he had reached the top of the crater so quickly. He tried to start the SEV, but it refused to move. He checked the vehicle's oxygen capacity, and saw that he needed to get moving soon or he would suffocate and asphyxiate. He willed himself to remain calm. It was no use cursing himself for having lost focus.

It was possible that he could walk to *Octavia* on foot, but he had no extra antirads and would be exposing himself to deadly amounts of radiation. He was also wary of having been followed. Given the conditions in the biodome, he suspected that if Silver was ambulatory again she might be able to survive the planet's atmosphere and could be tracking him. Unlike Silver, Hadley was still reliant on his space suit to keep him alive, and there was no back-up tank or spare suit in the SEV.

If he couldn't get the SEV working in the next few minutes, he would have to siphon the oxygen from the vehicle and head out on foot.

Hoping this wouldn't be necessary, Hadley checked each of the SEV's cameras. A huge dust storm had gathered just above him, and he realised that had he carried on driving, he may have steered the SEV in the wrong direction and lost traction, causing the vehicle to tip and roll down the crater. He had been fortuitous in stopping when he did, even if he didn't know why the SEV had ground to a halt.

He took a few deep breaths to clear his thoughts so he could work the problem in front of him. It was possible that one of the wheels was caught in a fissure in the ridge of the crater, but when he adjusted the cameras to check the ground around the SEV it looked fine. His path to *Octavia* was mostly clear now that the storm had passed, with just a few large boulders to traverse. He wondered if he had driven over a larger ventifact and caused some damage to the SEV. It might not be visible on the cameras, but it was odd that the control panel wasn't showing any malfunctions.

Before getting out to look, Hadley methodically ran through the other possible causes of the SEV's immobility. Beginning with the most likely problems that could be solved from within the SEV itself, Hadley dismissed each one in turn. Even in the spacesuit, he didn't want to spend any significant time outside of the SEV when there was such intense radiation all around.

With no good options presenting themselves, he assessed the control panel one more time. Although his eyes flickered over it again, he didn't register that the switch for the emergency brake lock was illuminated. A radiologic alert light flickered on, then off again, giving him pause. It was a bad idea to leave the relative safety of the SEV, especially if he was infected and the organism fed on radioactivity. He didn't see any other choice, though.

He checked the forward scanner, but saw nothing untoward. He checked his suit, and saw that his radiation patch had turned black, probably long ago.

His suit had just under thirty minutes of breathable air left, assuming minimal physical exertion and stress. It was unlikely to be enough to get him to *Octavia* by itself, so his best option remained fixing the SEV. Hadley tried to slow his breathing and calm his heart rate, then stepped out of the vehicle.

The red dust swirled slowly around Hadley as he lowered himself to the ground and took stock of his surroundings. He could see *Octavia* now, upright on her launch pad, but he was still too far away to make out the walkway that connected the ship with the station. He hoped that Aliyaah and Ansen were making good progress getting what remained of the crew to the ship. From his vantage point on the lip of the crater, he appreciated that the SEV could be seen from *Octavia*. He would be easy to locate if he called for assistance, but he didn't plan to do any such thing. They were busy preparing to launch, and if he didn't make it, well, then he was just one more casualty of the mission.

He turned around to face the SEV and lowered himself to the ground to look under the vehicle. There was no obvious obstacle, so he activated the flashlight on his scanner and crawled between the wheels. The dim sunlight was beginning to fade and the shadow of the SEV stretched out far across the Martian surface.

The underside of the SEV was covered with a tough metal plate to protect the complex mass of wiring and hydraulics that powered the vehicle. The metal was scratched and dented, but he couldn't see any major damage. He dragged himself further underneath, towards the back of the SEV and the light from his scanner bounced off something above the rear wheel arch. For a moment, he was hopeful that he could simply remove whatever was lodged there, and that there would be no permanent damage to the SEV. As he crawled closer, however, he saw a container strapped to the SEV's chassis.

He angled his light to get a clearer view and then recoiled, banging his helmet on the underside of the SEV. A glove was tangled around one of the hydraulic legs of the vehicle, and for a second it looked as if someone was hiding in the wheel arch, squeezing the cables. He sat up again and reached toward the glove, seeing that it had been used to hold something in place. He pried it loose and the object fell into his lap. It was an RMC, filled with what looked like a fibrous substrate coated with a film of the same material he had seen in the biodome.

He was tempted to toss it aside, but was wary of breaking the RMC. It had already been jangled about in the wheel arch.

The RMC couldn't have ended up there by accident, and it had been Aliyaah's team that had fixed the SEV after it got jammed on its return from *Octavia*. Perhaps he had been wrong to trust her. Giving himself a moment to think, he realised that anyone with access to the SEV could have planted the RMC, including the doctor and the missing engineers. He remembered what Aliyaah had said about the doctor's experiments and shuddered. This must be part of a deliberate attempt to spread the organism throughout the colony. If the SEV hadn't stopped, he would have driven the RMC right to *Octavia*. As he looked at the container, he saw that the seal was close to being compromised.

Carefully, Hadley used his foot to push the RMC to the edge of the switchback before kicking it off the side of the crater, back towards the biodome. As it disappeared from his view, he looked down into the valley below. With his back to *Octavia*, Hadley didn't see the light slowly making its way towards him.

FORTY-FIVE

When Hadley got back into the SEV he did a quick system check, toggled the brake switch without thinking, and then cautiously started the vehicle. The SEV jumped forward and he figured that the RMC had been the cause of the vehicle's sudden stop.

The radiological alarm sounded again and he scanned the landscape as he crept forward. There was nothing unusual in visual range and the alarm fell silent after a few seconds. He hoped it was just a residual radiation signature from the RMC, and not a sign that there was other undesirable cargo aboard the SEV. He had checked the other wheel arches as best he could before getting back into the vehicle, and had checked the interior, but found nothing else untoward.

He steered the vehicle slowly and carefully along the edge of the ridge. The short-lived dust storm had moved enough sand around to obscure the tracks left by Aliyaah on her earlier journey to *Octavia*, so he aimed the SEV towards one of the flattest spots on the ridge, from where he could begin his descent down the crater wall.

He focused on the screen that showed the ground immediately ahead of the SEV. His oxygen was running out, but he couldn't risk going any faster, nor could he ration his supply to stretch it out. Any cognitive impairment would increase the likelihood of him making a mistake and tipping the SEV down the side of the crater. His only option was to practice slow, regular breaths, keep physical exertion to a minimum, and go as fast as caution allowed.

In the dim light, he neared the beginning of the route down off the ridge to *Octavia*. He was about to turn when an alarm sounded. The low oxygen alert had been sounding for several minutes and for a second he conflated the two. When he realised it was the radiological alarm again, and that it hadn't stopped, he slowed the SEV and scanned the landscape.

The monitors in the SEV showed numerous hotspots amid a cloud of low level radiation just over the side of the crater. The edges of the radiation appeared to be growing closer and the hotspots kept vanishing and reappearing elsewhere. The effect was that of a high tide heading his way, with wave after wave rising and falling.

He was at a loss. It didn't seem that he could outrun whatever was heading his way, but he had no choice. He had to try to get to *Octavia*. He glanced at the oxygen monitor and saw he had just a few minutes left. The journey to the ship would take too long. He couldn't make it, either in the SEV or on foot.

He transferred the remainder of the SEV's oxygen supply to the tank on his suit and then climbed out of the SEV one last time. As he thought about the choices that had brought him to this point, he felt satisfied that there was little he would have done differently, if he had the chance. Despite its dusty, rust-red, inhospitable landscape, Mars had begun to feel like home in the last few months. Perhaps it was sheer arrogance to think humans could turn this place into a refuge from the changing climate on Earth. Perhaps his energies and talents would have been better employed back on that planet. Still, he had grown used to looking at the Earth from afar, and thinking of his life there as part of his history, not his future.

Hadley sat down on the lip of the crater, facing north. Biodome Three rose out of the ground below him. He had never seen it at dusk, and this was no ordinary sunset.

The surface of the dome was barely visible now. It was covered by a mass of shimmering filaments. The crystals caught the last of the sollight and channelled the light from the inner dome, creating a dazzling display. If this was where his life would end, he thought, at least he had a spectacular view.

He realised he had been holding his breath. He exhaled and

watched as the phosphorescence spread beyond the dome, creeping up the side of the crater towards him. He inhaled slowly, savouring the feel of the air before his oxygen ran out and he became frantic, hypoxic, and confused. He knew the feeling from decades of flying fighter jets, but that didn't mean he wasn't scared. He took another breath, shallower this time, then shallower again until he was still.

When Aliyaah reached the SEV it was sitting atop the ridge with the hatch open and no sign of Hadley inside.

She looked down at the ground and saw the imprints of his boots, slowly being covered over by dust. She followed the footprints to the edge of the crater and as the dust cleared for a moment she saw him sitting upright, his suit glowing orange in the last light of the sol. His eyes were closed, his body slumped forward, propped up only by the stiffness of the suit.

Working quickly, she connected the oxygen tank to Hadley's Primary Life Support Subsystem and lay him down on his back. She flooded his EV suit with oxygen and accessed the interface for his med pump. When his heart stopped, the interface protections automatically fell away and Aliyaah used the system to give him a shot of adrenaline before sending a current of electricity through his system.

Hadley's body jerked but his heart didn't start. Aliyaah tried again, sending a jolt via the circuitry surrounding his skin which reported his vital signs. This time, his body jerked and his eyes shot open. He took a breath, stared up at her, and began to gulp down air.

She helped him sit up and took a few breaths with him to help him regulate his breathing. As she watched him, she saw a change in the light reflected in his visor and turned to look at the biodome. There was an explosion of blinding light. A sudden expansion of the phosphorescence that burst high above the dome, then began to fall silently, like radioactive snow.

Aliyaah pulled Hadley to his feet and dragged him over the edge of the crater. The sky grew dark above them, filled with the material that had erupted from the giant cloud of light, and, tTogether, they scrambled down the side of the crater towards *Octavia*.

FORTY-SIX

Ansen watched from the top of *Octavia* as the dusky sky filled with a sudden eerie light. He could only assume that there had been some sort of explosion at Biodome Three: an explosion that had released millions of spores into the atmosphere, reflecting the last of the sol's sunlight.

It was just over an hour since Aliyaah had left the ship, and Ansen was leading the crew through one last round of checks. He felt confident that they were almost ready start the countdown to launch. Most of the crew had already settled into the sleeping units, with just five essential personnel remaining on duty. If Hadley, Aliyaah, and Silver returned, three of those men would likely spend most of the journey in the cryochambers with the others.

When the biodome blew, he felt his body flood with adrenaline and his thoughts become startlingly clear. He began to see how mechanical his actions had been since Aliyaah had left *Octavia*. As he looked around at the men nearest to him he recognised the same sudden realisation in their expressions. They had also paused for a moment, as if jolted awake by the explosion of light. He met the eye of a nearby engineer, and the man quickly looked away. Another engineer did the same, as if they had been caught sleepwalking on the job.

He tried to regulate his breathing and regain the sense of calm he had felt just moments before, but it was gone. The men began to talk among themselves, and the chatter seemed deafening. He realised that they had all been working in silence for the better part of an hour. There had been no need to vocalise their thoughts. Every man seemed to have

214

known exactly what the others were thinking, and what should have taken them hours had been done in less than half the time. He knew enough not to credit this efficiency to his leadership skills. Something, or someone, had been steering them all, as if they were mere rovers.

While this apparent invasion of his mind made him furious, he couldn't help but appreciate that in just under an hour they would be ready to go. He had a sudden, startling recollection of having spoken to CapCom. Communications with Earth had been restored while he and the men were in their strange stupor, and he had been given the go ahead for launch, or had he?

Not quite believing his memory, he checked the communications log and saw that there was a recording of the initial message from Mission Support. He replayed the transmission, with Mission Support urgently requesting updates. They ordered everyone remaining on the planet to board *Octavia* and recommended that non-essential crew and civilians be placed in cryo.

As he listened to the outgoing message, Ansen shook his head. It was clearly his voice, updating CapCom on the situation on the planet. Another transmission was timestamped seventeen minutes later and gave him the all-clear for launch, with some alterations to Hadley's proposed telemetry. They were to launch on the understanding that once they neared Earth they would have to stay in orbit until the Planetary Protection Agency was confident that the infection had been eradicated and posed no threat to the billions of people below.

It was still possible that they would all die in space, even if they got *Octavia* safely off the ground. There was no guarantee they would be cleared to land on Earth, or that NASA would send resupply ships to them in orbit. And that was assuming that they even made it back home. They had months of space travel ahead of them, limited supplies, and an aggressive organism on board, one that had already killed nearly everyone who had originally come to Mars on this mission.

He replayed CapCom's last message, received just ten minutes earlier. He needed to reassure himself that they really had approved the launch. He looked across the array of green lights on the cockpit control panel and saw that almost all systems had been checked and triple checked. They would soon be good to go, and he dearly hoped they would be launching on Hadley's command, not his.

As his thoughts returned to Hadley and the Chief, he remembered the RMC containers. The Chief had retrieved them from *Octavia* and handed them to him for disposal before she left. He hadn't questioned her at the time, but it dawned on him now that someone must have planted them on board. The containers had been stuffed with what he guessed was a substrate inoculated with the organism. The Chief had told him... no, a voice in his head had told him to put the RMCs in one of the wagons, and to move it back down the walkway before nicking the seal of each capsule, just enough that the elements would eventually break them open, exposing the organism to background radiation and fuelling its spread.

From his seat in the cockpit, he could see the wagon on the walkway, with its dangerous contents. It made no sense, but he didn't have time now to contemplate his actions. He had to do one final check of the ship.

As he climbed down through *Octavia's* belly he heard sounds coming from the medical unit. There was no reason for any of the men to be in there, so he moved as quietly as he could before turning the corner to look into the medical bay.

One of the engineers who should have been in cryo was instead organising an array of medications. There was a vial of blood in a rack in front of him and a selection of plant matter, presumably left over samples preserved from the on-board kitchen garden they had maintained during the flight. There were also several samples that had already been processed. The man looked up as Ansen entered the unit. His expression was one of confusion, as if he, too, had the feeling that he hadn't quite been in control of his actions over the previous hour.

"What is going on here?" Ansen asked.

"I had an idea, Sir. Antimicrobials, a broad-spectrum cocktail, combined with an extract from the Butterfly Pea," the man said.

"And the blood?"

The man reached out slowly, as if seeing the samples for the first time. Then he blinked and touched his arm. His sleeve was rolled up to the black CMO armband that indicated he was a Crew Medical Officer, and there was a Band-Aid over what Ansen figured was a fresh mark from a blood draw.

"I, I guess I ran some tests," the man said, looking at Ansen as if he had been caught poisoning their water supply. Ansen nodded. He had a pretty good idea of how the man felt, not quite being able to own these actions that seemed like they had stemmed from intuition.

"Are both vials yours?" Ansen asked, spotting a second vial labelled differently.

"It's the Chief's. She started genome sequencing before she left the ship."

Ansen wondered why the Chief would have left a sample of her blood. Then he realised that it was a contingency; the Chief wasn't sure that she and Hadley would make it back.

"The data is set up to go straight to Mission Support, Sir. They'll know what to do with it. At least, well, I think that's the idea," the CMO said, and Ansen nodded at him.

"And the medications? Are those for all the men?"

"Yes, Sir," he said, then added, after a brief pause, "But we might have to quarantine the Chief in cryo. She's the only woman left on the crew, and, I don't know why I know this, but there's something special about her, something that can help us figure out how to manage this thing."

Ansen considered this, and wiped his hand over his eyes. He also had the sense that the Chief held the answers to controlling this organism: not necessarily killing it, but working with it somehow. This idea, while lodged in his mind, seemed alien to him, and as his thoughts grew clearer, he began to think that it was downright dangerous to even consider not simply eradicating the infection.

"We can decide, with the Commander, what to do with the Chief when they get back," he said. "In the meantime, I'll override the ports on the cryochambers so you can distribute the meds to the men," he said, hoping that at least one of the drugs, or the combination, could keep the organism in check until they figured out how to kill the damn thing.

"And the children, Sir," the CMO said.

Ansen blinked, remembering Sofia and Ari. "Is it safe?" he asked.

"I, I don't know, Sir. But, it's got to be better than the alternative, right?"

He considered this, then shook his head. "Let's see how the others respond to treatment. If it looks good, we'll give the kids the drugs then. Their exposure has been limited, and they're not going to have high levels of testosterone in their systems. They might be fine for a while yet."

The CMO nodded, and Ansen left him to work, taking the long way back to the cockpit, through each cryo room.

When he reached the cockpit, Ansen took his seat and saw that all systems were now ready for launch. There was still no sign of the Chief or the Commander.

A visual scan of the crater's ridge confirmed that the SEV hadn't moved in some time. With the light floating above and around Biodome Three it was hard now to make out anything smaller than the SEV, so he opened a line to the Chief and was about to ask for an update when he spotted a light moving rapidly in the direction of *Octavia*. Through the gloaming, he could just make out two figures, running, stumbling, and then rolling down the side of the crater, just ahead of a growing cloud of swirling dust and spores.

Ansen threw off his harness and clambered down through the ship to the lower airlock, knowing there was no one down there to open the hatch.

Aliyaah and Hadley reached the ship just as Biodome Two exploded to the west. The spores dazzled with light as they shot into the sky, spreading out in the direction of the cloud already created by Biodome Three. The spores fell slowly, like snow catching the everchanging light of the aurora borealis. The top of the ridge was now covered in a fine layer of white filaments that clung to the planet's surface, taking root.

When he reached the lower airlock, Ansen cranked the handle to release the interior door, ignoring the shouts of the crew in his headset. Closing the door behind him, he ran to the exterior hatch, flipped down his visor and began spinning the handle. He heard the seal release and pushed open the door to see Hadley standing on the other side. The Chief was hidden in shadow a few steps behind the Commander.

"Sir," Ansen said, laughing with relief. He reached out his hand and the Commander took it, glad for the help. Ansen hauled him up into the airlock then reached out again to the Chief. His gloved hand hovered in the air and then he recoiled. Aliyaah had taken a step back and was suddenly illuminated from above by the cloud of phosphorescent spores.

Her visor was open and her face shimmered with light. The Commander moved Ansen aside and put out his hand. He nodded at Aliyaah and said, "Come with us."

She looked up at the oncoming cloud and grimaced. "It's too dangerous, Sir. I don't know if I can control it."

"We can quarantine you," Hadley shouted, his voice just audible over the sound of the hydraulics as the crew began retracting the ship's landing gear.

It's not safe to have me on board, Sir. Not yet. Aliyaah's voice was clear in the minds of both men, despite the surrounding noise.

Hadley looked at Ansen, knowing that Aliyaah was testing them both, seeing if they really could handle her being on board. Ansen thought about what the CMO had said, that the Chief might be the key to understanding this thing.

Both men held out their hands to the Chief, and Hadley shouted, "We need you, Chief. The rest we can figure out as we go."

Aliyaah looked up again, feeling the clouds above her, the ground under her feet. She felt the slow, soft wind on her face and she heard a tangle of indistinct voices, the greater consciousness made up of the other women and what was left of the minds of the men. Then, as clearly as she could hear her own thoughts, Aliyaah heard another voice in her mind.

Silver spoke softly, her voice calm and lilting. She described what she could feel in Aliyaah's mind, and asked her not to be scared. Their connection would fade as she moved farther from the red planet, but it would never be completely severed, not unless she wanted it to be.

They were entangled now, and as Silver spoke, Aliyaah could see how she had guided Ansen and the crew to ready *Octavia*, and had helped Hadley avoid the dust storm and get rid of the RMC. She knew Silver had sent her to rescue Hadley, and she could feel the weight of Silver's acceptance that she couldn't come with them. Silver communicated all of this in just a few seconds, and then asked Aliyaah to deliver a message to Cooper and Cosima. She hoped that people back on Earth would accept Aliyaah in her current form, but she knew it would be too frightening for them to see her as she was now.

Aliyaah's friend had changed too much to leave Mars. She was no longer a singular entity, but an excrescence deeply connected to the planet itself and to the others who had merged with the collective. They would never survive the trip back to Earth, not in their current state of being. Aliyaah was also part of this shared consciousness, but the peculiarities of the tissue in her brain had presented a challenge to full symbiosis. If Silver and the Doctor were right, Aliyaah could hold within her something remarkable for medical advancement back on Earth. Still, Aliyaah thought, she had to survive the journey home, relying on the crew accepting her in this changed form. And, even then, there was no guarantee she would be welcomed back on Earth.

"Come home, Aliyaah," Hadley said, interrupting her thoughts. With a last look overhead, and a final breath of sharp, rust-red air, Aliyaah smiled, flipped closed her visor, and took his hand.

ABOUT THE AUTHOR

Leigh Matthews lives in Vancouver, Canada, with a rambunctious border collie, and is the author of several works of fiction, non-fiction, and poetry.

To find out more about the author, go to leighmatthews.xyz

www.ingramcontent.com/pod-product-compliance
Lightning Source LLC
Chambersburg PA
CBHW060140130626
46556CB00006B/2423